Henry Woods

Elementary Palæontology

for Geological Students

Henry Woods

Elementary Palæontology
for Geological Students

ISBN/EAN: 9783337275518

Printed in Europe, USA, Canada, Australia, Japan

Cover: Foto ©Andreas Hilbeck / pixelio.de

More available books at **www.hansebooks.com**

ELEMENTARY

PALÆONTOLOGY.

London: C. J. CLAY AND SONS,
CAMBRIDGE UNIVERSITY PRESS WAREHOUSE,
AVE MARIA LANE.

Cambridge: DEIGHTON, BELL AND CO.
Leipzig: F. A. BROCKHAUS.
New York: MACMILLAN AND CO.

ELEMENTARY

PALÆONTOLOGY

FOR GEOLOGICAL STUDENTS

BY

HENRY WOODS, B.A., F.G.S.

CAMBRIDGE:
AT THE UNIVERSITY PRESS.
1893

Cambridge:

PRINTED BY C. J. CLAY, M.A. AND SONS,
AT THE UNIVERSITY PRESS.

PREFACE.

IN the following pages I have endeavoured to give an elementary account of Invertebrate Palæontology, adapted to the requirements of geological students. With this object in view, I have devoted the greater part of the space at my disposal to a consideration of those groups of fossil animals which are most useful to the stratigraphist, and have treated very briefly, those which are of interest mainly to the zoologist. My plan has been to give, in each group, first an account of its general zoological features with a full description of the hard parts, secondly the classification and characters of those genera which are important geologically, and thirdly a sketch of the present and past distribution of the group.

Since Palæontology can be learnt only by students who have access to a collection of fossils, I have purposely refrained from using figures to illustrate genera, and have confined myself to those required to explain structure and terminology.

For the benefit of those who may wish to obtain a more detailed knowledge of the subject, or of any special part of it, I have given at the end of the volume a list of some of the more important and easily accessible palæontological works.

I gratefully acknowledge my indebtedness to Professor McKenny Hughes and Dr G. J. Hinde for advice and help.

H. WOODS.

St John's College, Cambridge,
August, 1893.

CONTENTS.

INTRODUCTION.

Conditions necessary for the preservation of animals and plants as fossils. Structure and composition of the hard parts of animals and plants. Modes of fossilisation. Uses of fossils in geology. Imperfection of the palæontological record. Distribution of fossils. Classification.

THE fact that bodies resembling marine animals occur embedded in the rocks has been known from the earliest times. But for several centuries there were two views held respecting their nature. By some persons they were thought to have once formed part of living animals and consequently to indicate that the spot where they now occur was in past ages covered by the sea. Others, feeling it difficult to account for so much geographical change, considered that they were not of organic origin at all, but had been formed by some 'plastic force' within the earth, that they were in fact 'Sports of Nature.' But since these bodies resemble in every essential respect those now living, and since we can conceive of no other means by which they could have been formed except by animals, we may at once reject this hypothesis.

The remains of animals and plants thus preserved in the rocks are known as fossils, and their study forms the subject of Palæontology. The majority of fossils belong

to species which are not found living at the present day,
but at the same time a fossil is not necessarily now an
extinct form, thus in some of the later Cainozoic formations
as many as 90 per cent. of the species of mollusks are still
living.   On the other hand an extinct animal or plant is
not always a fossil, as for instance in the case of Steller's
Sea-cow, *Rhytina gigas*, which formerly lived in the seas
off Kamtschatka, Alaska, and the Kurile Islands, but of
which no remains are found in the rocks.

In order that an animal or plant may be preserved as
a fossil, two conditions are generally necessary: First, it
must possess a skeleton of some kind or other, since the
soft parts rapidly decompose, consequently such animals
as jelly-fishes can leave no trace of their existence, unless
it be the imprint of their exterior.   Second, it must be
covered up by a deposit, otherwise when exposed to the
air it will soon crumble to dust.   Now, since there are
comparatively few places on land where material is being
deposited to any extent, it follows that terrestrial animals
will stand but little chance of being preserved, the greater
number after death will remain on the surface, and, if not
devoured by other animals, will in a short time entirely
decompose.   A few, however, may become entombed in
peat-bogs, in the dust and ashes of volcanoes, in the sand
of sand-dunes, or by the falling of a landslip; some will
be sealed up in deposits of carbonate of lime, such as the
travertine thrown down by calcareous springs, or the sta-
lagmite formed on the floor of caves; and lastly, others
may be transported by running water and ultimately
buried in the bed of a river, of a lake, or of the sea.   But
all these are of comparatively rare occurrence.   With
aquatic animals the conditions are much more favourable,
since deposition is more universal in water than on land.

But of the aqueous deposits, those laid down in the sea will enclose by far the larger number of animals on account of the greater area which they cover. The structure and composition of the hard parts vary considerably in different groups of animals and plants, and as a result some are much more readily preserved as fossils than others. Thus in some, like *Argonauta*, the skeleton consists of a thin shell which is easily broken up; then again in some sponges it is formed of needles of silica which are held together by the soft parts only, and consequently become easily scattered after the death of the animal. But in other cases, as in most of the mollusks and corals, the skeleton is very strong and not easily broken up, and consequently these are abundant as fossils. Perhaps even more important than the structure, is the composition of the hard parts. These, in the case of insects and some hydrozoans consist of a horny substance known as chitin; in diatoms, in most radiolarians, and in many sponges, of silica; in the bones of vertebrates chiefly of phosphate of lime; in corals, echinoderms, mollusks and many other animals and some plants, of carbonate of lime; in most plants of woody or corky tissue. A larger or smaller amount of organic matter is always combined with the mineral. Of these substances, chitin is with difficulty dissolved. Silica in its ordinary crystalline condition is one of the most stable minerals, but when formed organically it is glassy and isotropic, and is dissolved with comparative case; so that such skeletons may disappear entirely, or another mineral may be deposited in the place of the silica, or the isotropic silica may become crystalline. In organisms with calcareous skeletons the carbonate of lime is easily dissolved by water containing carbonic acid, but the degree of solubility varies, according to the condition in which the carbonate of lime exists. In some animals it occurs as aragonite, in others as calcite. Of these two minerals, aragonite is the harder and heavier, its specific gravity being 2·93, whilst that of calcite is only 2·77. Aragonite is rhombic and optically biaxial, calcite is hexagonal and uniaxial. Fossil calcite shells (*e.g. Pecten opercularis*) are translucent, their surface is compact, but their interior porous; on the other hand the aragonite shells (*e.g. Pectunculus glycimeris*) are opaque, and have a chalky appearance and a compact structure throughout. When a shell of each kind, having the same size and weight, is suspended in water containing carbonic acid, it is found that the one composed of aragonite loses in the same time a much greater amount of matter than the one of calcite. And further, the calcite shell remains firm much longer than the aragonite, the latter soon coming to have the consistency of kaolin, and is then easily broken up and carried away by a stream of water. This difference, however, does not appear to be due directly to mineral composition, for Messrs Cornish and Kendall found that when ordinary crystalline calcite and aragonite were powdered and placed in carbonic acid solutions of the same strength, the aragonite was not acted on more rapidly than the calcite, and the same result was obtained with powdered fossil shells. From all these considerations, it is not surprising to find that in some strata the aragonite skeletons have entirely disappeared, whereas those formed of calcite remain. This will obviously be most likely to occur where the bed is pervious and where there is a flow of carbonated water. In the case of the mussel, *Mytilus edulis*, in which the inner layer of the shell is formed of aragonite and the outer of calcite, Dr Sorby found that specimens from the raised beach at

Hope's Nose, Torquay, had lost the inner layer but not the outer. In some cases aragonite is replaced by calcite, but then the organic structure is entirely destroyed, and we get merely a mass of calcite crystals. But calcite is never replaced by aragonite. The mineral character of the skeleton of the chief calcareous organisms is as follows:—

Foraminifera.—The vitreous forms consist of calcite, the porcellanous probably of aragonite.

Actinozoa.—The Alcyonarians mainly of calcite, but most of the Madreporaria of aragonite.

Echinodermata.—All of calcite.

Polyzoa.—Calcite and aragonite in layers, or sometimes perhaps mixed.

Brachiopoda.—All of calcite.

Lamellibranchiata.—Many consist entirely of aragonite, but *Ostrea* and *Pecten* of calcite. In *Pinna, Mytilus* and *Spondylus*, the inner layer is of aragonite, the outer of calcite.

Gasteropoda.—The majority are of aragonite, but *Scalaria* and some species of *Fusus* are of calcite. In some (*e.g. Patella, Littorina, Fusus antiquus*) the outer layer is of calcite.

Cephalopoda.—*Nautilus* and *Sepia* are mainly aragonite, as also were probably the Ammonites. The guard of *Belemnites* is calcite.

Crustacea.—The shell consists of calcite, with some phosphate of lime. In some cases there is a large amount of organic matter.

The conditions in which fossils occur depend, as we have seen, on their original composition and on the material in which they are embedded. The chief types are the following:—

1. *The entire organism preserved.* Occasionally the soft parts of the organism are preserved as well as the skeleton, the whole having suffered very little change. Instances of this are, (*a*) the woolly rhinoceros and mammoth frozen into the mud in Northern Siberia, and (*b*) insects and plants encased in fossil resin known as amber, found in the Oligocene beds on the Baltic shores of Prussia and in the Pliocene beds of Cromer.

2. *The skeleton preserved almost unchanged.* Sometimes when the skeleton alone is preserved, it remains almost in its original condition, except that it has lost its organic matter. Thus the shells in the Pliocene beds of England differ from living ones only in being lighter, more porous, and generally colourless. In some instances a certain amount of mineral matter, such as carbonate of lime, is added to the skeleton, making it heavier and more compact.

3. *Carbonisation.* In some plants, and in animals with chitinous skeletons, such as graptolites, the original material passes into a carbonaceous substance. The organism undergoes decomposition where there is but little access of air, it loses oxygen, and consequently the percentage of carbon increases.

4. *Incrustation.* The organism becomes coated over with a layer of carbonate of lime deposited from a calcareous spring, as in the case of those of Matlock: or of silica, as in the thermal springs formerly existing in New Zealand.

5. *A mould of the skeleton.* Sometimes the skeleton disappears entirely, a mould only remaining. This is especially the case with aragonite organisms embedded in porous strata. When the shell of a mollusk becomes covered up with sediment, after the soft parts have

decomposed, the interior also sometimes becomes filled. Water containing carbonic acid subsequently percolates through the rock and carries away the shell as bicarbonate of lime, so that there is left only a mould of the interior and of the exterior, the space between the two being that which was originally occupied by the shell and which if filled with wax will give an exact model of it. Excellent examples of this mode of fossilisation are seen in the mollusks *Cerithium portlandicum* and *Trigonia gibbosa* from the Portland Oolite. Sometimes after the shell has been removed, the space left becomes filled up with a secondary deposit of mineral matter, but this although having the form of the original skeleton will obviously not have its internal structure.

6. *Petrifaction.* In some deposits the fossils show the minute structure as well as the form of the organism, but the original material of the skeleton has been replaced by another mineral, so that it is truly 'petrified.' Thus we find fossil wood which in thin sections shows the cells and vessels just as in living trees, but with the walls formed of silica instead of cellulose. The change has gone on in such a manner that as each particle disappeared its place was taken by a particle of silica. The chief minerals which replace the original substance of organisms in this manner are :—

(i) Carbonate of lime ; calcite sometimes replaces the silica of sponges, and the aragonite of mollusks.

(ii) Silica; as in the fossils from the Blackdown Greensand, from the Thanet Sands near Faversham ; and the wood in the Purbeck dirt-bed in the Isle of Portland.

(iii) Iron pyrites ; *e.g.* ammonites from the Oxford Clay, Lias etc., some trilobites and graptolites.

(iv) Oxide of iron; in the form of limonite in some fossils from the Dogger (Inferior Oolite) of York-shire and the Lower Greensand of Pottou etc., and as hæmatite in fossils from the Carboniferous Limestone of Cumberland.

(v) In rare cases there are other replacing minerals, such as sulphate of lime, barytes, blende, galena, malachite, vivianite, and spathic iron.

7. *Infilling.* The interior of foraminifera and some other organisms soon after the death of the animal may become filled with mineral matter, such as glauconite (silicate of iron and alumina), calcite, or silica, subsequently the shell often disappears leaving only the internal mineral cast. Glauconite occurs in this way in the various greensand strata, and also in some of the deep-sea deposits at the present day. In the Cambridge Greensand the interior of the organism was filled with phosphate of lime.

8. *Imprints.* Some animals leave only their footprints, such as labyrinthodonts and reptiles from the Trias. In the Solenhofen Slates*, jelly-fishes have left the imprint of their exterior.

In Stratigraphical Geology fossils are of immense importance. By their aid alone, any formation may be identified in distant localities and under different lithological conditions. This depends on the fact that the genera and species of animals and plants are distributed through the rocks in a definite and regular order. In the geological record each great division (termed a System) is characterised by a particular assemblage of genera and species, some of which pass from one system to another, but a large number are confined to each one, and these

* These are really shaly limestones.

enable us to identify the division. In a similar manner, the smaller divisions of the system, the series and stages (or beds), are each characterised by possessing certain fossils which do not occur above or below. Further, it is found that the fauna of the smallest division (stage or beds) is not of uniform character throughout its thickness; although there may be no change in its lithological nature, some of the species which are abundant at one level will become rare or altogether extinct in passing to higher or lower horizons. Consequently, a set of beds may be divided into belts or zones, the general aspect of the fauna of each zone being somewhat different from that of the others, but between these divisions there will be no break either physical or palæontological. If then we have determined the order of succession of the formations in any one area by means of their relative positions, the newer resting on the older, it is easy in any other district, merely by examining the fossils, to refer any set of beds to their proper position in the geological record. But valuable as this law of the identification of strata by their organic remains is, it must not be used without some caution. For although two formations may have been deposited at exactly the same time, it does not necessarily follow that all the genera and species occurring in the two will be identical. Thus for instance in the seas at the present day the same forms of life do not occur in all parts. There is a distribution in provinces, depending largely on climatic conditions, each province possessing some forms peculiar to itself. So that the organisms now being entombed in deposits formed, say, off the British coasts, will as a whole be different from those off the Australian coasts, but still some of the species and many of the genera will be common to both areas, and sufficient to identify the two deposits as having been formed within the same general period, although not sufficient to say that they are absolutely synchronous. Then again there is a distribution of organisms according to the depth of the sea, and the nature of the sea-bottom, so that the fauna of a deep-water formation will necessarily be different from that of a shallow-water one, and that of a sandstone different from that of a clay.

In addition to their chronological value, fossils are also important in indicating the conditions under which the formations were deposited. In the case of the later beds, where most of the genera are still existing, it is easy to distinguish a marine deposit from a freshwater or terrestrial one. And even in the earlier, where most of the genera are extinct, it is not very difficult, since many of the groups of animals still have representatives at the present day, and these in some cases are entirely marine, as for instance the corals, echinoderms, and cephalopods. Then again none of the freshwater lamellibranchs possess one adductor muscle only; and very few of the land or freshwater gasteropods are siphonostomatous.

Fossils, especially plants, also furnish some evidence of the climate of past times. But the evidence afforded by marine animals is of comparatively little value, except when we are dealing with existing species. This is owing to the fact that at the present day the individual species of the same genus have often a very different range in space, some being tropical forms, others polar. But even in the case of extinct species, the assemblage of the genera is sometimes such as characterises some region at the present day, as for instance in the tropical mollusks of the London Clay.

The depth of the sea in which a formation was deposited

can also be told with any degree of certainty only in the case of species still living, or in the case of assemblages of genera which are now found at some particular depth. But in basing conclusions as to depth on fossils, it must be remembered that the fauna of any locality may include forms which have lived at higher or lower levels and have been transported from their original home after death. Perhaps the safest indication of shallow-water and the proximity of land is given by the occurrence of land animals and plants in a marine formation.

If all the plants and animals which have lived in past times had been preserved as fossils, we should have a complete record of the succession of life on the earth, and all questions of phylogeny could be easily answered. But we have already seen several reasons why this record—the palæontological record—must be imperfect. Thus, some animals have no skeleton. Others, particularly land animals, do not become entombed. And some rocks which originally contained fossils have had them dissolved by the percolation of water containing carbonic acid. In addition to this, the fossils in some of the older rocks have been obliterated by metamorphism. The palæontological record is also incomplete because of the imperfection of the geological record. Between some formations enormous masses of strata are missing, having been removed by denudation. And although these gaps may be filled up elsewhere, it does not render the record of life perfect, since in going from one district to another, we almost certainly pass into a different marine province, or into an area where the conditions of temperature, depth, or the sea-bottom have changed, and where as a result we shall meet with another assemblage of organisms.

The geological distribution of animals and plants varies considerably, some have a long range, others a short one. Thus a few species extend through several formations, as for instance, *Atrypa reticularis* from the Llandovery Beds to the Devonian, and *Orthis calligramma* from the Arenig to the Wenlock Limestone. Others have a short range, as in the case of many graptolites and ammonites, which are often confined to a single band of rock. Many instances of genera with long and with short ranges will be seen in the following pages; of the former we may mention *Lingula* extending from the Cambrian, and *Nautilus* from the Ordovician, to the present day. Of the latter *Belemnitella* found only in the Upper Chalk, *Cœnograptus* in the Upper Llandeilo, and *Tetragraptus* in the Lower Arenig. Often the genera which have a long range in time have also a wide distribution in existing seas, as in the case of *Lingula*, which lives off the coasts of Japan, China, Formosa, the Korean Archipelago, the Philippine Islands, the Sandwich Islands, Australia, and in the Indian Ocean.

With regard to the general succession of organisms, we find, as might be expected, that those in the earlier formations differ more from living animals and plants, than do those in the later. Thus, in the Palæozoic, some of the groups, many of the genera, and practically all the species are extinct. But as we pass to more recent times the proportion of extinct forms decreases, until in the newer Cainozoic rocks almost all the genera and very many of the species are still existing. The different groups of organisms also appear in the geological series in the order of their complexity of organisation, the lower forms preceding the higher and more specialized. Thus, taking the Vertebrata only, the Fishes first occur in the Silurian, the Amphibians in the Carboniferous, the Reptiles in the Permian, the Mammals in the Rhætic. The Birds are first found in the Solenhofen Slate (Upper Jurassic), but they must be left out of account, since owing to their mode of existence they rarely become preserved. And similarly in each of these smaller groups, the Fishes for instance, the genera of the earlier formations are simpler and more generalized than those in the later.

The animal kingdom may be divided into groups, the primary groups are termed sub-kingdoms, the members of each of these agreeing in the general arrangement of their parts. The sub-kingdoms are divided into classes, the classes into orders, and the orders into families. The animals included in each possess certain characters in common, which are not found in the other groups. The families are composed of genera, and the genera of species. The sub-kingdoms are :—1. Protozoa. 2. Porifera. 3. Cœlenterata. 4. Echinodermata. 5. Vermes. 6. Molluscoidea. 7. Mollusca. 8. Arthropoda. 9. Vertebrata. But the student must be warned against considering that this order of succession represents an increasing perfection of organisation. Some of the members of one sub-kingdom may be more highly developed than the lower members of another which as a whole occupies a higher position in the zoological scale. In other cases, owing to the difference in the general arrangement of the parts, it is difficult to determine which of two divisions is the higher.

SUB-KINGDOM I. PROTOZOA.

Classes.	*Orders.*	*Sub-Orders.*
	1. Foraminifera.	1. Imperforata.
		2. Perforata.
1. Rhizopoda......	2. Radiolaria.	
	3. Others not found fossil.	
2. Infusoria.		
3. Sporozoa or		
Gregarinida.		

THE Protozoa includes the lowest forms of animals, such as *Amœba, Vorticella* and *Globigerina.* The body consists in many cases of one cell only, in others of more than one, but the cells never become differentiated to form tissues as they do in all other animals, which are for this reason grouped together as the Metazoa.

In some protozoans the protoplasm is, with the exception of the nucleus, of uniform character throughout; these are characterised by having no definite external form, by being able to take in food at any part of their body, and by possessing the power of throwing out lobular or filamentous processes of protoplasm known as *pseudopodia.* In other forms the central uniform mass is surrounded by a denser cortical layer, which gives the animal a definite shape. In these the food is generally taken in at one permanent aperture which functions as a mouth. They never give out pseudopodia, but are in many cases provided with *cilia* or *flagella,* which are threads of protoplasm having a definite form and a rhythmic movement.

Reproduction in the Protozoa takes place asexually by

means of fission and by the formation of spores. But in some cases conjugation occurs, representing to some extent the sexual method of the higher animals. In some of the Protozoa there is no skeleton, but in others a shell, which may be calcareous, siliceous, or chitinous, is secreted.

The Protozoa can be divided into three classes, (1) the Rhizopoda, (2) the Infusoria, (3) the Sporozoa or Gregarinida. The Rhizopods are the only forms which have been definitely recognised in the fossil state.

CLASS. RHIZOPODA.

Protozoa which possess no cortical layer and which are able to throw out pseudopodia.

The Rhizopoda are divided into five or more orders, but only two of these have been definitely found fossil, namely, the Foraminifera (or Reticularia) and the Radiolaria.

ORDER. FORAMINIFERA.

The Foraminifera are characterized by giving out filamentous pseudopodia, which frequently branch and anastomose, and by possessing in most cases a shell or test, which may be calcareous, arenaceous, siliceous, or chitinous.

The calcareous forms are by far the commonest, and in these two kinds of test may be distinguished, namely, the *vitreous* and the *porcellanous*. In the vitreous, the test is glassy and transparent, and is perforated by innumerable tubes for the passage of the pseudopodia; in some forms (*e.g. Rotalia*) these tubes are as much as $\frac{1}{3000}$ of an inch in diameter, but in others (*e.g. Operculina*) they are only $\frac{1}{18000}$ of an inch. In the porcellanous forms, the test, when viewed by reflected light, is opaque and white, having the appearance of porcelain; it is perfectly homogeneous, and is not perforated by tubes, the whole of the pseudopodia passing out by one or two large apertures. Sometimes, however, the surface of the shell is pitted, producing at first sight the appearance of perforation.

In the arenaceous forms the shell consists of grains of sand united together by a cement, the appearance of the shell varying according to the material of which the grains are composed. The cement may be formed of chitinous, or of calcareous and ferruginous material. Usually the test is imperforate.

The chitinous forms do not occur as fossils. In one genus only is the test siliceous.

With regard to the form of the shell, in some genera it consists of a single chamber, when it is said to be *unilocular*, as in *Orbulina*, in which it is spherical, and in *Lagena* (fig. 2 *F*), in which it is generally flask-shaped. In other cases it consists of several chambers, which are usually placed in communication with one another by means of perforations in the walls (septa) between them*. The arrangement of the chambers in these *multilocular* forms is very varied, they may occur in a straight line as in *Nodosaria* (fig. 2 *H*), in a curved line as in *Dentalina*, in a plane spiral as in *Cristellaria* (fig. 2 *G*), or in a helicoid spiral as in *Rotalia* (fig. 2 *L, M*). In some spiral forms the earlier whorls are embraced partly or entirely by the later ones, so that sometimes the last whorl only is visible (*e.g. Cristellaria*); but when the later chambers are merely attached to the extremities of the earlier ones, all the whorls are visible (*e.g. Rotalia*).

---

* The communication in *Nodosaria* and its allies is through the mouth-aperture of the chambers which open into one another, and only to a small extent through perforations in the walls.

In the porcellanous and the lower vitreous forms the septum between the chambers (fig. 1 *A, b*) is formed entirely by the wall of the older chamber, but in the higher vitreous forms each chamber possesses a wall of its own, so that the septum (fig. 1 *B, b*) is formed of two lamellæ. Also in the higher vitreous forms the walls of the chambers are frequently strengthened by a deposit on

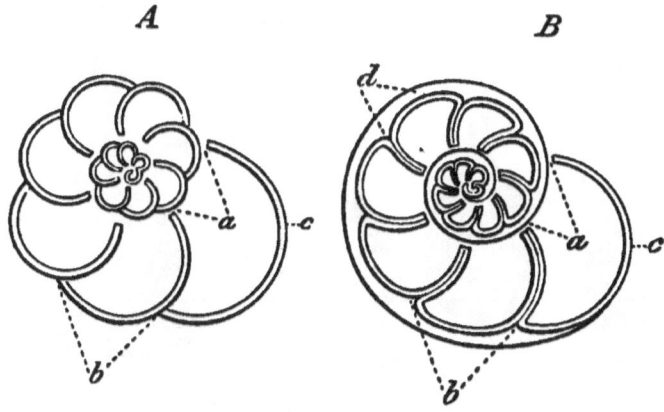

FIG. 1. *A*, section of a foraminifer in which each septum is formed of a single lamella. *B*, in which the septum is formed of two lamellæ. *a*, passages between the chambers; *b*, septum; *c*, anterior wall of last chamber; *d*, supplemental skeleton. (After Carpenter.)

their outer surfaces, filling up the outer hollows between the chambers; this deposit is often traversed by a system of canals, and is known as the *supplemental skeleton* (fig. 1 *B, d*).

The Foraminifera are divided into two sub-orders, (1) the Imperforata, (2) the Perforata.

SUB-ORDER 1. IMPERFORATA.

The test is not perforated by canals, but is provided with one or two large apertures, through which the whole of the pseudopodia pass out. The test is membranous, porcellanous, or arenaceous.

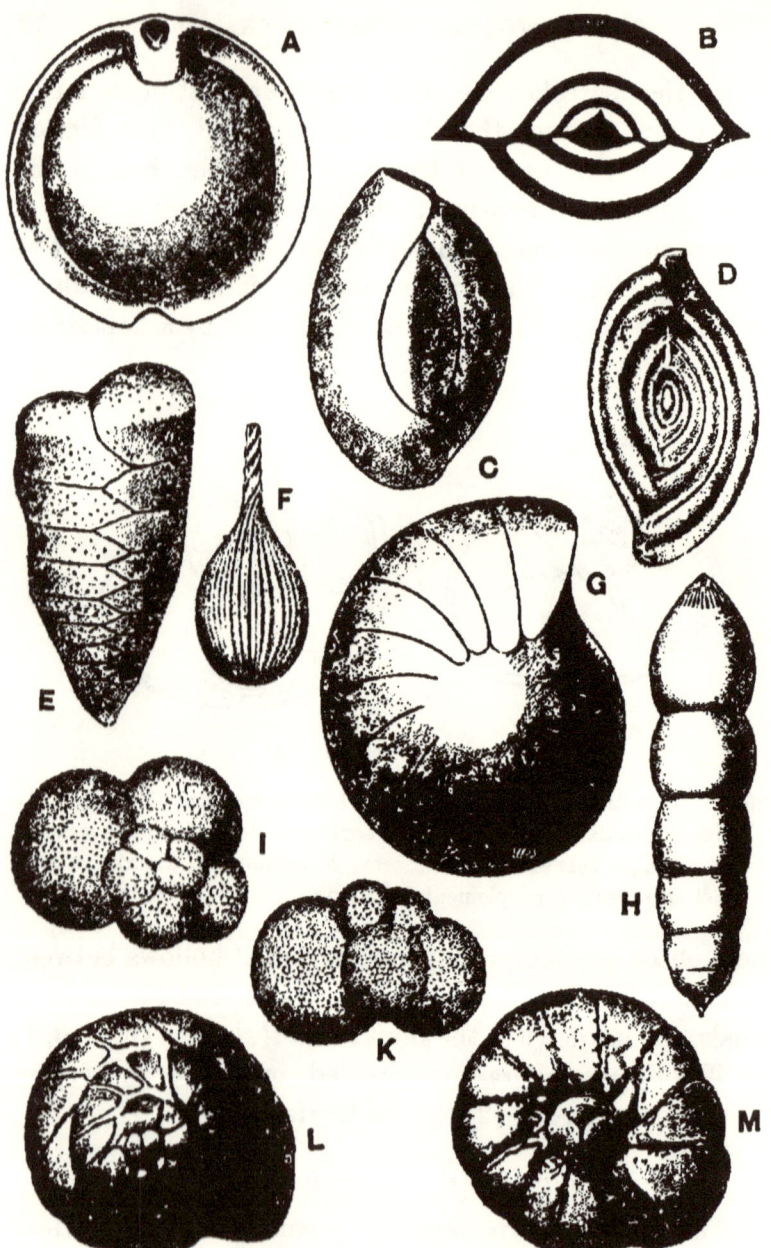

Fig. 2. Foraminifera (recent). *A, B, Miliola (Biloculina) depressa. B, section. C, Miliola (Miliolina) seminulum. D, Miliola (Spiroloculina) limbata. E, Textularia barretti. F, Lagena sulcata. G, Cristellaria rotulata. H, Nodosaria radicula. I, K, Globigerina bulloides. L, M, Rotalia beccari.* (After Brady, "Challenger" Report.)

Miliola. (fig. 2, *A—D.*) Test calcareous and porcellanous, multilocular, the chambers being coiled on an
elongated axis, each chamber forming half of a convolu-
tion. Sometimes all the chambers are visible externally
on both sides of the shell, at other times, owing to the
lateral prolongations of the chambers, only the last one or
two are seen, or it may be that more chambers are shown
on one side than on the other. The external features of
the shell consequently vary considerably, and on this
account the genus has been divided into a number of
subgenera. Trias to present day.

Saccamina. Test arenaceous, compact, thick, formed
of a single spherical, pyriform, or fusiform chamber, or of
a number of chambers united end to end. Surface smooth
or nearly so. Carboniferous and living.

SUB-ORDER 2. PERFORATA.

The test is perforated by numerous minute canals for
the passage of pseudopodia; it is usually calcareous and
vitreous, but sometimes arenaceous.

Lagena. (fig. 2, *F.*) Test unilocular, calcareous,
vitreous, very finely perforated. Form spherical, ovate
or flask-shaped. A single terminal aperture, sometimes
at the end of a long neck; rarely two apertures. Surface smooth, ribbed, or spinous. Wenlock Beds to present
day.

Nodosaria. (fig. 12, *H.*) Test vitreous, composed
of a number of chambers arranged in a straight line, and
separated by constrictions. Surface smooth or ornamented
with granules, spines, or ribs. Permian to present day.

Textularia. (fig. 2, *E.*) Test vitreous, sometimes
arenaceous; form variable, conical, pyriform, or cuneiform;

composed of numerous chambers in two alternating parallel series. Aperture slit-like on the inner edge of the last chamber. Carboniferous to present day.

Globigerina. (fig. 2, *I*, *K*.) Test calcareous, vitreous, perforated by large canals. Multilocular, chambers globular, few, arranged in a plane or helicoid spiral, each chamber opens by a large aperture into a large central cavity. No supplemental skeleton. Trias to present day.

Rotalia. (fig. 2, *L*, *M*.) Test calcareous, very finely perforated, multilocular. The chambers arranged in a helicoid spiral, so that on the upper surface all the whorls are seen, on the lower, only the last one. The aperture is in the form of a curved fissure on the lower surface of the last segment. The septa are generally double. A supplemental skeleton is sometimes present. Upper Jurassic to present day.

Nummulites. (fig. 3.) Test calcareous, lenticular in form, and composed of a large number of whorls coiled

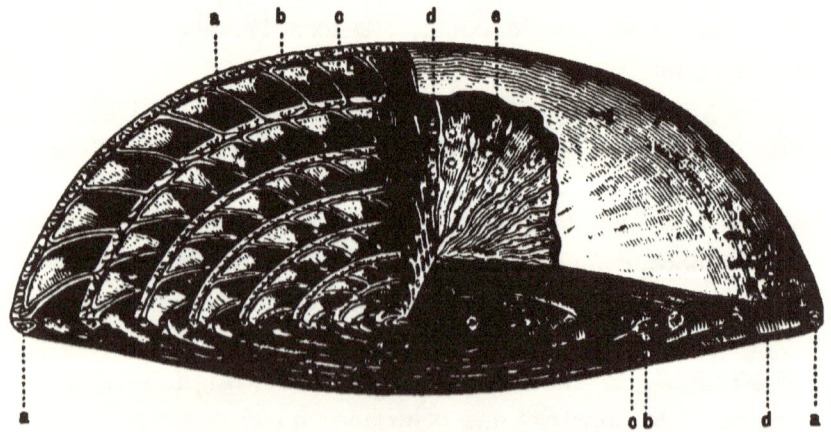

FIG. 3. *Nummulites*, showing vertical and horizontal sections. *a*, marginal cord, with system of canals; *b*, septum, with canals; *c*, chambers; *d*, test; *e*, pillars coming from the supplemental skeleton. (After Zittel.)

in a plane spiral. Each whorl completely encloses the preceding one, by means of the lateral prolongations of the chambers, so that externally only the last whorl of the shell is visible. The whorls are divided into chambers by septa which are slightly curved backwards; each chamber communicates with the neighbouring one by means of a median fissure placed next to the margin of the previous whorl. Each septum is formed by two lamellæ. A supplemental skeleton is present, the larger part of it forming what has been termed the 'marginal cord.' The general shell-substance is minutely perforated, and a system of canals also traverses the septa and supplemental skeleton. Carboniferous Limestone to present day. It attains its maximum in the Eocene, only one or two rather rare forms are living, one of which (*N. cummingi*) is found in shallow water in tropical and sub- tropical regions.

Eozoön. In the year 1864 the name *Eozoön canadense* was given by Dawson to a peculiar body found in the Laurentian rocks of Canada, and referred by Dr Carpenter and himself to the Foraminifera. Other 'species' were subsequently found in Bavaria, Bohemia, Silesia and elsewhere.

The Laurentian rocks of Canada consist of two divisions, an upper and a lower. The thickness of the lower is estimated at 20,000 feet; it is composed of gneisses and schists, with intercalated beds of crystalline limestone. In the latter, *Eozoön* occurs, frequently having the form of extensive sheets or masses; but according to Dawson, recently collected examples " have established the fact that the normal shape of young and isolated specimens of *Eozoön canadense* is a broadly-turbinate, funnel-shaped or top-shaped form, sometimes with a depression on the upper surface, giving it the appearance of the ordinary cup-shaped Mediterranean sponges."

A hand specimen of *Eozoōn* shows it to consist of alternating layers of a green mineral, serpentine, and a white mineral, calcite. In thin sections viewed under the microscope, the serpentine is seen to have at times a fairly regular and more or less beaded form. This layer is considered by Dawson and Carpenter to fill the space which was originally occupied by the soft parts of the animal (fig. 4, *b*), the serpentine having been introduced subsequently by infiltration, and thus forming a cast of the body chambers. On each side of the serpentine and between it and the layer of calcite, there may be seen in good specimens a thin lamina (*a*), said to be calcareous and perforated by numerous tubules; this lamina is com-

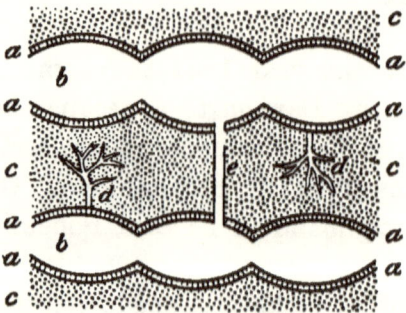

FIG. 4. Diagram to explain the organic theory of *Eozoön*. *a*, body-wall; *b*, body chamber; *c*, supplemental skeleton; *d*, canals in the supplemental skeleton; *e*, stolon-passages.

pared with the body-wall of the Foraminifera such as *Globigerina*, the tubules being the perforations for the passage of the pseudopodia. External to the body-wall is the thick layer of calcite (*c*), having the characteristic cleavage of that mineral; this is traversed by numerous branching canals (*d*), and by others which pass directly from one chamber to another placing them in communication. These canals are filled with serpentine or occasionally calcite. Since this layer comes between the body-walls, it will of course correspond to the supplemental skeleton, such as that which occurs in *Nummulina*; the branching canals will represent the complicated canal-system, and the canals passing between the chambers the stolon-passages (*e*).

If *Eozoön* be organic, it must certainly be placed among the Foraminifera, of which it will be a gigantic example. Several authors, however, especially King and Rowney in this country, and Möbius in Germany, have brought forward weighty objections to this view. They state that the chamber casts of serpentine are so extremely irregular in form that they cannot be compared with those of the Foraminifera, and they consider them to be merely granules of serpentine in a matrix of calcite. The body-wall is shown to be not calcareous but to consist of chrysolite, a fibrous variety of serpentine, derived from the alteration of the latter, and in some cases a gradual passage can be traced from the unaltered serpentine to the fibrous chrysolite. A layer of the same mineral is frequently found surrounding nodules of serpentine in ophites. Then again the fibres are often in actual contact, but if they represented the casts of the pseudopodial foramina, they ought to be isolated. With regard to the supplemental skeleton, this is found not to be of uniform structure throughout, but to contain masses of pyrites and other minerals, and in fact to correspond exactly to the matrix in which pargasite and coccolite occur. The branching canals are much too irregular both in form and distribution to be at all comparable to the canal system of a supplemental skeleton, and they are regarded merely as crystals of metaxite. Similarly the stolon passages are found to be simply crystals of pyrosclerite. The mode of occurrence of *Eozoön* also furnishes corroborative evidence. It has never been found in any unaltered rock, and no other fossils have been discovered in association with it. In the case of the specimens found at Chelmsford and Bolton, U.S.A., it has been shown that the limestone in which the *Eozoön* occurs was not formed at the same time as the gneiss with which it is associated, but that it has been introduced subsequently in the manner of a vein, so that here at any rate *Eozoön* cannot possibly be organic.

Distribution of the Foraminifera.

The majority of the Foraminifera are marine, most of them living on the sea-bottom. A few however, as for instance *Globigerina*, exist at or near the surface in the open ocean, and these few forms are very important on account of their great abundance. The earliest examples of the Foraminifera are found in the Ordovician rocks, but they are rare until we reach the Carboniferous, some of the limestones of which are formed largely of them, as for instance, the *Saccamina*-limestone of the North of England and Scotland, and the *Fusulina*-limestone of Russia, America etc. The order continues to be well represented throughout the Mesozoic formations, particularly in the Chalk, and it attains its greatest development in Tertiary and recent times. In the Eocene the genus *Nummulites* is extremely abundant, forming the massive Nummulitic Limestone of Southern Europe, Egypt, Asia Minor, and the Himalayas.

The genera and species of the Foraminifera have as a general rule a long range in time, as might be expected from their low organization; some of the species which occur in the Palæozoic are still living.

ORDER. RADIOLARIA.

In the Radiolaria the body consists of a central mass of protoplasm enclosed in a definite membrane, known as the *central capsule*. The intracapsular protoplasm contains one or more nuclei, and is continuous, through pores in the capsule, with a layer of protoplasm outside the capsule; this layer gives off filamentous pseudopodia, which occasionally anastomose. A skeleton is generally developed, which is composed either of silica, a silicate of carbon, or a peculiar horny substance known as acanthin. The skeleton may be entirely outside the central capsule or partly within, and it consists either of isolated spicules, or of a lattice-like structure frequently with projecting spines. The earliest British examples occur in the Ordovician rocks of Scotland, others have been found in the Carboniferous, and they become abundant in the Mesozoic and Cainozoic formations. Those forms in which the skeleton is composed of acanthin do not occur fossil.

SUB-KINGDOM II.   PORIFERA.

Orders.

1. Myxospongiæ.
2. Ceratospongiæ.
3. Monactinellidæ.
4. Tetractinellidæ.
5. Lithistidæ.

6. Hexactinellidæ.
7. Octactinellidæ.
8. Heteractinellidæ.
9. Calcispongiæ.

THE Porifera includes the Sponges. They are distinguished from the Protozoans by the body being always multicellular, by the cells being arranged in definite layers, and by the occurrence of sexual reproduction.

In a simple sponge the body has the form of a hollow sac open at the upper end, and in nearly all cases attached to the sea-bottom or to a foreign object, by the lower.

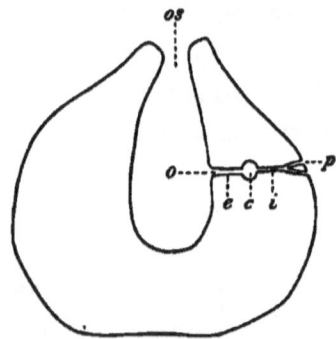

FIG. 5.   Diagram of the Structure of a simple Sponge, one canal only shown. *os*, osculum; *p*, pores; *i*, incurrent or inhalent canal; *c*, globular chamber; *e*, excurrent or exhalent canal; *o*, ostium.

In the living state a large number of small openings termed *pores* (fig. 5, *p*) may be seen on the surface, these in many forms are not permanent, disappearing and being replaced by others, they are the openings of canals leading to the interior, known as the *incurrent canals* (fig. 5, *i*). These dilate into globular chambers (*g*), from which canals pass to the central cavity of the sponge known as the *excurrent canals* (*e*), their openings on the inner surface being the *ostia* (*o*). The opening of the central cavity to the exterior is termed the *osculum* (*os*), in some cases there is only one, which is then placed at the summit of the sponge; in others there are several. A continual current of water flows through the canal-system, passing in by the pores and out by the osculum. By means of this the processes of respiration, nutrition and excretion go on.

The wall of the sponge is formed of three layers, the outer one is the *ectoderm* and consists of a single layer of flattened cells. The inner is the *endoderm*, it lines the globular chambers and the excurrent canals and is similar to the ectoderm, except in the chambers, where each cell is provided with a collar and a flagellum, the movements of the latter producing the current of water. Between the endoderm and the ectoderm comes the *mesoderm* which is much thicker than the other layers and forms the greater part of the sponge; in .it the skeleton is produced.

In nearly all sponges there is a skeleton, which serves to support the soft parts and to prevent the canals from closing. For systematic purposes its structure is found to be of immense importance, more especially since the external form of the sponge varies enormously even in the same species. The skeleton may consist of fibres of a horny substance known as *spongin*, or of needles (termed *spicules*) of various forms (fig. 6), composed of carbonate of lime or of silica, or it may consist of both siliceous spicules and spongin. It is only those forms which have either a siliceous or calcareous skeleton that are definitely known as fossils. In some groups the spicules are not united, as for instance the Monactinellidæ and Tetractinellidæ, but in others they are fused together or interlocked so as to form a complete scaffolding, and generally it is in these only that the external form of the sponge can be preserved in the fossil state. In most sponges, two kinds of spicules may be distinguished, the *skeletal-spicules* which go to build the main part of the skeleton, and the *flesh-spicules* which are smaller and isolated and are seldom preserved fossil. In the centre of each spicule, there is a tube known as the *axial canal* (fig. 6c), which in the living animal is occupied by a thread of organic matter. The spicules of recent siliceous sponges are characterised by the glassy appearance of their surface, and by the silica being colloidal, isotropic, and soluble in heated caustic potash. But in the fossil state the spicules have generally undergone considerable change, occasionally their silica is still colloidal but the surface has no longer the glassy appearance, and the axial canal is frequently filled with silica in a crystalline or crypto-crystalline condition, and is consequently easily distinguished between crossed Nicols when the spicule itself still remains colloidal and consequently isotropic; generally however the spicule has become crystalline or crypto-crystalline, and when this is the case the axial canals can rarely be detected since they are filled with material in the same condition. Sometimes however the silica of the spicules has been entirely removed, in some cases a hollow cast only remaining; in others its place is taken by another mineral, as for instance by calcite in the sponges from the Lower Chalk of Dover and Folkestone, by iron pyrites in *Protospongia* from the Menevian Beds of St Davids, by iron peroxide in the sponges of the Upper Chalk of the South of England, by glauconite in those from the Upper Greensand. Obviously then silica in the colloidal state in which it occurs in recent sponge spicules is anything but a stable substance, thus differing widely from its crystalline and crypto-crystalline condition.

The spicules of the calcareous sponges are usually smaller than those of the siliceous forms, and their material is not in an isotropic state, each one being optically a crystal of calcite but having the external form and internal structure of a spicule, consequently in polarised light they are readily distinguished from the siliceous forms. Then again the fossil calcareous spicules have undergone much less chemical change than the siliceous ones, generally they are still composed of carbonate of lime, it is only in rare cases that this is replaced by silica, but at the same time the external form of the individual calcareous spicules has very often disappeared.

The canal-system is indicated in the skeleton of both recent and fossil forms, by spaces in the spicular framework, but these spaces represent only the larger canals, the smaller existing in the soft parts alone.

Reproduction in the sponges takes place by budding or gemmation, and sexually.

The Porifera may be divided into the following nine orders.

ORDER 1. MYXOSPONGIÆ. Sponges with no skeleton or occasionally a few isolated siliceous spicules. Not known in the fossil state.

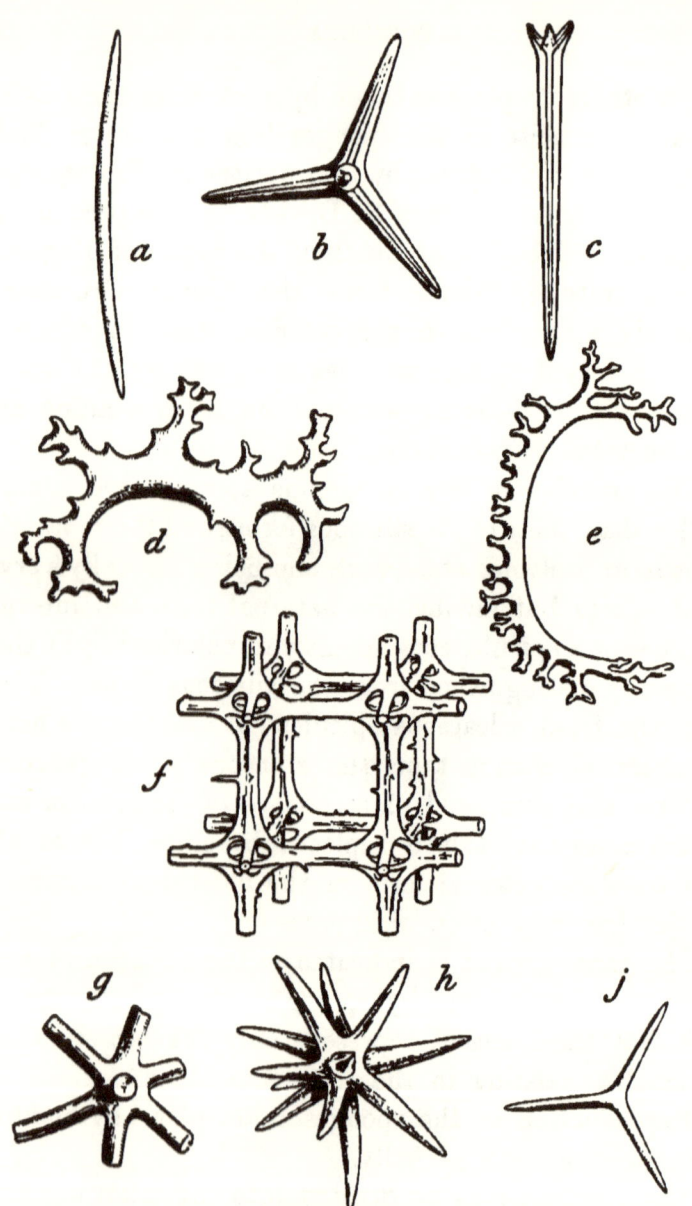

Fɪɢ. 6. Sponge spicules (skeletal). *a*, monactinellid, *Halichondria panicea*, Recent. *b*, tetractinellid, *Pachastrella* sp. Upper Green-sand. *c*, tetractinellid, *Geodites* sp. Eocene. *d*, lithistid, *Scytalia radiciformis*, Chalk. *e*, lithistid, *Seliscothon mantelli*. *f*, hexactinellid *Cæloptychium agaricoides*, Chalk. *g*, octactinellid, *Astræospongia* sp. Silurian. *h*, heteractinellid, *Asteractinella expansa*, Carbo-niferous. *j*, calcisponge, *Grantia compressa*, Recent. All magnified.

ORDER 2. CERATOSPONGIÆ. Sponges with a skeleton composed of a fibrous network of spongin. This includes the ordinary bath sponges. A few siliceous spicules are occasionally present. Not definitely known in the fossil state.

ORDER 3. MONACTINELLIDÆ. Sponges in which the skeleton consists of spongin and siliceous spicules. The spicules (fig. 6, a) are uniaxial, that is to say, they consist of a single rod or axis; they vary considerably in shape, being straight or curved, and with sharp or blunt ends. Flesh-spicules may also occur. Since in this order the spicules are only united by decomposable material, it is extremely rare to find the form of the sponge preserved fossil, usually detached spicules only occur. The earliest forms belonging to this order are found in the Silurian, they become more abundant in the Carboniferous where the genus *Reniera* occurs. The freshwater form *Spongilla* is found in the Purbeck Beds of the South of England. A large number of examples are still living.

ORDER 4. TETRACTINELLIDÆ. The spicules (fig. 6, b, c) are siliceous and are held together by spongin, they consist of four rays given off from a common centre, the angle between each of the rays being 120°. The rays may be equal or unequal in length, frequently one is very much elongated, and sometimes their terminations are bifurcated. Like the Monactinellids, the Tetractinellids are seldom preserved in anything like a perfect condition as fossils. The oldest forms occur in the Carboniferous Limestone, where they are represented by the genus *Geodites*.

ORDER 5. LITHISTIDÆ. Sponges with thick stony walls and very variable external form. The spicules (fig. 6, *d, e*) are siliceous and consist of four rays, or are irregular in form, the extremities of the rays branch or expand and firmly interlock with one another but do not fuse together. In addition to the skeletal-spicules there is generally a surface layer of trifid spicules or of discs. Flesh-spicules are also present. Several different types of canal-system occur. Owing to their solidity the Lithistids are preserved abundantly as fossils. They are rare in the Palæozoic, the earliest form being *Archæoscyphia* found in the Upper Cambrian; in the Ordovician and Silurian we get *Astylospongia*. No forms belonging to this order have been found in the Devonian, Permian, or Trias, they are numerous in the Jurassic, attain their maximum in the Cretaceous, and are scarce in the Tertiary.

Siphonia. (fig. 7.) Pear-shaped, usually provided with a stalk, which is given off from the broad end of the body and terminates in rootlets. The incurrent canals are small, slightly curved, and extend radially from

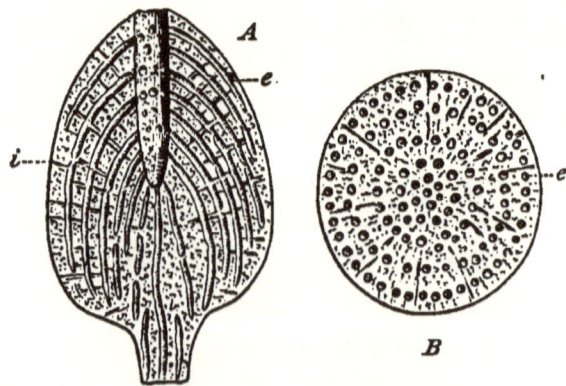

FIG. 7. *Siphonia tulipa.* Upper Greensand, Warminster. *A*, vertical section. *B*, horizontal section. *e*, excurrent canals; *i*, incurrent canals. Two-thirds natural size.

the centre of the sponge to the surface. The excurrent canals are larger, and are arranged parallel to the surface of the sponge, extending from the base to the summit, where they open into the large central cavity by means of a series of parallel ostia. The skeletal-spicules possess four rays with bifurcated and expanded extremities, by means of which they interlock. Upper Greensand to Upper Chalk.

ORDER 6. HEXACTINELLIDÆ. The spicules (fig. 6, *f*) are siliceous and consist of six rays (three axes) at right angles to one another. Each ray is traversed by an axial canal, and these unite at the point of junction of the six rays. In some cases one ray is longer or shorter than the others, or almost absent. The spicules are united so as to form a framework of skeleton cubes, either by being fused, or simply held in position by the soft parts. Flesh-spicules are abundant, but rare as fossils. The canal-system is usually simple. The earliest form is *Protospongia* from the Menevian Beds of St Davids. In the Ordovician and Silurian we get the genera *Dictyophyton* and *Phormosella*; in the Carboniferous *Hyalostelia*. There are none in the Permian and Trias, but they become abundant in the Jurassic, especially in the upper part, and also in the Cretaceous ; they are rare in the Tertiary. The sponge-character of the genera *Ischadites, Receptaculites*, and *Sphærospongia*, from the Silurian and Devonian is now disputed.

Protospongia. Form unknown but probably cup-shaped. Spicules cruciform, owing to the reduction of one axis, and arranged in a quadrate manner, the larger ones forming a framework, in the squares of which are smaller spicules of two or three sizes, arranged in the same regular way, so that the larger squares enclose

W. P. 3

four or five series of smaller ones. The spicules were either free or probably partly fused together. Menevian Beds and Lingula Flags.

Ventriculites. Simple, form variable, but usually cup-shaped, funnel-shaped, or cylindrical. Central cavity large and deep. Walls folded so as to form a series of vertical grooves and ridges. Canal-system well developed, the radial canals are large and start from the surface of the central cavity, but end before reaching the outer surface, others start from the outer surface and end before reaching the central cavity. Spicules six-rayed and fused with one another so as to form a mesh-work. The node where the axes of the spicule cross is hollow, having the form of a negative octahedron, the central part of each face of which is absent; the axial canals cross in the centre of the space. The sponge was provided with a root consisting of siliceous fibres. Upper Chalk.

ORDER 7. OCTACTINELLIDÆ. Spicules siliceous (fig. 6, *g*), consisting of eight rays, six of which are in one plane diverging at equal angles, the other two are at right angles to this plane, forming a vertical axis. Frequently, however, the vertical axis is only slightly developed or altogether absent. The spicules are not united. The only genus is *Astræospongia* found in the Silurian and Devonian.

ORDER 8. HETERACTINELLIDÆ. Spicules siliceous and unusually large (fig. 6, *h*), the number of rays varying from six to thirty. The body spicules are not fused, but there is a dermal layer in which the spicules are interwoven and more or less fused. The only genera are *Tholiasterella* and *Asteractinella* found in the Carboniferous rocks of Ayrshire.

ORDER 9. CALCISPONGIÆ. Spicules composed of carbonate of lime (fig. 6, *j*); usually much smaller and less varied in form than those of the siliceous sponges; there are three kinds, the simple uniaxial, the three-rayed, and the four-rayed; they are never fused with one another, and they are either arranged close together so as to form fibres, or they are loosely distributed. The earliest forms in Britain occur in the Carboniferous rocks of Fifeshire.

Peronella. Cylindrical, simple or branched; central cavity tubular and extending from the summit to the base. Walls thick and with no definite canals, the current of water having probably passed through the irregular spaces between the spicular fibres. Spicules three or four-rayed forming anastomosing fibres. Carboniferous (possibly also Devonian) to Cretaceous; most abundant in the Jurassic and Cretaceous.

Distribution of the Porifera.

The Sponges are all aquatic, and, with the exception of the Monactinellid genus *Spongilla*, and its allies, all marine. They are found in the seas of all parts of the world, many of the genera and species having a very wide distribution. All the orders except the Octactinellidæ and the Heteractinellidæ are still living. The Lithistids are found mainly between 10 and 150 fathoms, but some species occur at greater depths. The Hexactinellids are deeper water forms than the Lithistids, being found down to a depth of 2900 fathoms, but they are most abundant between 100 and 200 fathoms. The Calcispongiæ are mainly shallow water forms.

The fossil forms are comparatively rare in the Palæozoic rocks, until we reach the Carboniferous; and throughout

the geological formations they are much less abundant
in argillaceous than in calcareous and arenaceous rocks.
Sponges are first found in the Cambrian System, the
earliest form being *Protospongia* from the Menevian Beds
and Lingula Flags. In the Tremadoc the Hexactinellid
Hyalostelia occurs, ranging onwards as far as the
Chalk. In the Ordovician we have in the Llandeilo
Beds the first appearance of *Ischadites* associated with
Hyalostelia. In the Bala Beds we meet with *Astylospongia*. The most abundant Silurian form is *Ischadites;*
Astræospongia and *Hyalostelia* also occur. Sponges
are rare in the Devonian, but *Sphærospongia* and *Receptaculites* have been recorded. In the Carboniferous
rocks, sponges become much more common, the siliceous
spicules often forming thick beds of chert: the Monactinellids are represented by *Reniera*, the Tetractinellids
by *Geodites*, the Lithistids by *Doryderma*, the Hexactinellids by *Hyalostelia*, and the Heteractinellids by the
two component genera. Sponges appear to be absent in
the Permian and they are rare in the Trias, except in the
St Cassian Beds of the Tyrol, where Calcispongiæ are
numerous. In the Jurassic sponges are extremely abundant; the only Monactinellid is *Spongilla* from the Purbeck
Beds; Lithistids and Hexactinellids although abundant
in Germany and Switzerland are rare in England; the
Calcispongiæ are fairly numerous in this country as well as
in France and Germany. But of all the systems, it is the
Cretaceous in which sponges are most abundant. They are
found chiefly at four horizons:—(1) in the Lower Greensand
of Faringdon, Upware, Kent, and Surrey; (2) in the Upper
Greensand and Chloritic Marl of Warminster, Blackdown,
Haldon, and the Isle of Wight; the Lithistids being here
very abundant, exceeding the Hexactinellids; the Calci-

sponges are also common in some places; (3) in the
Lower Chalk of the South of England, the Calcisponges
are however not represented here; (4) in the Upper
Chalk, where the siliceous sponges are very common, the
Calcisponges rare. Lastly in the Tertiary formations few
sponges have been found.

SUB-KINGDOM III. CŒLENTERATA.

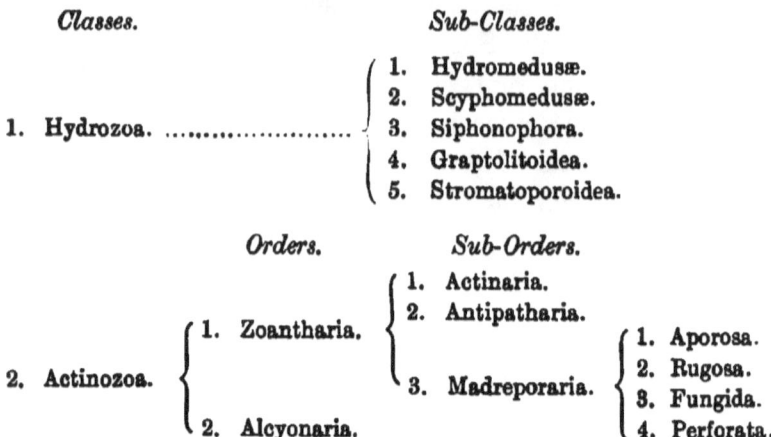

Classes.	Sub-Classes.
1. Hydrozoa.	1. Hydromedusæ.
	2. Scyphomedusæ.
	3. Siphonophora.
	4. Graptolitoidea.
	5. Stromatoporoidea.

Orders.	Sub-Orders.	
2. Actinozoa.	1. Zoantharia.	1. Actinaria.
		2. Antipatharia.
		3. Madreporaria. 1. Aporosa. 2. Rugosa. 3. Fungida. 4. Perforata.
	2. Alcyonaria.	

THE Cœlenterates include the jelly-fishes, corals, and allied forms. They differ from the sponges in the absence of a canal-system, in the middle layer of the body wall being very thin, and in the presence of thread-cells or nematocysts. This sub-kingdom can be divided into two classes, (1) the Hydrozoa, (2) the Actinozoa.

CLASS. HYDROZOA.

The Hydrozoans are characterised by not having the digestive tract separate from the general cavity of the body (cœlenteron), and by the latter not being divided into compartments by partitions (mesenteries). The simplest form of hydrozoan is the common freshwater *Hydra*. In this the body consists of an elongated sac, at one end of which there is an opening, serving as the mouth, the animal being attached by the opposite end. The interior of this sac is hollow and undivided, it is produced above into a row of tentacles surrounding the mouth; the whole body is very contractile and constantly changing its shape. Multiplication takes place (1) by the giving off of buds which ultimately separate from the parent, (2) by fission, and (3) sexually, by the production of ova and spermatozoa. The sexual elements are developed in the ectoderm. In many hydrozoans however, the sexual elements are produced in another individual (medusa), so that there is an alternation of a sexual with an asexual generation. In a large number of forms there are no hard parts whatever, others possess a skeleton which is produced by the ectoderm, and may be chitinous as in *Sertularia*, or calcareous as in *Millepora*. A simple hydrozoan, like *Hydra*, is known as a *polyp*, but many forms are compound, consisting of a number of polypites united together. All the hydrozoans, except *Hydra* and *Cordylophora* are marine. They may be divided into five sub-classes, (1) Hydromedusæ (or Hydroidea), (2) Scyphomedusæ, (3) Siphonophora, (4) Graptolitoidea, (5) Stromatoporoidea.

The Hydromedusæ includes such modern genera as *Tubularia* and *Sertularia*. Although there is frequently a chitinous or calcareous skeleton, this sub-class is but poorly represented in the fossil state. The living form *Hydractinia* is found in the Cretaceous and later formations. Probably the genera *Dendrograptus* found in the Cambrian and Ordovician, and *Dictyonema* which ranges from the Cambrian to the Devonian, also belong to this

group. The Hydrocorallinæ in which the skeleton is
calcareous, are also placed here, *Millepora* being the best
known form, it ranges from the Eocene to the present day.

The Scyphomedusæ includes such jelly-fishes as
Aurelia, Rhizostoma, and *Pelagia,* but as they possess no
hard parts it is not to be expected that they should be
found fossil; nevertheless the impressions of some forms
(*e.g. Rhizostomites*) have been found in the Lithographic
Slate of Solenhofen.

The Siphonophora includes *Physalia* ('Portuguese
Man-of-War'), *Physophora,* and other forms, and is
unknown in the fossil state.

SUB-CLASS. GRAPTOLITOIDEA.

The Graptolitoidea includes the graptolites; these are
altogether extinct, being found only in the Lower Palæozoic
rocks, where owing to their abundance and to the limited
range in time of both genera and species, they are of
immense importance to the stratigraphical geologist.
They occur most commonly in argillaceous rocks, especially
in black shales, whilst they are rare in sandstones and
limestones. The graptolites were, like the modern
Sertularia, compound animals, consisting of a number of
polypites united by a common *cœnosarc,* the whole being
protected by a skeleton of chitin. But the original
material of the skeleton is never preserved in the fossil
state, its place being taken by carbon or iron pyrites.
The entire skeleton is termed the *polypary;* this in a
simple form like *Monograptus,* consists of the following
parts. A more or less cylindrical tube known as the
common canal (fig. 8 b, c), extends the whole length of
the animal, the wall being termed the *periderm.* From

one side of the common canal a row of small cups or tooth-like projections is given off, these are the *hydrothecæ* (fig. 8 b, *h*), and each one opens on the one hand into the common canal and on the other to the exterior; the latter aperture, known as the *mouth* (*m*) of the hydrotheca, is

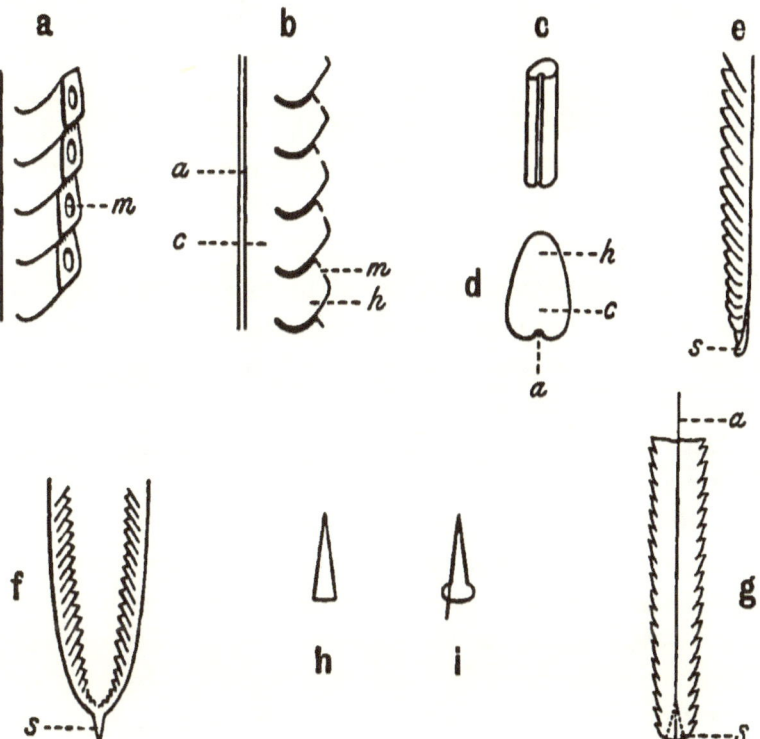

Fig. 8. Morphology of Graptolites. a, Portion of *Monograptus perso-natus*; b, vertical section of the same; c, *Monograptus* showing the dorsal groove in which the sicula was placed; d, transverse section of *Monograptus* with dorsal groove and virgula; e, *Monograptus colonus*, Coniston Grits, with sicula; f, *Didymograptus murchisoni*, Llandeilo Beds; g, *Diplograptus foliaceus*, Llandeilo Beds, with the position of the embedded sicula indicated; h, sicula of *Diplograptus*, the earliest stage; i, the same with virgula and two buds developed. (All enlarged except f.)

a, axis or virgula; *c*, common canal; *h*, hydrotheca; *m*, mouth of hydrotheca; *s*, sicula.

frequently circular, but sometimes quadrangular or slit-
like. On the dorsal side of the polypary, that is, opposite
the hydrothecæ, there is on the outer surface of the
periderm a longitudinal groove (fig. 8 c), in which is
placed a chitinous thread or rod, termed the *axis* or
virgula (fig. 8 d, *a*); in some cases this is solid, in others it
appears to be hollow. In some species of *Monograptus*
the virgula projects beyond the distal end of the common
canal. At the proximal end of the polypary there is a
small elongated cone-like body, of an embryonic nature,
termed the *sicula* (fig. 8 e, *s*).

With regard to the soft parts of the animal, speaking
from analogy with recent allied forms, we may suppose,
that each hydrotheca lodged an individual polypite, and
these were connected by means of the cœnosarc which
occupied the common canal.

In the form just described (*Monograptus*) the polypary
is always simple, but in many genera it is compound,
consisting of two or more branches. When the branches
are given off from a common centre, their proximal
parts are sometimes enclosed in a horny sheath termed
the *central disc*[1], as in some species of *Tetragraptus*.
In some cases (*e.g. Monograptus*, fig. 8 e) the polypary
possesses only a single row of hydrothecæ, such forms are
said to be *monoprionidian*; others however (*e.g. Diplograptus*, fig. 8 g) possess two rows on opposite sides of
the polypary, these are the *diprionidian* forms, and they
may have a single common canal (*e.g. Retiolites*), but
more usually there are two (*e.g. Diplograptus*), and when
this is the case, the polypary appears to consist of two
monoprionidian forms united by their dorsal surfaces. In

---

[1] In some simple forms (*e.g. Climacograptus bicornis*) there is frequently a similar disc at the proximal end.

the genus *Dicranograptus*, however, there is a transition between these two types, its proximal end being diprionidian, whilst its distal end is monoprionidian. The hydrothecæ vary considerably in different genera, and even in different species of the same genus; but in the same species they are similar, except that they diminish in size towards the proximal end of the polypary; they may be rectangular (*e.g. Phyllograptus*), tubular (*e.g. Rastrites*), conical (*e.g. Monograptus spiralis*), or recurved (*e.g. Monograptus lobiferus*). They may be in contact throughout their entire length (*e.g. Phyllograptus*), at their bases only (*e.g. Cœnograptus*), or entirely separate (*e.g. Rastrites*). Frequently they are provided with one or more spines near the mouth. By most authors the hydrothecæ are said to communicate freely with the common canal, in this respect differing from the allied living forms, in which there is a constriction, or a diaphragm, at the base of each hydrotheca separating it from the common canal. But McCoy and Hopkinson state that in some specimens, as for instance *Didymograptus extensus*, *Didymograptus patulus*, and *Tetragraptus serra*, from the Skiddaw Slates, there is a distinct septum between the hydrothecæ and the common canal, and moreover in some cases the common canal itself is divided up by transverse septa.

The periderm of the graptolite is said by some authors to be formed of three layers. In the genus *Retiolites* the two inner layers are modified so as to form a fibrous network, upon which the outer layer is stretched as a kind of epiderm.

We saw that in *Monograptus*, the virgula sometimes extends beyond the distal end of the polypary; in some genera (*e.g. Diplograptus*) it sometimes also extends beyond the proximal extremity. In the majority of cases the vir-

gula is single, and is placed dorsally in the monoprionidian
genera, but in the diprionidian it is central, being situated
in the middle of the wall separating the two common
canals.   Occasionally, however, it is double, as in *Retiolites*, in which the axes are separated and placed in the
wall on opposite sides of the common canal.   The position
of the sicula also varies.   In *Monograptus* it is united
to the dorsal surface of the polypary, the pointed end
being directed distally (fig. 8 e, *s*).   In *Didymograptus* its
broad end only is united to the polypary, the pointed
end being directed downwards (fig. 8 f, *s*).   In *Dicellograptus*, in which there are two branches diverging at
a wide angle, it forms a kind of axial spine.   In *Diplograptus* it is enclosed by the hydrothecæ (fig. 8 g, *s*).
Lastly, in some forms it does not persist in the adult
state.   In those genera which have two branches, the
term *angle of divergence* is applied to the angle between
the hydrothecal margins.

The appearance of even the same species of graptolite
varies considerably according to its mode of preservation.
Frequently it is flattened to a film, and when this is the
case we may get a side view, a front view showing the
mouths of the hydrothecæ, or a back view; in the two
latter cases the margins will be parallel.   But when the
original material has been replaced by iron pyrites, the
natural form of the polypary is preserved.

The reproduction of the graptolites appears to have
been similar to that which takes place in some modern
hydrozoans.   In a few diprionidian forms (fig. 9) sac-like
bodies have been found attached to the sides of the
polypary, these appear when perfect to be pear-shaped,
and in some cases at any rate, they are connected with
the virgula by means of fibres.   These bodies resemble

in many respects the *gonangia* of living Sertularians, and very probably represent them. In the latter the

Fɪɢ. 9. *Diplograptus whitfieldi*, with reproductive sacs. (After Hall.)

gonangia are chitinous sacs, within which in the calypto-blastic hydroids[1], the *gonophores* are developed, and these give rise directly to the generative elements. The earliest condition of the graptolite at present known, is the *sicula* (fig. 8 h), this probably arises indirectly from the sac-like bodies which have been supposed to be gonangia. The first change which takes place in the sicula, is the forma-tion of the virgula in the wall of one side; this frequently projects beyond one or both ends (fig. 8 i). Next there appears a bud on one face of the sicula, frequently near its broader extremity but sometimes near the point; this developes into the first hydrotheca, and is soon

[1] These include such genera as *Plumularia*, *Sertularia* and *Campanu-laria*.

followed by other buds, which in like manner pass into hydrothecæ. In the diprionidian forms the buds are produced on two sides of the sicula; they are sometimes directed towards the point of the sicula, at other times away from it. When two series are formed they may either remain free or be united by their dorsal surfaces.

Owing to the fact that the soft parts of the graptolites are entirely unknown, it is difficult to speak of their affinities with any degree of certainty. There can be no doubt, however, that they belong to the Hydrozoa; and Allman and others have referred them doubtfully to the Hydromedusæ, being nearest to such forms as *Sertularia* and *Plumularia*, with which they agree in the general arrangement of the hydrothecæ, and in having gonangia. But they differ from them in possessing a virgula, in being free forms, in the diminution in size of the hydrothecæ towards the proximal end of the polypary, and in the free communication which exists in many, if not all, cases between the hydrothecæ and the common canal. The graptolites also resemble slightly some forms of Polyzoa, as for instance *Rhabdopleura*, which possesses a chitinous axis.

Monograptus. (fig. 8 e.) Polypary simple, unilateral, monoprionidian, straight, curved or spiral. Hydrothecæ vary in form in different species. The pointed end of the sicula is thrown back upon and attached to the dorsal side of the proximal end of the polypary. Lower Llandovery to Lower Ludlow.

Rastrites. Polypary similar to *Monograptus*, but the common canal is very narrow, and the hydrothecæ are long and widely separated. Lower Llandovery to Tarannon.

Cyrtograptus. Polypary similar to *Monograptus*, but

always curved and with branches given off from the hydrothecal margin. Upper Tarannon to Lower Ludlow.

Cœnograptus. Polypary bilateral, monoprionidian. The central non-celluliferous portion bent into an S-shape, giving off branches from the convex portions. Hydrothecæ in contact only, not overlapping. Sicula median, triangular. Upper Llandeilo.

Didymograptus. (fig. 8 f.) Polypary bilateral, monoprionidian, consisting of two simple branches diverging at an angle which varies from 0° to 180° in different species. Hydrothecæ rectangular, in contact. The pointed end of the sicula directed downwards. Lower Arenig to Upper Llandeilo.

Tetragraptus. Polypary bilateral, monoprionidian, consisting of four simple radiating branches. Hydrothecæ rectangular, in contact. A central disc may or may not be present. Lower Arenig.

Dicranograptus. Proximal portion of the polypary diprionidian, but dividing distally into two monoprionidian branches. Terminations of the hydrothecæ isolated and incurved. Upper Llandeilo to Lower Bala.

Dicellograptus. Like *Dicranograptus*, but monoprionidian throughout, the two branches united by the sicula only. Angle of divergence greater than 180°. Upper Arenig to Upper Bala.

Diplograptus. (fig. 8 g.) Polypary diprionidian. Hydrothecæ overlapping, and placed obliquely. Virgula prolonged beyond the distal and sometimes also the proximal extremity of the polypary. Sicula imbedded. Lower Arenig to Tarannon.

Climacograptus. Polypary diprionidian. Hydrothecæ placed vertically and separated by deep depressions. Virgula prolonged beyond both extremities. Lower Arenig to Taraunon.

Phyllograptus. Polypary leaf-like, formed of four monoprionidian branches united along the whole of their dorsal surfaces. Hydrothecæ rectangular, in contact throughout their entire length, and furnished with two strong spines. Arenig.

Retiolites. Polypary simple, diprionidian, narrower at the ends. There are two virgulas, which are feebly developed, one being placed in each of the lateral faces of the polypary. Hydrothecæ rectangular, alternating, given off from a single common canal. Inner layer of the periderm is in the form of a chitinous network. Lower Bala to Wenlock.

Distribution of the Graptolitoidea.

The oldest graptolites in Britain occur in the Tremadoc Beds, where we get the genus *Bryograptus*; in the *Olenus*-shales of Gothland, *Dichograptus* and *Clonograptus* also occur. These forms are also found in the lower part of the Arenig Beds, but other genera are associated with them and soon become abundant, such as *Tetragraptus* and *Didymograptus; Phyllograptus* also occurs here. The Llandeilo graptolites are transitional between the Arenig and Bala forms, *Phyllograptus* has died out, *Didymograptus* is fairly common in the lower part, and the genera *Dicellograptus*, *Dicranograptus*, *Diplograptus* and *Climacograptus* now appear for the first time. In the Bala Beds, these four last-mentioned genera become much more abundant, and with them occur *Leptograptus* and *Pleurograptus*. The only genera which pass up from the Bala to the Silurian are *Climacograptus, Diplograptus*, and *Retiolites*; not a single Bala species (except perhaps a variety of *Climacograptus scalaris*) is found in the Llandovery Beds, so that between the Ordovician and Silurian there is an enormous break in the graptolitic succession. As a whole the Silurian formations are characterised by the presence of the family *Monograp-tidæ*[1], which appears first at the base of the Llandovery Beds. In the lower part of the Llandovery the genera *Diplograptus* and *Climacograptus* are fairly abundant, but they become extinct in the Tarannon, and in the Wenlock and Ludlow Beds the only forms are *Monograptus, Cyrto-graptus*, and *Retiolites*. The last traces of graptolites occur in the Downtonian Beds, but they are too imperfect for determination.

SUB-CLASS. STROMATOPOROIDEA.

In the Stromatoporoids the skeleton is calcareous, and very variable in form; it may be hemispherical, spheroidal, dendroid, encrusting, or altogether irregular, frequently forming large masses. It consists of a series of concentric laminæ separated by interlaminar spaces; both are crossed at right angles by a series of rods or pillars, which give off horizontal processes at definite intervals, and these joining together really form the porous laminæ. The stromatopo-roids were compound animals, the polypites in some cases simply occupying pores in the external lamina, in others there were definite tubes. The Stromatoporoids are most closely related to such living forms as *Hydractinia*

---

[1] This includes the genera, *Monograptus, Rastrites* and *Cyrtograptus*.

and *Millepora.*   They are found only in the Ordovician,
Silurian, and Devonian Systems, being most abundant in
the last; frequently they are of considerable importance
as rock-builders.   Some of the best known genera are
Labechia, Stromatopora, Actinostroma, and *Clathrodictyon.*

CLASS.   ACTINOZOA.

This includes the corals and sea-anemones.   They
differ from the Hydrozoa (1) in possessing an alimentary
tube, the œsophagus, which is distinct from the cœlenteron
but at the same time communicates freely with it; (2) in
the cœlenteron being divided up into chambers by vertical
radiating partitions known as mesenteries; (3) in the
reproductive elements being developed within the polyp
and never on a medusa.

In a typical actinozoan, such as the common sea-
anemone *Actinaria,* the body has a more or less cylindrical

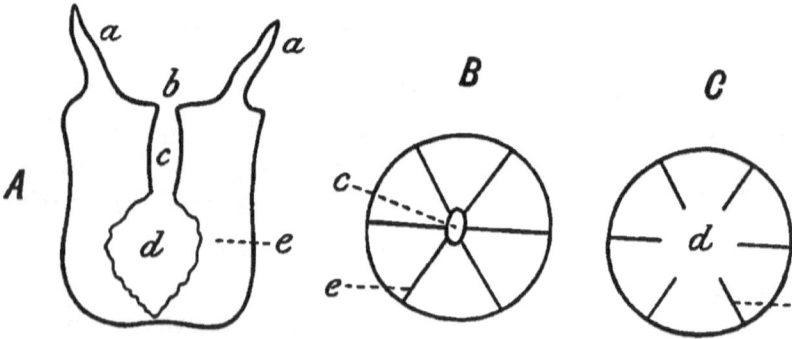

Fig. 10.   Diagram-sections of a sea-anemone.   *A,* vertical.   *B,* horizontal, through the upper part of the polyp.   *C,* through the lower
part.   *a,* tentacles; *b,* mouth; *c,* œsophageal tube; *d,* cœlenteron;
e, mesenteries.

form, and is attached by one end, the other having an
opening, the mouth (fig. 10 *b*), surrounded by tentacles (*a*).
The mouth leads into the *œsophageal tube* (*c*), which opens

at its lower end into the body-cavity (d). The latter is divided into chambers by folds of the endoderm, the *mesenteries* (e); in the upper part of the polyp, their inner edges join the œsophageal tube, in the lower part they remain free, so that a section in the former region (fig. 10 B) will show the body wall and also the œsophageal wall, but in the latter (C) the body wall only. The tentacles are placed immediately above the intermesenteric chambers, and the space in each tentacle is continuous with that of the chamber below. In *Actinaria* as in the other sea-anemones there is no skeleton, but the majority of actinozoans possess one, which in many cases is external to the body, being formed of carbonate of lime, secreted by the ectoderm; this is said to be *sclerodermic*: in others it is formed internally and consists of calcareous spicules, or there is a cœnosarcal axial rod of horny or calcareous material, this last being a *sclerobasic* skeleton. The Actinozoa can be divided into three orders, (1) Zoantharia, (2) Alcyonaria, (3) Ctenophora. The Monticuliporoidea may also perhaps belong to this class, but they are considered by several authors to be Polyzoa.

ORDER. ZOANTHARIA.

In the Zoantharia, the tentacles and mesenteries are generally numerous and are never eight in number as is the case in the Alcyonaria, but frequently a multiple of six or sometimes four. The tentacles are always simple. A skeleton is usually present and it may be calcareous or horny.

There are three sub-orders (1) the Actinaria, including the sea-anemones, which possess no skeleton and are consequently unknown in the fossil state; (2) the Antipatharia, in which the skeleton consists of an internal horny rod; these are also not found fossil; (3) the Madreporaria, including the well-known stony corals, in which the skeleton is calcareous, these are very abundant as fossils.

SUB-ORDER. MADREPORARIA.

There is a sclerodermic skeleton, consisting of carbonate of lime, secreted by the ectoderm of the lower part of the polyp. The entire skeleton is spoken of as the *corallum*; it may be simple or compound, in the latter case each individual is termed a *corallite*.

In a typical simple coral, the skeleton has a more or less conical form, the base of the cone is depressed and termed the *calyx*, in it the polyp was placed. The wall bounding the corallum is known as the *theca* (fig. 11 *A, d*) sometimes there is outside this, another calcareous layer,

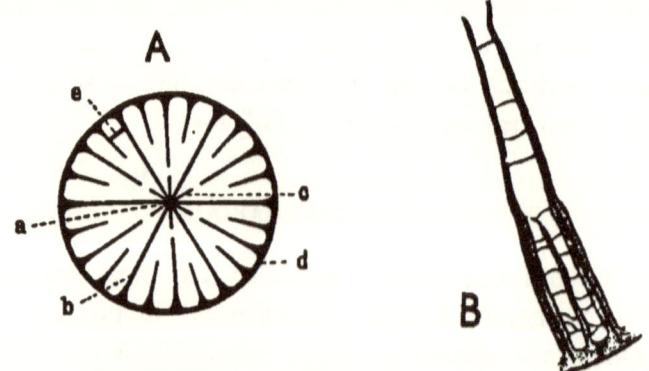

Fig. 11. *A.* Diagram-section (horizontal) of a simple coral. *a*, columella; *b*, primary septa; *c*, pali; *d*, theca; *e*, dissepiments.
B. Portion of a horizontal section of *Cyathophyllum murchisoni*, Carboniferous Limestone, showing the septa composed of a thin middle layer with a thicker layer on each side (magnified).

the *epitheca*. The whole space enclosed by the theca is termed the *visceral chamber*; this is divided up by numerous calcareous partitions, the most important of which are the *septa* (fig. 11 *A, b*). These are vertical plates running from the theca towards the centre, and alternating with the mesenteries. They are of different sizes, some reaching the centre, others going only part of the distance; they frequently occur in cycles, of which three or more may often be distinguished, the largest being the *primary* (*b*), the others the *secondary, tertiary* and so on. In some forms one or more of the primary septa are absent, and we have what are known as *septal fossulæ*. When the septa project upwards above the edge of the theca, they are said to be *exsert*. Sometimes they are only feebly developed, being represented by rows of spines. When seen in section the septa are frequently found to consist of three layers (fig. 11 *B*), the middle being darker and thinner than the outer, and apparently representing the original septum, the outer layers having been formed subsequently. In the centre of the visceral chamber, where the larger septa come together, there is often a vertical rod, which extends from the base of the chamber to the bottom of the calyx, this is the *columella* (figs. 11 *A, a*; 13 *c*). Its structure varies considerably; when it is solid and ends in a knob or point in the calyx, it is termed *styliform*; if the top is porous, it is said to be *spongy*; when it consists of twisted laminæ it is termed *trabeculate*; if formed by the twisting together of processes given off from the inner edges of the septa, it is *false*; and lastly in some forms it is altogether absent. Another set of vertical partitions somewhat similar to the septa are the *pali* (fig. 11 *A, c*), these are radiating plates attached to the columella and placed opposite the inner edges of some of the shorter septa, but not joining them. Passing from one septum to another, there are often rods known as *synapticulæ.* Similarly uniting two septa, there are plates, which may be horizontal or oblique, straight or curved, these are the *dissepiments* (figs. 11 *A, e*; 13 *d*). Lastly we have the *tabulæ* (fig. 13 *B, t*), which instead of merely passing across the space between two septa, cut across several, in a typical case going right across the visceral chamber horizontally; but frequently they extend only partly across. The tabulæ are arranged one above the other, so that the visceral chamber is divided into horizontal compartments. On the outside of the wall of the coral there are in some forms vertical ridges, which may be smooth or spiny, these are known as the *costæ*, and they usually correspond with the septa.

A simple coral like that just described may become compound either by budding or by fission. Three kinds of budding may be distinguished, (1) the *lateral* (fig. 12 *A*), in which the buds are given off from the sides of the

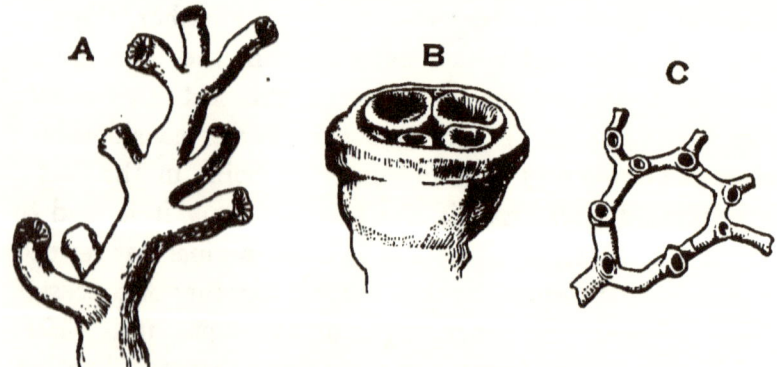

Fig. 12.   *A. Dendrophyllia nigrescens,* showing lateral budding, Recent, (reduced one-half). *B. Cyathophyllum truncatum,* showing calicular budding, Wenlock Limestone, (natural size). *C. Syringopora,* showing basal budding, Carboniferous Limestone, (natural size).

polyp, (2) the *calicular* (fig. 12 *B*), in which they arise from the calyx, (3) the *basal* (fig. 12 *C*), in which the buds spring from branches or stolons, which are given off from the base of the corallite. Fission commences by the mouth becoming slightly constricted, this goes on until two mouths and two polyps are formed; and this division is of course repeated in the skeleton. When in a compound form, the individual corallites are free from one another, the corallum is termed *dendroid* (fig. 12 *A*); when they are in contact, it is *massive*. Sometimes the spaces between the individual corallites are filled up with calcareous material formed by the cœnosarc, and known as the *cœnenchyma*.

The Madreporaria[1] are divided into four sections (1) Aporosa, (2) Rugosa, (3) Fungida, (4) Perforata.

Section I. Aporosa.

The theca and septa are not perforated but solid. Dissepiments, and sometimes also tabulæ and synapticulæ, are present. The septa are generally in multiples of six.

Montlivaltia. Corallum simple, fixed or free; turbinate, cylindrical, or discoidal. Epitheca well developed, theca feeble. Columella absent. Septa numerous, strong and dentate, often exsert. Dissepiments abundant. In England, Lias to Corallian; foreign, Trias to Recent.

Isastræa. Compound, massive; calyces polygonal. Walls of the corallites fused along their entire length. Columella rudimentary or absent. Septa thin and close

---

[1] Until recently one of the divisions of the Madreporaria was the *Tabulata*. This was characterised by the well-developed tabulæ, and the rudimentary septa; but it is now considered to be an artificial group and its genera are placed in the Aporosa, Perforata, and Alcyonaria. It included amongst others the following, *Heliolites*, *Favosites*, *Syringopora*, and *Halysites*.

together.   Dissepiments fairly abundant.   Lias to Upper Greensand.

Holocystis.   Compound, massive, convex; calyces polygonal.   Columella small, styliform.   Corallites united by their walls or by costæ.   The four primary septa are much better developed than the others.   Tabulæ present. Lower Greensand.

Thecosmilia.   Compound, branching or rarely almost massive.   Multiplication by fission.   Margin of calyces irregular.   Columella rudimentary or absent.   Septa, strong, dentate, and more or less exsert.   Dissepiments abundant.   Epitheca thick and folded, but often not preserved.   Lias to Corallian.

Section II.   Rugosa.

The corallum is compact and imperforate, and generally bilaterally symmetrical.   The septa are usually in multiples of four, there being four primary septa.   In most cases the septa are of two sizes, the longer alternating with the shorter.   Dissepiments are abundant and tabulæ are often present.   One or more septal fossulæ usually occur.   There is no cœnenchyma.

Cyathophyllum.   Simple or compound; branching or massive.   Septa numerous, of two sizes, alternating, the longer giving rise to a false columella.   Tabulæ small, occupying the central part only of the visceral chamber. Dissepiments form an extensive peripheral zone of vesicular tissue.   Bala to Carboniferous Limestone.

Acervularia.   Compound, massive; corallites with two walls, the outer polygonal, frequently hexagonal, the inner circular.   Septa well developed, reaching the centre.

Columella absent. Tabulæ extending across the central part of the visceral chamber. Dissepiments form a peripheral vesicular zone. Budding calicular. Silurian to Devonian.

Lithostrotion (fig. 13). Compound, massive or dendroid. When massive the corallites are prismatic, when dendroid they are cylindrical. Septa well developed, alternately long and short. Columella styliform, laterally compressed. Peripheral zone of dissepiments narrow. Tabulæ wide, occupying the centre of the visceral

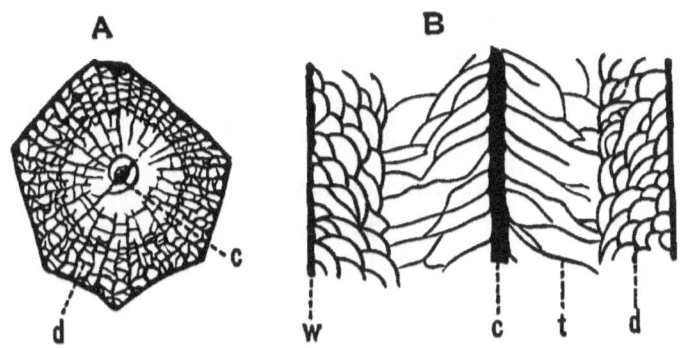

Fig. 13. *Lithostrotion basaltiforme*, Carboniferous Limestone. *A*. Horizontal section of a single corallite, × 2½. *B*. Vertical section, × 5; *c*, columella ; *t*, tabulæ ; *d*, dissepiments ; *w*, theca.

chamber. Septal fossulæ well marked. Carboniferous Limestone.

Omphyma. Simple, turbinate. Septa numerous, alternately long and short, but extending only a short distance into the visceral chamber, the central part being occupied by the tabulæ. The four primary septa are placed in shallow fossulæ. Peripheral zone of dissepiments narrow. The theca gives off root-like processes. Bala to Lower Ludlow.

Zaphrentis. Simple, free, bilateral ; turbinate, conical or cylindrical, often curved ; calyx deep. A well marked septal fossula, containing a septum which is generally small. Septa numerous. Tabulæ well developed, extending quite across the visceral chamber. Dissepiments few, never forming a peripheral vesicular zone. Columella absent. Theca thick. Wenlock Limestone to Carboniferous Limestone.

Calceola. Simple, conical or slipper-shaped, one side is flat, the opposite convex; calyx very deep and closed by a semi-lunar operculum, which has on its inner surface a strongly marked median ridge and several less prominent lateral ridges. Septa rudimentary, being represented by striæ. An epitheca is present. Middle Devonian.

Section III. Fungida.

The corallum is simple or compound. The calyces are united by their costæ. Synapticulæ are present, and sometimes also a columella and dissepiments. Septa generally solid.

Thamnastræa. Compound, massive; convex or laminar. Walls of the corallites indistinct. Calyces shallow. Septa of adjoining corallites confluent. Columella variable. Dissepiments and synapticulæ present. In England, Lias to Upper Greensand; foreign, Trias to Miocene.

Section IV. Perforata.

The corallum is porous or reticulate. The visceral cavities of adjoining corallites are placed in communication with one another by means of perforations in their walls. The septa sometimes consist of trabeculæ, or are represented by spines only. Dissepiments and tabulæ may or may not be present.

Litharæa. Compound, massive. Calyces more or less polygonal. Septa well developed, the faces spiny, the upper edges dentate. Walls of the corallites reticulate. Columella trabecular. In England, Bracklesham Beds; foreign, Eocene to Miocene.

Favosites. Compound, massive, sometimes branched. Corallites long and polygonal, the walls are in contact but not fused, and they are perforated by pores arranged in a row along each face, known as 'mural pores.' Tabulæ numerous, regular, generally extending quite across the visceral chamber. Septa represented by rows of spines. Bala to Carboniferous Limestone.

Syringopora. Compound, fasciculate; corallites tubular, for the most part not in contact. The visceral chambers of the different corallites are placed in communication by means of horizontal connecting tubes. Tabulæ numerous, funnel-shaped. Septa feebly developed, generally represented by rows of spines. Budding basal. Llandovery to Carboniferous Limestone.

ORDER. ALCYONARIA.

There are eight mesenteries and eight tentacles, the latter being pinnate. The skeleton varies considerably, it may consist of isolated calcareous spicules in the soft parts (*e.g. Alcyonium*), of an internal axial rod formed of horny material (*e.g. Gorgonia*) or of carbonate of lime (*e.g. Pennatula*), or of both (*e.g. Isis*), or it may be external in the form of calcareous tubes (*e.g. Tubipora*).

Heliolites. Corallum compound, massive or branching, not spicular, formed of tubes of two sizes, the larger circular ones are known as autopores, between these come the smaller polygonal siphonopores. Tabulæ occur in both, and in the autopores there are septa also, which may be lamellar, spiny, or rudimentary, and are usually twelve in number. Bala to Devonian.

Halysites. Compound, corallites long and tubular, arranged in a single row and united at their sides so as to form laminæ, which intersect; in some species the corallites are of two sizes. Epitheca thick. Septa absent or represented by spines. Tabulæ well developed, horizontal or concave. Llandeilo to Wenlock.

Distribution of the Actinozoa.

From the point of view of their distribution at the present day, the Madreporaria may be divided into two groups, the solitary and the reef-building. Each of these includes representatives of the three sections, Aporosa, Fungida, and Perforata. The solitary corals are almost entirely confined to deep water, occurring down to at least 2,900 fathoms, and are found in almost all latitudes. The species likewise have a wide distribution, apparently not being affected by conditions of temperature and depth. It might therefore be expected that they would also have a long range in time; this however is not the case, for existing forms extend but a short way back into the geological record, thus not a single living species is found fossil in the English Cainozoic formations. The distribution of the reef-building corals unlike that of the solitary forms is limited by both depth and temperature. Thus they are found only in shallow water, not usually extending lower than depths of 20 or 30 fathoms, and only where the temperature of the ocean is not less than 68° F., flourishing best in water even warmer than this. Like the solitary corals, the reef-building genera of the present day have but a very limited geological range. As a general rule, corals can only exist in salt water, there are however one or two exceptions, thus *Cylicia rubeola* flourishes in the river Thames, New Zealand. Clear water is likewise generally necessary, but one species, *Porites limosa*, thrives in muddy situations. In geological times the reef-building corals had a much wider geographical range than they have at the present day. Thus they occur abundantly in various formations in temperate and also in polar regions. But it does not necessarily follow from this, that these forms required the same temperature as their living representatives.

The only extinct section of the Madreporaria is the Rugosa; this is confined to the Palæozoic period, ranging from the Ordovician to the Carboniferous. The Aporose corals also appear first in the Ordovician system, the earliest genus being *Columnaria*; but they are very much more abundant in the Mesozoic and Cainozoic periods than in the Palæozoic. The Perforata commence in the Ordovician and range on to the present day, but the forms occurring in the Palæozoic are almost entirely confined to that period. The Palæozoic families of the Alcyonaria are also almost entirely unrepresented in later formations, and very few of the modern forms occur fossil, but *Corallium* is found in the Jurassic, and forms allied to *Pennatula* and *Gorgonia* occur in the Cretaceous. The Ctenophora do not occur fossil. The Monticuliporoids (regarded by some as Polyzoa) range from the Ordovician to the Permian, and they include *Monticulipora, Fistulipora* and other forms. From all these considerations it follows that there must be a marked contrast between the coral faunas of the Palæozoic and the Neozoic periods.

Fossil corals are most abundant in calcareous rocks

and comparatively rare in argillaceous and arenaceous beds; this is indeed what might be expected, since existing forms can, as a general rule, live only in clear water; consequently very many limestone rocks are formed almost entirely of coral remains. In North America corals are abundant in the Ordovician, but in England only a few forms have been found; they are much more abundant in the Silurian, especially in the Wenlock Limestone, the chief genera being *Halysites*, *Omphyma*, *Acervularia*, *Favosites*, *Heliolites*, and *Cyathophyllum*. In the Devonian, the last four are still well represented; *Zaphrentis* and *Calceola* also occur. The genera *Lithostrotion*, *Amplexus*, and *Michelinia* are confined to the Carboniferous System in England, and the following do not extend beyond it, *Zaphrentis*, *Syringopora*, *Favosites*, and *Cyathophyllum*. In the Permian and Trias corals are rare. In the Lias a few forms have been found, such as *Montlivaltia*, *Thamnastræa*, *Thecosmilia*, and *Isastræa*. In the Oolites, these four genera become extremely abundant in England, and many others also occur. In the Cretaceous formations, corals become much rarer, the chief being *Holocystis*, *Micrabacia*, and *Parasmilia*. Corals are also rare in the English Cainozoic; *Litharæa*, *Dendrophyllia*, and *Oculina* occurring in the Eocene, *Madrepora* in the Oligocene, and *Flabellum* in the Pliocene.

SUB-KINGDOM IV. ECHINODERMATA.

Classes.		*Orders.*
1. Asteroidea............	{	1. Encrinasteriæ.
		2. Eusasteroidea.
2. Ophiuroidea.		
3. Echinoidea.	{	1. Palæechinoidea.
		2. Euechinoidea.
4. Holothuroidea.		
5. Crinoidea.	{	1. Palæocrinoidea.
		2. Neocrinoidea.
6. Cystidea.		
7. Blastoidea.		

THE animals included in this sub-kingdom are all
marine; they comprise the starfishes, brittle-stars, sea-
urchins, sea-lilies, sea-cucumbers, and the extinct blastoids and cystideans. The body is very often radially
symmetrical, the symmetry being generally pentamerous.
But in many cases there is a more or less well-marked
bilateral arrangement of parts. Unlike so many of the
cœlenterates the echinoderms are never colonial forms.
In the majority of cases the alimentary cavity terminates
in an anus. A distinct vascular system is present, and
also a set of vessels containing a watery fluid, known as
the *water-vascular system*. This consists of a ring round
the œsophagus from which five radiating trunks are given
off, and it functions generally in locomotion, and probably

also in respiration. A nervous system is also found having a distribution similar to that of the water-vascular system.

In all the echinoderms there is a dermal skeleton. This is calcareous and consists of isolated pieces, or more usually of rods or plates, often forming a complete exoskeleton, which may be either flexible or rigid; spines

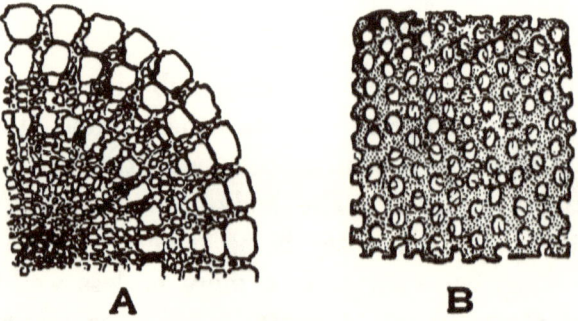

A   **B**

Fig. 14. *A*. Portion of transverse section of a spine of a sea-urchin *Echinometra*, Recent (magnified). *B*. Section of interambulacral plate of recent *Cidaris* parallel to the surface (magnified).

and other processes are also often present, attached to the plates. When examined microscopically each part of the skeleton is found to be formed of a network of calcareous rods (fig. 14). The details of the structure vary in different forms, depending on the size and shape of the spaces between the rods. In the spines of the sea-urchins the network of rods is frequently arranged so as to form radiating perforated plates (fig. 14 *A*), which are united by rods placed at right angles to them. The axial portion of the spine often has a coarser structure than the other parts. Another characteristic feature of the skeleton is that each component part shows a uniform optic orientation, being in fact a crystal of calcite, differing only from an ordinary crystal in not having crystal contours and in possessing the netted structure. In a plate the principal crystallographic axis is at right angles to the surface, in a spine it is parallel to the length. In fossil forms the spaces in the network of rods generally become filled with calcite, this being deposited in crystalline continuity with that forming the plate or spine. In such cases the characteristic cleavage of calcite becomes well marked, so that when the plate or spine is broken, the fracture passes along the cleavage planes, instead of being irregular as in the recent forms. By the infiltration of calcite and the development of cleavage, the organic structure in the fossils is sometimes more or less completely destroyed.

Reproduction in the echinoderms is mainly sexual, and as a rule the sexes are separate, but they do not differ externally. The Echinodermata are divided into the following seven classes :—(1) Asteroidea; (2) Ophiuroidea; (3) Echinoidea; (4) Holothuroidea; (5) Crinoidea; (6) Cystidea; (7) Blastoidea.

CLASS. ASTEROIDEA.

The star-fishes constitute the class Asteroidea. In these the body is sometimes pentagonal in outline as in *Goniaster*, but in the majority of cases it is more or less star-shaped, consisting of a central part, the *disc*, which is produced into five *arms* or *rays*. In a few forms there are more than five arms, as in *Solaster papposus* which has thirteen.

On the under surface of the animal are placed the mouth and tube-feet. The mouth is in the centre of the disc, and along the arms are rows of tube-feet, these are tubular processes connected with the radial water-vascular vessel.   This surface then is the *oral, ambulacral,* or *ventral.*   The upper surface is *aboral, anti-ambulacral,* or *dorsal*; on it occurs the anus, a small opening placed near the centre of the disc.   In some forms the anus is absent. Also on the dorsal surface between two of the rays there is a porous plate, the *madreporic tubercle*; sometimes more than one is present.

On the ventral surface of each arm, there is a deep longitudinal groove, the *ambulacral groove*; this is formed by two rows of plates known as the *ambulacral ossicles,* (fig. 15 *a*) which are inclined to each other so as to form

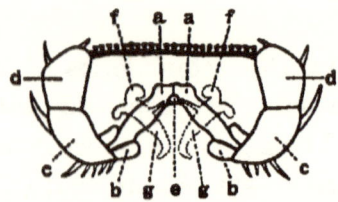

Fɪᴏ. 15.   Section of the arm of a star-fish (*Astropecten*).   *a,* ambulacral ossicles; *b,* adambulacral plates; *c,* inferior marginal plates with spines; *d,* superior marginals; *e,* radial water vessel : *f,* ampulla ; *g,* tube-feet.

an obtuse angle; the ossicles on opposite sides of the groove are movably articulated at their dorsal surfaces.   Along each row of ambulacral ossicles, there is a row of pores, each pore coming between two plates and being formed by the apposition of two notches on the oral and distal faces of adjoining plates; generally the pores are arranged in a straight line, but in some forms as in the common star-fish, *Asterias rubens,* they are zigzag, being alternately near to, and distant from, the middle of the ambulacral groove.   External to the rows of ambulacral ossicles there is on each side of the groove, another row of plates, the *adambulacral plates* (*b*).   In some forms beyond this row, and coming between the dorsal and ventral surfaces of the arms there are one or two rows known as the *marginal plates* (*c, d*). The dorsal surface of the skeleton is formed of a meshwork of calcareous rods with membranous inter- spaces. Short spines are often abundant on the plates. Pedicellariæ also occur, especially on the dorsal surface; they are spines having a pincer-like termination, and probably serve to remove excrement from the surface of the body. Projecting into the mouth at the angles formed by the ambulacral grooves are five pairs of plates, which give the mouth a star-shaped form. The mouth leads into the globular stomach, from which a small projection passes a short way into each arm, the stomach narrows and passes into the pentagonal pyloric sac, from the angles of which five processes are given off, and pass into the arms near the aboral surface and soon divide. From the pyloric sac a short narrow intestine leads to the anus. The water-vascular system consists of a vessel forming a ring round the mouth (fig. 16 *a*), from which five branches (*b*) radiate off, one down each arm, placed in the ambula- cral groove and consequently outside the skeleton. Each of these radial vessels gives off two rows of processes on opposite sides, which pass on the one hand through the pores between the ambulacral ossicles into vesicles situ- ated dorsally to the ossicles and known as the *ampullæ* (*g*), and on the other hand into the tubular processes known as the *tube-feet* (*f*), which project along the ventral surface of the arm and are provided at their extremities with sucking discs. It is by means of these tube-feet that the animal moves. The ampullæ contract, forcing water into the tube-feet, which then expand and become attached to some foreign object, afterwards the ampullæ become distended causing the tube-feet to contract. The

water-vascular system is placed in communication with
the sea-water by means of a canal (fig. 16 d) passing from
the circular vessel to the dorsal surface of the disc and

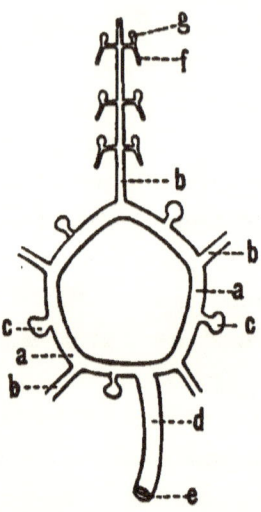

Fig. 16.   Diagram of the water-vascular system of a starfish. a, circular
    vessel round the mouth; b, radial vessels; c, Polian vesicles;
    d, stone-canal; e, madreporic plate; f, tube-feet (only a few shown);
    g, ampulla.

ending in the madreporic tubercle.   This is known as the
stone-canal on account of the deposit of carbonate of lime
in its walls.

The distribution of the nervous system is similar to
that of the water-vascular system.   It consists of a ring
round the mouth from which a branch goes down the
ambulacral groove of each arm, being situated immediately
under the epidermis, and external to the water-vascular
vessel ; each radial nerve terminates at the end of the ray
in an eye.   The blood vascular system consists of a dorsal
and a ventral ring, one round the mouth and the other
round the anus, from each of which radial branches are

given off; these two circular vessels are connected by means of a tube passing along the stone-canal, and sometimes regarded as a heart*. The genital glands occur in pairs at the base of each arm and they open to the exterior between the rays on the dorsal surface.

ORDER. ENCRINASTERIÆ.

The ambulacral ossicles alternate on either side of the ambulacral groove.

Palæaster. Arms five, thick, convex, short or of moderate length. The dorsal surface formed of rows of small ossicles provided with spines. There is a row of adambulacral plates and also a row of large marginal plates. Madreporic tubercle small. Bala Beds to Carboniferous.

ORDER. EUASTEROIDEA.

The ambulacral plates are placed opposite each other.

Astropecten. Body flattened. Arms five, long. Two rows of marginal plates, the ventral row carries spine-like scales, which increase in size outwards and terminate in long spines; the dorsal row granulated and often spinous. Dorsal surface of the disc and rays furnished with small appendages which are covered with bristly prolongations. Anus absent. Lias to present day.

Distribution of the Asteroidea.

The Asteroidea have a wide distribution in the ocean at the present day; they are most abundant at moderate depths, but also occur in abyssal regions.

The fossil forms do not differ greatly from the modern

* A different interpretation of the vascular system has been given by Cuénot.

ones. The Encrinasteroidea are confined to the Palæozoic. A few Euasteroids occur in the Devonian and Carbon- iferous, but they are mainly Neozoic forms. The star-fishes occur first in the Bala Beds, where we get the genus *Palæaster.* They are more abundant in the Silurian, where *Palæaster, Palæasterina,* and *Palæocoma* occur. *Palæaster* and other forms are found in the Devonian; in the Jurassic, *Uraster, Solaster, Astropecten, Plumaster, Oreaster* and *Goniaster.* The two last also occur in the Cretaceous. In the Cainozoic rocks star-fishes are rare.

CLASS. OPHIUROIDEA.

In the Ophiuroids or brittle-stars, the body consists of a disc and arms. The arms are generally five in number, usually simple, but in some cases branched; they are much smaller than in the star-fishes and are merely appendages of the disc and not prolongations. Usually they are long, cylindrical and very flexible, serving for locomotion by means of movements which take place chiefly in a horizontal direction. Unlike the arms of the star-fish they do not contain any prolongations of the alimentary canal, and the ambulacral groove is not open to the exterior. The arrangement of the nervous, the water-vascular, and the vascular systems is similar to that found in the Asteroidea; but the tube-feet are not pro- vided with sucking-discs and there are no ampullæ. There is no anus and pedicellariæ are absent.

Generally there is a well-developed skeleton, but in some cases granules only are found. In a typical case the following parts are found. Encasing the arms, there are four rows of plates (fig. 17), one dorsal, one ventral and two lateral. The lateral are provided with rows of spines.

Between the lateral plates and the ventral there are apertures for the passage of the tube-feet. The greater part of the space enclosed by the four rows of plates is filled up by a longitudinal row of ossicles (*d*); each ossicle consists of two halves fused together along the median vertical line and in this part is immovable. But each ossicle in the row articulates with the preceding and succeeding one, so that the arm is flexible. On the

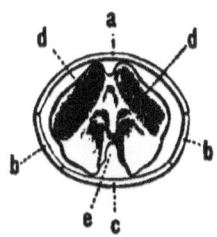

Fig. 17.   Section of the arm of an Ophiuroid (*Ophioglypha*). *a*, dorsal plate; *b*, lateral plate; *c*, ventral plate; *d*, ambulacral ossicles fused along the median vertical line; *e*, ambulacral groove.

ventral surface of the row there is a groove (*e*) in which the radial vascular and water-vascular vessels, and the nerve cord are placed; this corresponds to the ambulacral groove of the star-fish and the plates above to the ambulacral ossicles.

Coming now to the disc, this is usually round or pentagonal. On its ventral surface (fig. 18 *A*) the arms are prolonged so as to reach the mouth. The last pair of ambulacral ossicles,—those next the mouth, instead of being fused like the others, become free, and each one unites with that of the adjoining arm. The parts of the disc that come between the arms are known as the *inter-brachial areas*; these are covered mainly with scales and granules, but in each of the areas there is a large plate, the *buccal plate* (*b*), and other smaller plates, projecting into the mouth, giving it a stellate form. One of the buccal plates serves as the madreporic plate. The genital openings (*g*) also occur on the ventral surface of the disc, they are in the form of slits in the interbrachial areas, usually two in each, situated near the bases of the arms; occasionally there are four. The dorsal surface of the

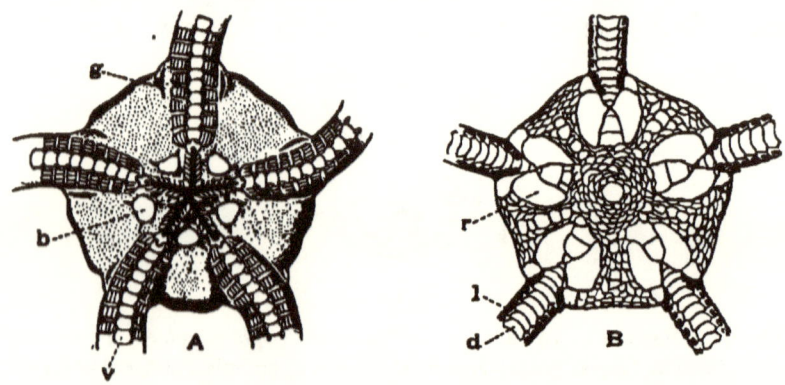

Fig. 18. *A, Ophioderma longicauda,* Recent. Ventral surface of disc and part of the arms, *b,* buccal plates; *g,* genital slits; *v,* ventral plates of arms. *B, Ophioglypha,* Recent. Dorsal surface, *r,* radial plates; *l,* lateral plates of arms; *d,* dorsal plates of arms.

disc (fig. 17 *B*) is covered with scales or granules; and usually there is at the bases of the arms on each side, a large plate, the *radial plate* (*r*); the arms end abruptly at the margin of the disc.

Ophioderma (fig. 18 *A*). Arms long, round, smooth; the lateral plates provided with short spines or papillæ. Four genital slits in each area, two near the border of the disc, two near the mouth arranged radially. Buccal plates undivided. Dorsal surface of the disc finely granulated. Lias to present day.

Distribution of the Ophiuroidea.

The majority of the Ophiuroids at the present day occur in shallow water, more than half of the known species being found above a depth of 30 fathoms, and most of these not extending lower. Other forms occur at greater depths, as many as 69 species being found below 1000 fathoms. Ophiuroids are rare as fossils, the earliest form occurs in the Bala Beds, and belongs to the genus *Protaster*, this ranges on to the Silurian, where *Eucladia* and other forms appear. In the Mesozoic we get *Ophioderma*, *Ophiolepis*, and *Geoconia*. All the Eocene genera are still living.

CLASS. ECHINOIDEA.

The Echinoids or sea-urchins have usually a globular, heart-shaped, or discoidal body. The soft parts are enclosed in a shell or test, which is formed in the mesoderm and is covered by a thin ectoderm. This test consists of numerous calcareous plates, which in the majority of cases, are immoveably united. There is nothing corresponding to the ambulacral groove of the star-fish, the water-vascular system being internal, as a result the tube-feet in order to reach the exterior, must pierce the plates of the test. The mouth is always on the inferior surface and often central, but when excentral it is placed anteriorly. The anus is either at the summit of the test or posterior to it, somewhere along a line drawn from the summit to the mouth. In the test we may distinguish two parts, a small patch of plates placed at the summit, known as the *apical disc*, and the remainder of the test termed the *corona*. The apical disc represents the whole of the dorsal surface of the starfish, and the corona the ambulacral surface.

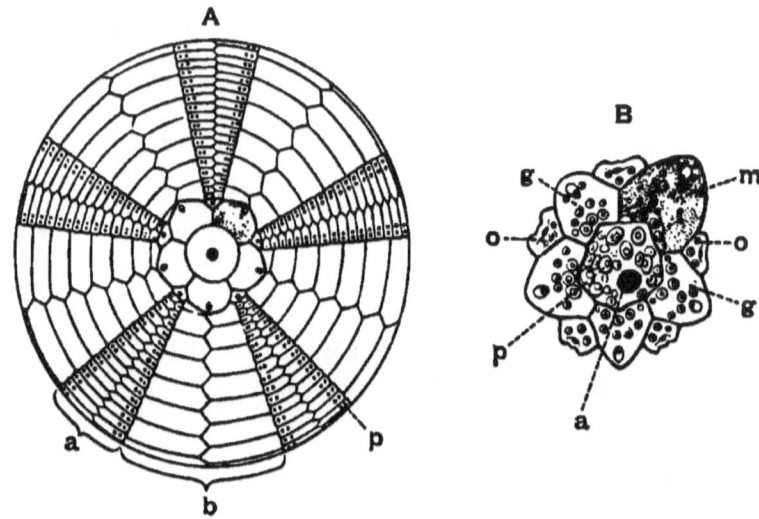

FIG. 19. *A*. Diagram of the upper surface of a regular echinoid, with the tubercles and spines omitted. *a*, ambulacral areas; *b*, interambulacral areas; *p*, pores in the ambulacral plates. *B*. Apical disc of *Echinus esculentus*, Recent; *a*, anus; *p*, periproct; *g*, genital plates, each with a pore; *m*, madreporic plate; *o*, ocular plates, each with a pore.

In a typical regular echinoid (*e.g. Echinus*) the anus is placed within the apical disc (fig. 19), which then consists of the following parts. At or near the centre is the anus (*a*), this is surrounded by a membrane covered with scaly plates and known as the *periproct* (*p*). The periproct is encircled by a ring formed of ten plates, five called *genital* (*g*) and five *ocular* (*o*). The genital plates form the inner part of the ring, they are often more or less hexagonal in outline, and are provided with a pore which serves as the opening for the genital ducts. In some cases one or more of the plates is imperforate, and one has a porous structure serving as the madreporic plate (*m*). Outside the genital plates and alternating with them come the ocular plates, these are smaller than the genital and usually triangular or pentagonal and they each have a perforation for the eye-spot. In the irregular echinoids, the anus is not placed within the apical disc, which then becomes more compact. In some forms it is considerably elongated, as in *Collyrites*, in which two of the ocular plates are placed some distance posterior to the other portion of the disc.

The corona consists of twenty rows of plates, each row extending from the apical disc to the mouth. The plates are of two kinds, *ambulacral* (fig. 19 *A, a*) and *interambulacral* (*b*) and they are arranged in pairs, there being five double rows of ambulacrals separated by five double rows of interambulacrals, each double row being termed an *area*. The former end against the ocular plates, the latter against the genital, and in each case fresh plates are developed next the apical disc. In each area the plates alternate on either side, and since their inner ends are triangular, the line between the two rows is zig-zag. The ambulacral plates are smaller and more numerous than the interambulacral, and they are perforated by pores (*p*) for the passage of the tube feet to the exterior, a radial water-vessel being placed under each ambulacral area. The pores may be round or elongated and they are situated in the outer portion of the plates and are almost always in pairs, sometimes there is one pair on each plate, sometimes more. When there is one pair, the pores are said to be *unigeminal*, two pairs *bigeminal*, three pairs *trigeminal*. In the two latter cases the pairs are arranged obliquely. Sometimes the pores in each pair are united by a groove, they are then termed *conjugate*. In some

sea-urchins the rows of pores extend from the apical
disc to the mouth without any important alteration, the
ambulacral areas are then said to be *simple* (*e.g. Cidaris*).
In others the rows of pores diverge soon after leaving
the apical disc, and then come together again, so as to
form a rosette on the upper surface of the corona, the
pores only being irregularly developed on the lower, the
ambulacral areas are then termed *petaloid* (*e.g. Scutella*),
and when the rows of pores diverge but do not come in
contact at their lower ends they are *sub-petaloid* (*e.g.
Echinobrissus*). The plates of both the ambulacral and
interambulacral areas are often provided with rounded
elevations known as *tubercles* and *granules.* The tubercles
are of various sizes, the largest being the primary. In

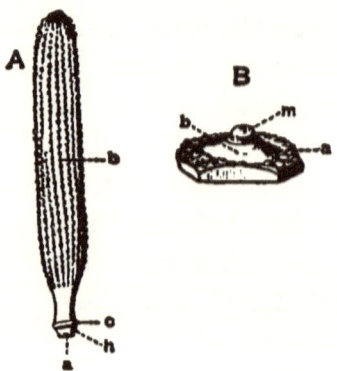

Fig. 20.   *A.*   Spine of *Cidaris florigemma*, from the Corallian Rocks.
a, acetabulum ; *h*, head ; *c*, collar ; *b*, body or stem.   *B.*   Ambulacral plate of *Cidaris* (recent) with a large primary tubercle and
secondary tubercles. In the primary tubercle, *m*, mamelon ; *b*, boss ;
a, areola.

these the following parts may be distinguished; at the
summit there is a spheroidal piece, which is sometimes
perforated, this is the *mamelon* (fig. 20 *B, m*).   The
mamelon rests on a short pillar termed the boss (*b*), the

upper margin of which is sometimes smooth, sometimes crenulated. The base of the boss is frequently surrounded by a smooth excavated space known as the *areola* (*a*). The granules are smaller than the tubercles.

Attached to the tubercles are the *spines*, these are of different sizes and shapes in different genera and species and even in the same individual, being needle-like, rod-like, or flask-shaped. At the end of the spine where it articulates with the mamelon there is a rounded cavity, the *acetabulum* (fig. 20 *A*, *a*), above this comes the *head* (*h*), this is limited above by a ring or collar (*c*) which may be smooth or crenulate and which serves for the attachment of the muscles that move the spine. Beyond the collar and forming the greater part of the spine is the *stem* or body (*b*), which may be smooth, or ornamented with ridges or rows of spiny processes. Pedicellariæ also occur. On the surface of some sea-urchins, there are nearly smooth bands covered with very minute tubercles, bearing slender modified spines, these bands are termed *fascioles*, sometimes they form a ring beneath the anus (*e.g.* *Micraster*) when they are said to be *sub-anal*, at other times they encircle the rosette formed by the petaloid ambulacra (*e.g. Hemiaster*) and are said to be *peri-petalous*.

The mouth is placed in the centre of a membrane, which is covered with plates or granules, and is known as the *peristome.* Consequently the aperture in the corona of fossil specimens does not represent the mouth but the peristome. The shape of the peristome varies in different forms, it may be circular, oval, pentagonal, or decagonal. In some genera there is at the commencement of the alimentary canal, a complicated calcareous apparatus, which functions in mastication; this is connected with arches, known as *auricles*, placed over the ambulacra just within the peristome.

In the irregular echinoids there is a well-marked bilateral symmetry; a plane which passes through the anus (which is posterior), the apical disc, and the mouth, will divide the body into two similar parts. The ambulacra are often markedly dissimilar, the anterior one differing from the others which are paired. The bilaterality is quite inconspicuous in the regular sea-urchins, but the plane of symmetry may be found by means of the madreporic plate, which is always placed at the upper end of the right anterior interambulacral area.

ORDER. PALÆECHINOIDEA.

The number of rows of plates forming the test varies. In each interambulacral area there is one, or more than two; in each ambulacral two or many. The plates frequently overlap, giving the test a certain amount of flexibility. All the genera, except *Echinocystites*, are regular. In the genital plates there are from three to five pores, in the oculars two or none. Jaws are present.

Palæechinus. Test spheroidal, rigid. Apical disc central, enclosing the anus. Five large genital plates, each with three perforations, one may have one only. Ocular plates, five, small, each with two perforations. Ambulacral areas narrow, with two rows of plates, pores unigeminal. Interambulacral areas wide, with four to eight rows of plates at the equator, fewer towards the poles, plates hexagonal, except those next the ambulacral area, which are pentagonal; surface of plates covered with granules. Spines small. Upper Silurian to Carboniferous Limestone.

The test is always formed of twenty rows of plates, two in each area. The plates very rarely overlap. Regular and irregular forms occur. There is usually one pore only in each genital and ocular plate. Jaws are present in some forms, absent in others.

(a) Regular Euechinoids.

The test is radially symmetrical and generally spheroidal. The apical disc encloses the anus. The mouth is central. The ambulacral areas are simple. Jaws present.

Cidaris. Test spheroidal, the summit and base equally flattened. Apical disc very large, rarely preserved fossil, ocular plates large. Ambulacral areas narrow, undulating, pores unigeminal, between the rows of pores are vertical rows of small tubercles and granules. Interambulacral areas wide, plates few, each with a primary tubercle which is generally perforated, and may be crenulated or smooth; areola large, surrounded by secondary tubercles, beyond which are granules. Peristome rounded. Spines large, of various forms, generally ornamented with rows of granules. Lias to present day.

Peltastes. Test circular in outline, somewhat depressed. Apical disc very large, prominent, containing one extra plate, the sur-anal, placed in front of the periproct; the madreporic plate has an oblique fissure. Ambulacral areas narrow, straight or slightly flexuous, with small tubercles; pores unigeminal except near the mouth. Interambulacral areas wide, with large primary tubercles, which are imperforate, and may be crenulate. Peristome slightly notched. Lower Greensand to Gault.

Hemicidaris. Test spheroidal, inferior surface flattened. Apical disc small. Ambulacral areas narrow, slightly flexuous, with two rows of tubercles on the under surface, which pass into granules on the upper. Pores unigeminal, but bigeminal or trigeminal near the mouth. Interambulacral areas broad; plates large and few, each with a large perforated and crenulated tubercle, and also smaller tubercles and granules. Spines cylindrical, long. Peristome large, decagonal. Inferior Oolite to Purbeck Beds.

(b) Irregular Euechinoids.

The test is bilaterally symmetrical. The anus is placed outside the apical disc. The mouth is central or excentral. Ambulacra simple or petaloid. Jaws may be present or absent.

Echinoconus (= Galerites). Test conical, or almost hemispherical, inferior surface flat, outline pentagonal or oval. Apical disc small, with four genital plates. Ambulacral areas, narrow, straight, simple; pores bigeminal, trigeminal near the mouth. Interambulacral areas with broad plates, tubercles very small, perforated and crenulated. Peristome small, central, decagonal. Jaws absent. Periproct marginal or submarginal. Upper Greensand to Upper Chalk.

Holectypus. Test hemispherical, depressed, base excavated. Apical disc small. Ambulacral areas narrow, straight, simple; pores unigeminal, tubercles small. Interambulacral areas with rather large plates, tubercles small. Peristome central, decagonal. Jaws present.

Periproct large, placed between the peristome and the posterior margin of the test. Inferior Oolite to Corallian.

Pygaster. Test large, depressed, outline pentagonal or circular, base concave. Apical disc small, madreporic plate large. Ambulacral areas straight, simple; pores unigeminal; tubercles in vertical rows. Interambulacral areas wide, tubercles perforate, crenulate or not. Peristome central, large, decagonal. Jaws present. Periproct very large, placed behind the apical disc. Inferior Oolite to Cretaceous.

Echinobrissus (= *Nucleolites*). Test depressed; outline oval or quadrilateral, rounded anteriorly, truncated and broadest posteriorly; inferior surface concave. Apical disc compact, four perforate genital plates, and one imperforate. Ambulacral areas subpetaloid, pores unigeminal, the outer pore elongated. Interambulacral plates wide, tubercles small. Peristome oval or pentagonal, excentric, a little anterior. Jaws absent. Periproct placed in a sulcus on the dorsal surface. Inferior Oolite to Recent.

Echinocorys (= *Ananchytes*). Test very convex above, inferior surface flattened, outline oval. Apical disc a little elongated; the four genital plates perforated, the two anterior separated from the two posterior by two ocular plates. Ambulacral areas simple, pores unigeminal. Interambulacral plates large, tubercles small. Peristome bilabiate, placed anteriorly. Jaws absent. Periproct oval, inframarginal. Upper Chalk.

Holaster. Test cordiform, inferior surface more or less flattened, superior surface with a broad shallow groove anteriorly. Apical disc elongate, the two pairs of genital plates separated by the two oculars. Ambulacral areas large, simple; pores unigeminal, round or elongate, the anterior ambulacrum in the groove. Interambulacral areas with small tubercles and granules. Peristome excentric and elliptical. Jaws absent. Periproct supramarginal. Upper Greensand and Lower Chalk; also Tertiary in Australia.

Micraster. Test cordiform or oval. Apical disc small, excentric. Ambulacral areas subpetaloid, placed in sunken areas, the subpetaloid part of the two anterior-lateral longer than the two posterior-lateral; pores unigeminal. The anterior unpaired ambulacrum in a deep groove, pores round. Interambulacral areas with large plates; tubercles small, perforate and crenulate. Subanal fasciole. Peristome excentral, near the anterior border, with a projecting lip. Jaws present. Periproct supramarginal. Middle and Upper Chalk; also Tertiary in Australia.

Distribution of the Echinoidea.

Some Echinoids live at great depths in the ocean, one species being found at 2900 fathoms, but by far the larger number occur near the coasts in shallow water. They are most abundant where the sea-bottom is rocky, sandy, or calcareous, and less common where it is muddy; consequently fossil forms are rare in clayey strata. Those found in deep water have a much wider range in space than those found in shallow water, and many of the genera, especially those with a considerable range in depth, have also a long range in time, some extending back to the Cretaceous period and even further.

There is a marked contrast in the distribution of the two orders of the Echinoidea. The Palæechinoids are found almost exclusively in the Palæozoic, only one genus occurring in the Neozoic, viz. *Anaulocidaris* from the Trias. The Euechinoids are nearly confined to the Neozoic; *Eocidaris* from the Permian, being the only genus found in the Palæozoic.

The earliest echinoid is the genus *Bothriocidaris* from the Ordovician rocks of Esthonia in Russia. In the Silurian we get *Palæechinus* and *Echinocystites*; in the Devonian, *Lepidocentrus*; in the Carboniferous, *Palæechinus*, *Melonites*, and *Archæocidaris*. In the Jurassic the echinoids are much more numerous, relatively to the other groups of animals, than in the earlier formations, they are rare in the Lias and the other clayey divisions, but very abundant in the calcareous beds, especially in the Inferior Oolite and Coral Rag. The genera which are best represented in the Jurassic are, of the regular group, *Cidaris*, *Hemicidaris*, *Acrosalenia*, *Pseudodiadema*, and *Stomechinus*; of the irregular group, *Collyrites*, *Echinobrissus*, *Holectypus*, and *Pygaster*. In the Cretaceous the echinoids are even more abundant than in the Jurassic; many of the genera found in the Lower Cretaceous occur also in the Upper Jurassic. The most important genera are, (1) regular, *Cidaris*, *Pseudodiadema*, *Cyphosoma*, *Peltastes*, *Salenia*, (2) irregular, *Discoidea*, *Echinoconus* (= *Galerites*), *Hemiaster*, *Micraster*, *Cardiaster*, *Holaster*, *Echinocorys* (= *Ananchytes*). Between the Cretaceous and the Eocene there is an enormous break in the succession of the echinoids, not a single species being common to the two systems, and the genera also are mostly different. This change is due in part to the great difference in the conditions under which the deposits were formed, the Chalk being a comparatively deep water formation, and the Eocene beds, shallow water; but the

Eocene forms differ much more from those of the Upper Chalk than they do from those of the Chalk Marl, the latter being a shallower water deposit. Throughout the English Tertiaries the echinoids are much rarer than in the Cretaceous; thus in the Cretaceous there are thirty genera, in the Eocene seven, in the Pliocene eleven. In the Eocene this can be accounted for largely by the fact that the sea-bottom was for the most part muddy; in the Pliocene by the lower temperature of the ocean. The London Clay echinoids belong to tropical or sub-tropical genera. The commonest Eocene forms are *Hemiaster* and *Schizaster*. The Pliocene forms present a considerable affinity to those now living in the West Indian seas, indicating the existence of shallow water between Europe and America in which migration could take place. The most important genera in the Pliocene are *Echinus, Echinocyamus, Spatangus,* and *Temnechinus.*

CLASS. HOLOTHUROIDEA.

This includes the sea-cucumbers. They possess an elongated cylindrical body provided with a circle of tentacles around the mouth connected with the water-vascular ring; from the radial vessels tube-feet are given off, except in the genus *Synapta.* The integument is leathery, and the calcareous skeleton is very poorly developed, consisting of minute isolated pieces of various shapes, such as spicules, anchors, and wheels. At the present day the Holothurians are widely distributed, but owing to the nature of their hard parts, they are rarely found fossil. The earliest forms occur in the Carboniferous rocks of Scotland, and a few have also been recorded from the Jurassic and later formations.

CLASS. CRINOIDEA.

The Crinoidea includes the sea-lilies or feather-stars. Unlike the star-fishes and sea-urchins, these have the oral surface directed upwards and the dorsal surface downwards. In very many forms the animal is fixed by means of a stem given off from the dorsal surface, but in others this is only found in the young state, the adult form being free. The skeleton consists of a *stem*, and of a cup or *calyx* formed of calcareous plates closely united and arranged in a regular manner; from the margin of this, branches or *arms* are given off.

The soft parts consist of a central mass known as the *disc*, placed in the calyx, and of *arms* which come off from the disc; these may be five in number or there may be as many as two hundred produced by repeated branching. The whole of the alimentary canal is situated within the disc, the mouth and anus being on the upper surface. On each side of the arms there is a row of small appendages, which alternate; these are the *pinnules*. On the upper surface of each pinnule and of each arm there is a groove, which is continued on to the disc, where they unite, ultimately forming five main channels which meet in the mouth, this being usually central. The grooves are lined with cilia, by the movements of which food particles are conveyed to the mouth. The anus is placed in one of the spaces between the main channels on the disc, usually at the end of a tubular process. In some forms the surface of the disc is covered with small calcareous plates, in others there are only isolated granules. Immediately under the groove of each arm there is a radial nerve cord, these like the grooves unite to form larger trunks at the margin of the disc and ultimately join as a ring round the mouth.

The blood-vascular system has a similar distribution, the radial vessels being immediately under the nerve cord; but there is in addition to this a bundle of blood vessels situated in the axis of the disc and known as the central plexus, this gives off branches to the oral ring and elsewhere; dorsally it is connected with what is known as the *chambered organ*, which is placed in the centro-dorsal plate, or sometimes between the basal plates of the calyx. In addition to the nervous system already mentioned, there is another placed dorsally, consisting of a fibrous sheath surrounding the chambered organ, and of cords given off from it, which pass through canals in the plates of the calyx to the arms and pinnules. The fibrous sheath is also prolonged into the stem when present and contains in its centre a vessel from the chambered organ. The water-vascular system consists of radial vessels placed dorsally to the blood vessels and of a ring round the mouth; from the latter, tubes hang down and open into the body-cavity, which communicates with the water of the exterior by means of pores. In connection with the radial vessels are tubular processes, the tentacles, which form a row on each side of the food-grooves, and correspond with the tube feet of the star-fish, but do not function in locomotion.

We come now to the structure of the skeleton. In the majority of crinoids a stem is present, this is more or less flexible and is sometimes several feet in length. It is formed of a number of circular or pentagonal (occasionally elliptical) plates, articulated by their broad surfaces. Each plate is pierced in the centre by a canal which is circular or pentagonal and contains a prolongation of the chambered organ and its fibrous sheath. The articular faces of the plates are often provided with radiating striæ or with ridges in the form of a rosette. From the stem small branches known as *cirri* are sometimes given off, these have a structure similar to that of the stem and are also pierced by a central canal. The inferior part of the stem often expands and branches in a root-like manner, and serves to fix the animal. Sometimes the plates near the top of the stem become very much larger than the others.

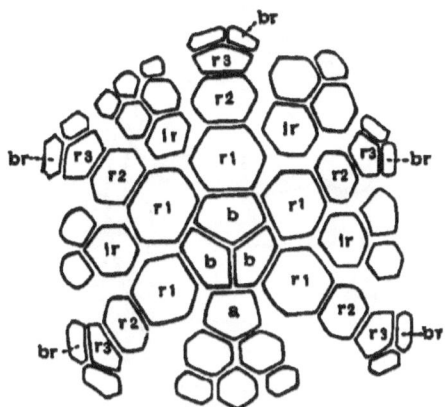

Fig. 21. Diagram of the plates of *Actinocrinus triacontadactylus*, Carboniferous Limestone. *b*, basal plates; *r*1, first cycle of radials; *r*2, *r*3, second and third cycles of radials; *br*, brachial plates; *ir*, interradials; *a*, anal inter-radial.

Resting on the topmost joint of the stem is the calyx (figs. 21, 22), this consists at its base of a cycle of five (sometimes fewer) plates, known as the *basals* (*b*), occasionally these are not visible, being covered by the radials. In some forms there is below the basals and alternating with them another cycle of plates, termed the *underbasals*, and the base is then said to be *dicyclic*; when basals only are present, it is *monocyclic*. Above the basals and alternating with them, comes a cycle of five *radial* plates (*r*1); often there are two or three cycles of radials (*r*2, *r*3), in

which case the plates are placed vertically above one
another. In some genera there are between the rows of
radials, other smaller plates, the *inter-radials* (fig. 21, *ir*);
and in the inter-radius which leads up to the anus there
is an extra series of plates, the *anal inter-radials* (fig. 21, *a*).
From the highest row of radials the arms arise; these are
generally movable, they have a groove on the upper
surface, and are formed either of a single row of plates,

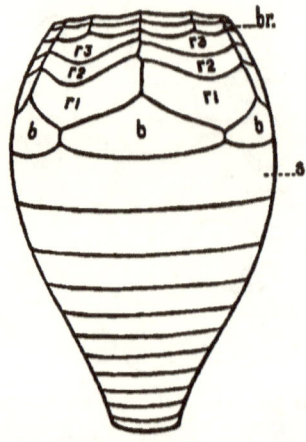

Fig. 22. *Apiocrinus parkinsoni*, from the Bradford Clay. *s*, topmost
plate of the stem; *b*, basal plates; *r* 1, *r* 2, *r* 3, first, second and
third cycles of radial plates; *br*, brachial plates. (Three-quarters
natural size.)

the *brachials* (*br*), or of a double row, in which case the
plates alternate. The pinnules also consist of calcareous
plates, with an arrangement similar to those of the arms.
It has already been stated that the upper surface of
the disc is sometimes furnished with small plates, but
these are seldom preserved fossil; they do not however cover over the food grooves or mouth, which are
still visible externally. But in most of the Palæozoic
crinoids there is also a more or less complete roof of

plates over the upper surface of the calyx, hiding the grooves and the mouth. This roof is in some genera provided with a conical process, the *anal proboscis*, at the summit of which is the anus. In these forms, as well as in a few others, the grooves in the arms are also roofed over with plates.

There are two orders, (1) Palæocrinoidea, (2) Neocrinoidea.

ORDER. PALÆOCRINOIDEA.

The calyx is large and the arms small, relatively. Inter-radials are generally present. On the ventral surface there is a roof of plates hiding the food grooves and the mouth.

Actinocrinus. Calyx variable in form, pear-shaped, ovoid, or more or less spherical; monocyclic. Basals three, forming a hexagon. Three cycles of radials firmly united, the first high, the third bearing the double series of brachials. Inter-radials present and also the anal inter-radial, the first plate of the latter resting on the basals. The ventral roof formed of thick, tubercled, hexagonal plates; anal proboscis sometimes present. Arms ten to thirty, with two rows of plates. Stem circular, canal pentagonal. Silurian to Carboniferous Limestone.

Crotalocrinus. Dicyclic. Underbasals five, small, pentagonal. Basals very large. One cycle of radials, very large. Inter-radials absent, except a small anal inter-radial. Arms five, with a single row of plates; dichotomous, the branches uniting so as to form lamellar expansions or networks, which are enrolled. Ventral roof formed of small plates; in the centre five large oral plates. Anal proboscis marginal. Stem thick, circular; canal pentagonal; roots thick. Wenlock Limestone.

ORDER. NEOCRINOIDEA.

The calyx is small and the arms large, relatively. Usually monocyclic, basals five. Inter-radials are seldom present, there is no anal inter-radial. The radials of the higher cycles are generally movable. There is no ventral roof of plates.

Apiocrinus. Calyx pear-shaped. Basals five, thick. Three cycles of low radials, excavated on their upper surfaces, all the plates firmly united. Arms ten, bifurcating once or twice, formed of a single row of plates. Stem long, cylindrical, base expanded; the articular surfaces of the plates radiately striated. The plates of the upper part of the stem are in contact at the periphery only, leaving a space between each plate. The upper part of the stem expands and passes gradually into the calyx, the upper surface of the last plate is provided with five radiating ridges between which the basals lie. Lias to Lower Cretaceous.

Marsupites. Calyx large, globular, plates large and thin. Dicyclic. Stem absent. Base formed of a large central pentagonal plate, the centro-dorsal plate. Under-basals five, pentagonal. Basals five, hexagonal. Radials five, pentagonal. Arms bifurcating, formed of a single row of plates. Ventral surface of calyx covered with small plates. Anus sub-central. Upper Chalk.

Distribution of the Crinoidea.

In comparison with its abundance in former times the class Crinoidea is but poorly represented at the present day. The most important family is the Comatulidæ (*e.g.*

Antedon, Actinometra), this has a wide range in space and depth, the genus *Antedon* being found from the shore down to 2900 fathoms. The stalked crinoids are much less abundant than the Comatulidæ, and are found mainly at great depths. In most cases the species of crinoids have only a limited distribution in space.

The Palæocrinoids are found only in the Palæozoic formations, the Neocrinoids only in the Neozoic and at the present day. In the Palæozoic the crinoids are much more numerous than the other Echinoderms, their remains in some cases forming the main part of some limestone beds (crinoidal limestone), as for instance in the Carboniferous. None of the other classes are ever sufficiently abundant to be of importance as rock-builders.

The crinoids occur first in the Tremadoc Beds; in the Upper Ordovician *Glyptocrinus* and a few others have been found. In the Silurian they become very much more abundant, attaining their maximum development, the most important genera being *Cyathocrinus, Ichthyocrinus*, and *Crotalocrinus*. In the Devonian, *Cyathocrinus, Actinocrinus* and others are common; in the Carboniferous, *Actinocrinus, Poteriocrinus*, and *Platycrinus*. Crinoids are rare in the Permian. In the Trias we meet with a new phase in their development, the Palæocrinoids being replaced by the Neocrinoids; the characteristic form is *Encrinus*. In the Jurassic we get *Antedon, Pentacrinus, Extracrinus, Apiocrinus*, and *Millericrinus*, the first two living on to the present day. In the Cretaceous the chief forms are *Marsupites* and *Bourgueticrinus*. In the Cainozoic, crinoids are very rare.

CLASS. CYSTIDEA.

The Cystideans in general appearance resemble the crinoids. They consist of a calyx and generally a stem, the latter as a rule being very sho·ˑ The calyx is in most cases more or less spherical or ovate, with a depression at its base for the articulation of the stem. It is formed of plates which vary in number from thirteen to a hundred or more, these are not arranged in a regular manner as they are in crinoids, and at best the calyx shows but little radial symmetry. Arms are present, and vary from three to five in number, but they are very feebly developed or sometimes quite rudimentary; in some forms they are free, but in other cases fused to the calyx. Or they may be represented merely by scattered filaments, articulated to the calyx by sockets on some of the plates. At the summit of the calyx (fig. 23 *A*) either at or near the centre, there is an aperture (*a*) from which

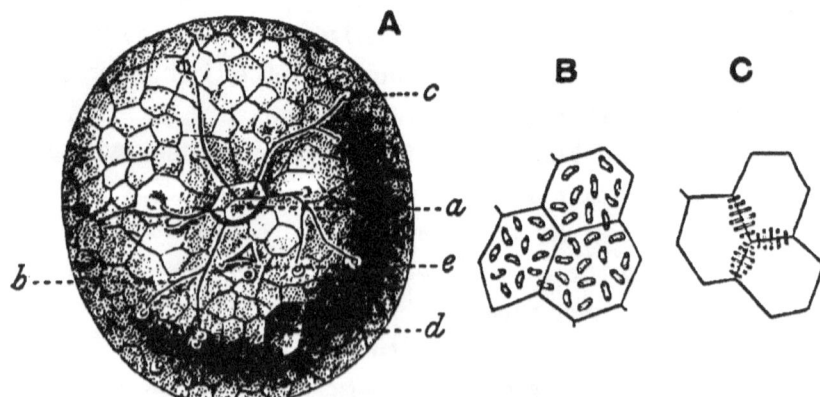

Fig. 23. *A, Glyptosphærites leuchtenbergi,* from the Ordovician of Russia. *a*, mouth covered by oral plates; *b*, ambulacral grooves; *c*, socket for the armlet; *d*, anus; *e*, ovarian aperture, (after Volborth). *B*, a few plates of the same enlarged, showing double pores. *C*, Plates of *Echinosphærites*, with pore-rhombs.

radiate food-grooves (*b*), this may therefore be regarded as the mouth. On the upper surface also there is another opening regarded as the anus (*d*), it is covered with plates which form a cone. In some forms, near the mouth there is a smaller aperture, which may be a genital pore (*e*). A characteristic feature of the plates of the calyx is the presence of pores which pass right through the plates. In a few forms they are absent. They may either be arranged in pairs (fig. 23 *B*) placed in oval depressions or on elevations; in other cases they form what are known as *pore-rhombs* (fig. 23 *C*), these consist of rhombic figures, the outline of which is formed by the pores, half the rhomb being on one plate, and half on the adjoining, and the pores of the two plates are united by grooves. The number of these pore-rhombs varies considerably in different genera.

The cystideans then resemble the crinoids in the general form of the calyx and stem, in the position of the mouth and anus, and in the possession of food-grooves and arms. But they differ in having the arms feebly developed, in the irregular arrangement of the plates and in the presence of pores.

Lepadocrinus (= *Pseudocrinites*). Calyx ovate, rhombic in outline, with rounded edges; at the base is a cycle of four plates followed by three cycles of five plates each. Mouth central. Two to four straight food-grooves, extending to about the middle of the calyx, and with projecting edges. Anal aperture near the summit, covered with six triangular plates. Three pore-rhombs, one near the base, two on the upper surface of the calyx. Stem thick, circular, rather long, becoming thinner towards the lower extremity. Silurian.

Distribution of the Cystidea.

The Cystideans are comparatively rare fossils, they range from the Menevian Beds to the Carboniferous Limestone, and attain their maximum development in the Upper Ordovician. In the Menevian we get *Protocystites*; this also occurs in the Tremadoc, and with it *Macrocystella*. In the Upper Ordovician we get amongst others, *Echinosphærites*, *Ateleocystites*, and *Pleurocystites*; in the Silurian *Lepadocrinus* and *Ateleocystites*. In the Devonian there are fewer, and in the Carboniferous only one or two genera are known.

CLASS. BLASTOIDEA.

In the Blastoids, as in the cystideans and many of the crinoids, the body consists of a stem and calyx, but the former is rarely found attached. The calyx may be spherical, oval, pear-shaped, or bud-like; it is formed chiefly of thirteen plates, arranged in a regular manner. True arms are not present.

In a typical form (*Pentremites*) the calyx (fig. 24) has

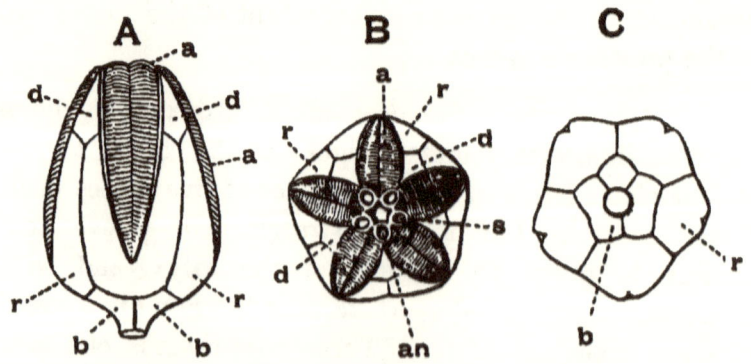

Fig. 24. *Pentremites godoni*, Carboniferous. *A*, lateral; *B*, upper surface; *C*, under surface. *a*, ambulacral areas; *b*, basal plates; *r*, radials; *d*, deltoids; *s*, spiracles around the mouth; *an*, anus. (Twice natural size.)

the following structure.   The dorsal part is formed of a cycle of three plates—the *basals* (*b*), two of which are alike, and the third smaller.   Above the basals, comes a cycle of five *radial plates* (*r*), these are larger than the basals and form the main part of the calyx.   At the upper end of each there is a deep incision, which serves for the reception of the ambulacral area (*a*).   Above the radials and alternating with them comes a cycle of smaller plates —the *deltoids* (*d*).   The mouth is placed at the summit of the calyx, in the centre, and around it are five other apertures termed *spiracles* (*s*), one of which is larger than the others and includes the anus (*an*).   From the summit the five ambulacral areas (*a*) radiate towards the dorsal surface, they are bordered partly by the deltoids but mainly by the radials.   Each ambulacral area (fig. 25)

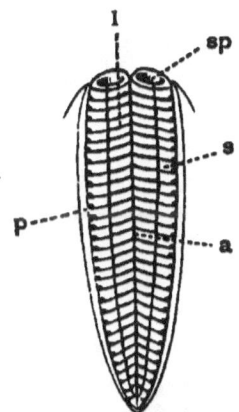

FIG. 25. Ambulacral area of *Pentremites godoni*, Carboniferous. *l*, lancet plate; *s*, side plate; *p*, pore; *a*, ambulacral groove; *sp*, spiracle. (Three times natural size.)

consists of the following plates.   Occupying the middle is a long pointed plate (*l*), the *lancet plate*, which is traversed by a longitudinal canal, in which the radial vessel of the water-vascular system was placed. On each side of the lancet plate is a row of small plates, the *side plates* (*s*). Extending down the middle of each ambulacral area is a groove, the *ambulacral groove* (*a*); this in some specimens is covered over by a roof of small calcareous plates. At right angles to the ambulacral groove, on each side of it, are numerous transverse grooves. Along the outer margin of the side plates there is a row of pores, the *marginal pores* (*p*), formed by spaces between adjoining plates. When

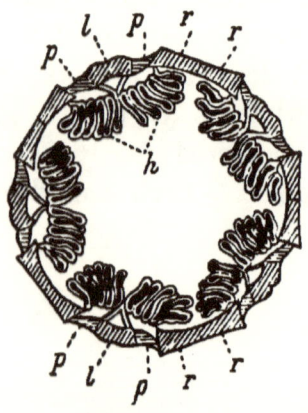

Fig. 26. *Pentremites sulcatus*, Carboniferous. Horizontal section of the calyx. *l*, lancet plate; *p*, side plates; *r*, radial plates; *hy*, hydrospires. (After Zittel.)

the lancet plate and the side plates are removed from an ambulacral area, we find underneath, in the middle line, an elongated trough-like plate, known as the *under lancet plate*. At the sides of this may be seen the edges of the *hydrospire*. The latter consists (fig. 26 *h*) of a flattened and folded calcareous tube, communicating with the exterior by means of the marginal pores, and also ventrally by the spiracles. A current of water probably passed in through the former openings and out by the latter. In well preserved specimens, the mouth, as in many crinoids, is not visible externally, but is covered over by a roof of small plates. Arms are represented by pinnules only, which are given off from the margins of the ambulacral areas.

The other blastoids differ from the one described mainly in the relative sizes of the plates, in the distance which the ambulacra go towards the base, and in the amount of folding of the hydrospires.

Granatocrinus. Calyx elliptical, oval, or more or less spherical, in section pentagonal or round. Basals small, not seen in a side view. Radials of variable size. Deltoids generally rhombic, large in some species, small in others. Ambulacra narrow, straight. Lancet-plate narrow. Hydrospires simple, often not folded, dilated at the end. Spiracles round or oval, piercing the apices of the deltoids, the posterior one including the anus. Carboniferous Limestone.

Distribution of the Blastoidea.

In England the Blastoids range from the Devonian to the Carboniferous, being most abundant in the latter. But in North America they are also found in the Silurian. The English Devonian forms are rare and but little known. In the Carboniferous Limestone the blastoids attain their maximum, ten genera are represented, the most important being *Granatocrinus* and *Codaster*. *Pentremites* does not occur in Britain.

SUB-KINGDOM V. VERMES.

Classes.	*Orders.*
1. Platyhelminthes.	
2. Nemathelminthes.	
3. Rotifera.	

4. Annelida .... { 1. Chætopoda .... { 1. Polychæta.
2. Oligochæta.
2. Gephyrea.
3. Hirudinea.

THE worms include a large number of animals which differ considerably in their plan of organisation and thus form a very artificial group. The body is bilaterally symmetrical and has generally an elongated form. In some it is unsegmented, in others it is divided into somites. Lateral appendages are often present, but they differ from those of the Arthropods in being unsegmented. A nervous system and generally a blood vascular system and alimentary canal are present. A large number possess no skeleton and consequently the palæontological history of the sub-kingdom is extremely imperfect.

The worms may be divided into four classes, (1) Platyhelminthes, (2) Nemathelminthes, (3) Rotifera, (4) Annelida. The Platyhelminthes and Rotifera are unknown in the fossil state, the former includes the liver-fluke, tape-worms etc. (*e.g. Distomum, Tænia, Planaria*), the latter the wheel-animalcules. The Nemathelminthes includes the thread-worms (*e.g. Ascaris*), only two or three forms are found fossil.

CLASS. ANNELIDA.

The body is segmented and generally the segments are similar. There is a ventral nerve cord and a ring round the œsophagus. A vascular system is generally present.

There are three orders (1) Chætopoda, (2) Gephyrea, (3) Hirudinea.

The Gephyrea includes *Sipunculus, Echiurus*, etc.; the Hirudinea includes the leeches. Both these orders are represented in the fossil condition by doubtful examples only.

ORDER. CHÆTOPODA.

The Chætopoda possess bristle-like appendages termed setæ. There are two sub-orders (1) Oligochæta, (2) Polychæta. The Oligochæta is unknown in the fossil state, it includes the common earth-worm *Lumbricus*.

SUB-ORDER. POLYCHÆTA.

The members of this sub-order are nearly all marine, they are characterised by the possession of numerous setæ which are placed on special processes termed *parapodia*. Tentacles are present on the head. Many forms live in tubes, which may consist of carbonate of lime, of chitinous material, or of grains of sand cemented together by a secretion. On account of the possession of this tube the polychætous annelids are often found fossil. Other forms, which do not live in tubes, are provided with minute chitinous jaws, and in some formations, especially the Ordovician and Silurian, these are abundantly preserved.

Serpula. Tube calcareous, long, round, angular or flattened; straight, curved irregularly, or sometimes spiral, closed at one end; generally attached to some foreign object by a portion of its surface. Carboniferous to present day.

Spirorbis. Tube calcareous, small, spiral, attached by one side. The spiral either left-handed or right-handed, the last whorl often produced into a free tube. Ordovician to the present day.

Distribution of the Vermes.

Practically all the worms found fossil belong to the Polychæta, the earliest examples occurring in the Cambrian beds. In addition to the worm-tubes and jaws, we find in the rocks numerous trails and burrows which are regarded as having been formed by worms, but it is impossible to speak definitely of the affinities of these forms. And in many cases it is quite probable that the tracks may have been made by other animals such as crustaceans and gasteropods.

SUB-KINGDOM VI. MOLLUSCOIDEA.

Classes.	Sub-Classes.	Orders.	Sub-Orders.
1. Polyzoa.......	1. Ectoprocta.	1. Phylactolæma.	
		2. Gymnolæma.	1. Cyclostomata.
			2. Cheilostomata.
			3. Ctenostomata.
	2. Entoprocta.		
	3. Aspidophora.		

Orders.

2. Brachiopoda. { 1. Inarticulata.
{ 2. Articulata.

WHETHER the two classes Polyzoa and Brachiopoda are very closely related to one another is rather doubtful. They have affinities on the one hand with the worms and on the other with the mollusks. For the present they may be retained as a separate sub-kingdom.

CLASS. POLYZOA.

With the exception of the genus *Loxosoma*, all the Polyzoa are colonial animals, numerous individuals living in association. The colony may be arborescent, laminar, almost massive, or encrusting shells and stones. A dermal skeleton, consisting of calcareous or chitinous material, is usually present. The entire colony is known as the

zoarium, and each individual of the colony as a *polypide*.
The entire skeleton is termed the *cœnœcium*, and the
skeleton of each polypide a *zoœcium*.

The polypide (fig. 27 *A*) has a sac-like form; at the
upper end there is a platform or disc, the *lophophore*, on
which tentacles (*t*) are placed, arranged either in a circle

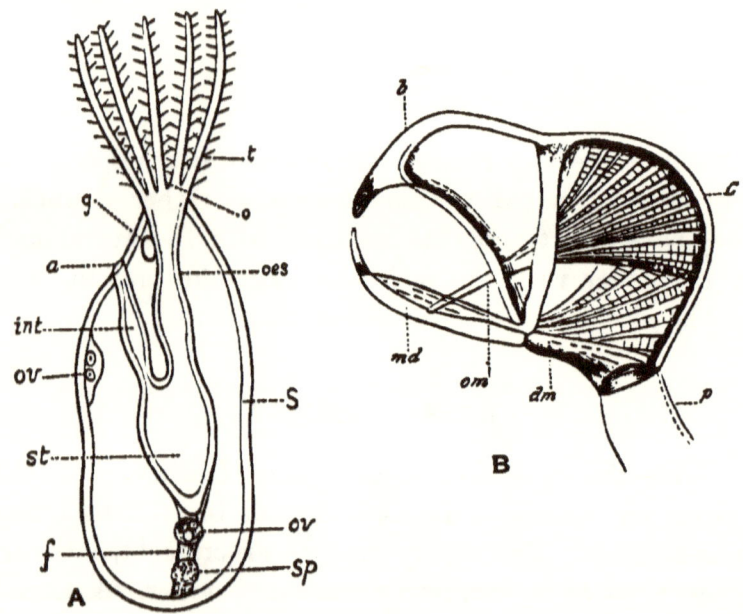

A

B

Fig. 27.   *A*, Diagram of the structure of a single polypide of a
Polyzoan. *s*, body-wall; *t*, tentacles; *o*, mouth; *œs*, œsophagus;
st, stomach; *int*, intestine; *a*, anus; *g*, ganglion; *f*, funiculus;
ov, ovary; *sp*, testis. *B*, Avicularium of *Bugula*, enlarged. *b*, beak;
md, mandible; *C*, chamber; *p*, peduncle; *om*, occlusor muscles;
dm, divaricator muscles. (After Hincks, Brit. Mar. Polyz.)

or in the form of a horse-shoe. The tentacles are not contractile, but they are provided with cilia, which produce
a current of water that conveys food to the central
mouth (*o*). The anal aperture (*a*) is near the mouth,
generally below the lophophore, but in some forms within

the circle of tentacles. On account of this approximation of the mouth and anus the alimentary canal is bent into a U-shape, and in it may be distinguished œsophagus (*œs*), stomach (*st*) and intestine (*int*). Between the alimentary canal and the body wall there is a considerable space, filled with fluid, this is the *body-cavity* or *cœlom*. The nervous system consists of a single ganglion (*g*) placed on the side of the œsophagus facing the intestine. The polyzoan multiplies sexually and by budding; generally the polypide is hermaphrodite, the ovary and testis occurring in the same individual. Blood vessels and excretory organs are absent in almost all forms.

The outer layer of the body wall in the lower part of the polypide generally becomes hardened by calcareous or chitinous matter, and after the death of the animal, this alone remains, constituting the zoœcium. The zoœcium therefore is not distinct from the body wall, but is merely its outer hardened layer. The anterior part of the polypide can be withdrawn by means of longitudinal muscles into the zoœcium, just as the finger of a glove can be pulled into the hand. In some Polyzoa (the Cyclostomata

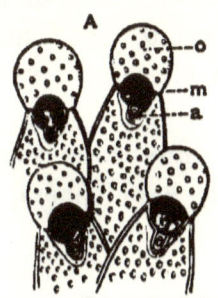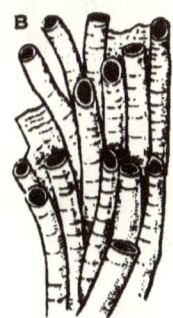

FIG. 28. *A*, Portion of *Smittia landsborovi*, a Cheilostomatous Polyzoan, Recent. *o*, oœcium; *m*, aperture of the cell; *a*, avicularium. *B*, Portion of *Tubulipora fimbria*, a Cyclostomatous Polyzoan, Recent. Enlarged.

fig. 28 *B*) the zoœcium is tube-like, the aperture is at the end and is of the same diameter, or nearly so, as the rest of the tube. In others (the Cheilostomata, fig. 28 *A*) the zoœcium is more or less oval, the aperture (*m*) is contracted and is not terminal, but is situated in front near the anterior end, and is provided with a movable lid or operculum. In many of the Cheilostomata, there is at the anterior end of the zoœcium, above the aperture, a projecting chamber (*o*), into which the ova pass, termed the *oœcium*. Many of the Cheilostomata also possess appendages to the zoœcia, termed *avicularia* (fig. 27 *B*) and *vibracula*, but these are rarely preserved fossil. The avicularium may be sessile or placed on a peduncle (*p*), and in the more specialized forms, has somewhat the appearance of a bird's head, consisting of a chamber (*C*) produced into a beak and provided with a mandible (*md*) which is kept constantly snapping by means of muscles in the chamber. The vibraculum consists of a long seta kept in motion by means of muscles at its base. The individual polypides of a colony may communicate with one another, either directly, or by means of *communication-plates*; these are portions of the zoœcium which are thinner and perforated. The surface of the zoœcium may be smooth or punctate, or ornamented with spines, granules, or ribs.

The Polyzoa are divided into three sub-classes, (1) Ectoprocta, (2) Entoprocta, (3) Aspidophora. The Ectoprocta are the only forms found fossil.

SUB-CLASS. ECTOPROCTA.

The anal aperture is not placed within the area of the lophophore. There are two orders, (1) Phylactolæma, (2) Gymnolæma.

ORDER. PHYLACTOLÆMA.

The lophophore is horse-shoe shaped. There is a tongue-shaped lobe in front of the mouth, known as the epistome. The forms included in this order are found only in fresh-water and do not occur fossil.

ORDER. GYMNOLÆMA.

The lophophore is circular. An epistome is present. There are three sub-orders, (1) Cyclostomata, (2) Cheilostomata, (3) Ctenostomata. The last is not known in the fossil state.

SUB-ORDER. CYCLOSTOMATA.

The zoœcia are tubular, their apertures are round and terminal, not constricted and not provided with opercula. Vibracula are absent, and generally also avicularia and oœcia.

Fenestella. Zoarium funnel-shaped or fan-shaped. Branches straight, united by cross-bars, so as to form a network. The cross-bars do not bear zoœcia. On each branch there is a median ridge or carina, on the sides of which the zoœcia occur. Openings of zoœcia round. Silurian to Permian.

Fascicularia. Zoarium large, generally massive and globose. Zoœcia in the form of long tubes, with horizontal tabulæ, in contact laterally, and forming bundles which are either distinct and radiate from the base to the periphery, or fuse into laminæ which intersect. Coralline Crag.

SUB-ORDER. CHEILOSTOMATA.

The zoœcia are more or less oval, never tubular, their apertures are contracted and provided with a movable operculum. Avicularia, vibracula, and oœcia are often present.

Membranipora. Zoarium encrusting, generally irregular in form. Zoœcia quincuncial, or arranged irregularly, their margins raised, the anterior part depressed and more or less membranous. Chalk to present day.

Distribution of the Polyzoa.

By far the larger number of the Polyzoa are marine, they occur both in shallow and in deep water. The deep-water forms belong mainly to the Cheilostomata, the Ctenostomata being but poorly represented. The Cyclostomata are comparatively rare at the present day, except in the Northern seas.

The earliest Polyzoa occur in the Ordovician rocks. Practically all the Palæozoic genera are extinct, and they belong almost entirely to the Cyclostomata. The Cheilostomata do not become abundant until we reach the Cretaceous, and in the Tertiary they are more important than the Cyclostomata. Very many of the Pliocene forms belong to species still living.

The chief genera found in the Palæozoic are *Fenestella*, *Ptilodictya*, *Glauconome*; in the Jurassic, *Stomatopora*, *Spiropora*, *Berenicea*, *Idmonea*; in the Cretaceous, *Ceriopora*, *Heteropora*, *Stomatopora*, *Membranipora*, *Eschara*; in the Eocene, *Hornera*; in the Pliocene, *Membranipora*, *Eschara*, *Hornera*, *Fascicularia*.

CLASS. BRACHIOPODA.

In the Brachiopods the soft parts of the animal are enclosed in a shell which is formed of two parts termed *valves*, one is placed on the dorsal surface, the other on the ventral. The interior of the shell is lined by a membrane, the *mantle*, which is divided into two lobes, one occurring in each valve, and the space between the two is known as the *pallial chamber*. The margin of the mantle is thickened and carries numerous chitinous setæ. The alimentary canal is placed in a portion of the body-cavity (cœlom) in the posterior part of the shell; the mouth (fig. 29, *v*) opens into the pallial chamber, and leads into an œsophagus which is followed by a stomach

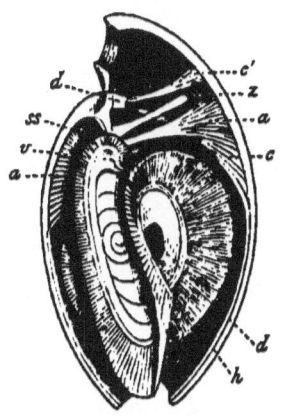

Fig. 29. *Waldheimia flavescens*, Recent. Longitudinal section. *d*, arms; *h*, cirri; *a*, adductor muscle; *c*, *c'*, divaricator muscles; *ss*, septum; *v*, mouth; *z*, terminal part of alimentary canal. (After Davidson.)

surrounded by liver-lobes, and an intestine; in the articulate brachiopods the latter is short and ends blindly, in the inarticulate it is long and ends in an anus which opens into the pallial chamber. The nervous system consists of a ring round the œsophagus, with ganglionic enlargements from which nerves are given off to the arms, mantle, etc. The part of the body-cavity which surrounds the alimentary canal communicates with the pallial chamber by means of two or four funnel-shaped canals. The body-cavity extends into the mantle as a series of spaces or sinuses; these produce slight depressions on the interior of the valves, and can often be traced in casts of the interior of fossil specimens as ridges (fig. 40). The body-cavity is filled with a fluid which is kept in motion by means of cilia. A heart appears to be absent, but a vesicle on the dorsal surface of the stomach has been described as such.

The brachiopods are never colonial animals. Reproduction takes place sexually, never by budding or fission. The genital organs are placed in the body-cavity, in the sinuses of the mantle, or in both. Some forms are hermaphrodite, others diœceous.

The greater part of the pallial chamber is occupied by two long processes, the *arms* (fig. 29, *d*), given off from the sides of the mouth. These are covered with cirri (*h*), and they, with the mantle serve as organs of respiration. The cirri also produce a current of water, which carries food to the mouth.

Of the two valves of the brachiopod, the ventral is always larger than the dorsal, and it is produced into a beak or *umbone*, the termination of which is generally perforated by a *foramen* (fig. 32 A, *f*). Each valve is equilateral, that is to say, a line drawn from the umbone to the opposite margin of the shell divides the valves into two equal and similar parts. This character, combined with the inequality in the size of the valves, renders it easy to distinguish the shell of a brachiopod from that of a lamellibranch. In many forms the two valves are joined together by means of a hinge, these constitute the group *Articulata*; in others they are held together by muscles only, these form the *Inarticulata*. The hinge consists of two short curved processes or teeth given off from the

ventral valve near the umbone, which fit into corresponding sockets in the dorsal valve. The line near the teeth
on which the two valves move in the opening and closing
of the shell, is termed the *hinge-line* (fig. 30, *g—h*). In
some genera (*Terebratula*) this is short and curved, in
others (*Spirifera*) it is long and straight. The posterior
part of the shell is that near the hinge (fig. 30, *a*), the

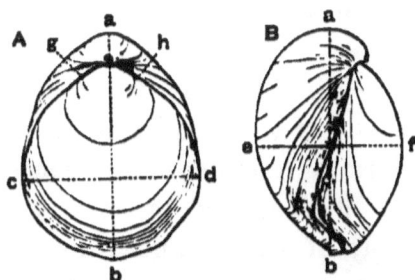

Fɪɢ. 30. *Terebratula obesa*, Upper Chalk. *A*, dorsal view. *B*, lateral
view. *a*, posterior; *b*, anterior; *a—b*, length; *c—d*, breadth; *e—f*,
thickness; *g—h*, hinge-line. Two-thirds natural size.

anterior is the opposite margin (*b*). The length of the
shell is measured from the posterior to the anterior
border (*a—b*). The breadth is at right angles to this, from
one side of the shell to the other (*c—d*). The thickness is
measured from one valve to the other perpendicular to the
length and breadth *e—f*. In some genera (*e.g. Terebratula*)
the length is greater than the breadth, in others (*e.g.
Strophomena*) the bread this greater. Between the hinge-
line and the umbone, there is in some brachiopods (*e.g.
Cyrtia*, fig. 31) a flat or slightly concave portion of the
shell, usually triangular, on which the ornamentation of
the rest of the shell is absent, the surface being either
smooth or striated; this is known as the *area*. It is

generally found on the ventral valve, but may also occur
on the dorsal. The margin of the foramen is sometimes

Fig. 31. *Cyrtia exporrecta*, Wenlock Limestone.   *abc*, area; *b—c*,
hinge-line. Natural size.

formed partly or entirely by the *deltidium* (fig. 32 *A, d*).
This consists usually of two small plates; in *Rhynchonella*
the two plates form a triangle, in the centre of which is
the foramen; in *Waldheimia* the two plates form the
lower margin only of the foramen; in *Terebratella* the
two plates are completely separated by the foramen.

Almost all living brachiopods are fixed to a foreign
object, but some of the fossil forms were free. The
attachment takes place very often by means of the *peduncle*; this is a cylindrical process, sometimes long,
sometimes short, connected with the mantle, and passing
either through the foramen, or between the apices of the
valves. The peduncle consists of horny material, with at
times some muscular layers also. Some forms (*e.g.*
Strophalosia) are fixed by spines given off from the surface
of the shell; others (*e.g. Crania*) by means of one valve
which is soldered to the rock or other object.

The two valves of the brachiopod can be opened and
closed by means of muscles (fig. 29), those which open them
are called the *divaricators* (*cc'*), those which close them,
the *adductors* (*a*). When the soft parts of the animal have
been removed the places where the muscles were attached
to the interior of the shell are indicated by a difference in

the surface such as striation, or by slight depressions or elevations, these markings are termed the *muscular impressions*. In the articulate brachiopods there are generally five or six pairs of muscles. In the genus *Waldheimia* there are two pairs of divaricators (fig. 29 *A, c, c'*) and one of adductors (*a*). Both pairs of the former are attached to a process (the *cardinal process*, fig. 32 *B, c, c'*)

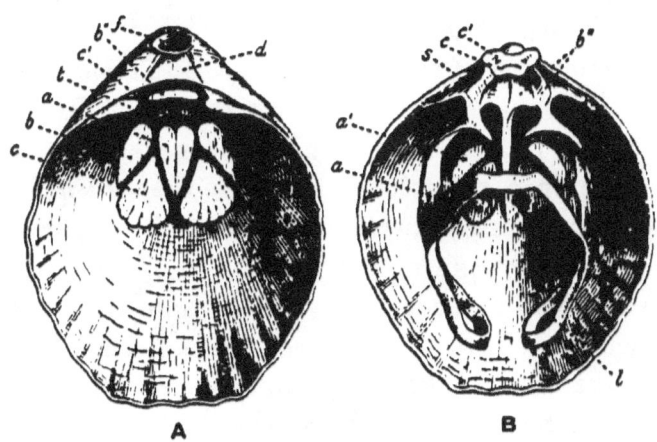

A   B

FIG. 32. *Waldheimia flavescens*, Recent. *A*, Interior of ventral valve. *f*, foramen; *d*, deltidium; *t*, teeth; *a*, impressions of adductor muscles; *c, c'*, impressions of divaricator muscles; *b, b''*, muscles of the peduncle. *B*, Interior of dorsal valve. *c, c'*, cardinal process; *b''*, hinge-plate; *s*, dental sockets; *l*, loop; *a, a'*, adductor impressions; *c*, point of attachment of the smaller divaricator. (After Davidson.)

on the dorsal valve between the teeth sockets, and one pair of these joins the ventral valve near its centre (fig. 32 *A, c*), and the other, which is smaller, is attached nearer the posterior border (*c'*). Hence these two pairs of muscles form with the shell a lever of the first order. The adductor muscles are united to the ventral valve near the centre (fig. 32 *A, a*) and form a single impression divided by a median line; these muscles bifurcate before reaching the dorsal valve and there form four impressions (fig. 32 *B, a, a'*). In the Inarticulata the muscles are much more complicated.

The arms, already mentioned as occupying the main part of the pallial chamber, are generally coiled up. In some forms they can be protruded a greater or shorter distance. Sometimes they are supported on a calcareous framework—the *brachial skeleton*—which is attached to the posterior part of the dorsal valve. In *Rhynchonella* it consists of two short curved processes. In *Terebratula* (fig. 42) the processes are longer, ribbon-like, and united so as to form a short loop. In *Stringocephalus* (fig. 43) the loop is more extensive and forms a band parallel to and near the margin of the valves. In *Waldheimia* (fig. 32 *B*) the loop extends nearly to the anterior margin of the shell and is then bent back upon itself. In other genera, the brachial skeleton is in the form of two spiral ribbons; in *Spirifera* (fig. 38 *A*) the apices of the spirals are directed towards the lateral margins of the shell, in *Glassia* they point inwards, in *Atrypa* (fig. 39 *A*) upwards to the centre of the dorsal surface.

The largest brachiopod is *Productus giganteus* from the Carboniferous Limestone, which has a breadth of twelve inches; the size varies from this down to about a quarter of an inch. Generally the shell is very thin, but in some forms (*e.g. Productus llangollensis*) it is thick and massive, leaving but little space for the soft parts of the animal. The external form varies immensely, it may be globular, ovoid, hemispherical, quadrilateral, or triangular. Usually both valves are convex, but in some, one is plane the other convex, or one may be concave and the other convex, and in the last case the space in the

interior is small. Sometimes there is a depression or
sulcus on one valve (generally the ventral) and a corresponding ridge on the other valve. The surface of the
shell is sometimes quite smooth, or it may be punctate,
or ornamented with striæ or ribs, which generally radiate
from the umbones, but are occasionally concentric. A
few forms possess spines.

In the Articulata the shell is mainly calcareous. In
the genus *Waldheimia* it is formed of three layers (fig. 33),
the inner (*a*), next the mantle, is the thickest and most

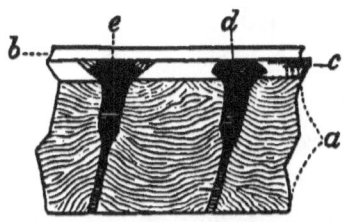

Fig. 33. Vertical section of shell of *Waldheimia flavescens*, Recent.
a, prismatic layer; *b*, epidermal layer; *c*, outer calcareous layer; *e*, *d*,
canals traversing the calcareous layers. Magnified. (After King.)

important, it consists of flattened calcareous prisms,
arranged obliquely to the surface of the shell, each prism
being encased in a chitinous membrane, which of course
has disappeared in the fossil examples. The middle layer
(*c*) is lamellated and also calcareous. The outer (*b*) is the
epidermal layer and consists of chitinous material. The

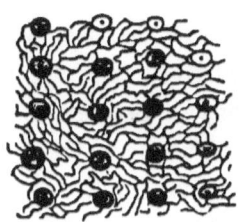

Fig. 34. Horizontal section through the prismatic layer of *Terebratula
maxillata*, from the Great Oolite, showing prisms and canals.
Magnified.

inner and middle layers are traversed by canals (fig. 33, *e*, *d*, 34) running at right angles to the surface of the shell, and contain prolongations of the mantle. The shell is secreted by the mantle, its outermost border producing the epidermal layer, a zone just within this producing the lamellated layer, and the remainder producing the prismatic layer which gradually encroaches on the preceding. So that the last layer is the only one which can subsequently increase in thickness. In many forms the lamellated layer is absent; and some (*e.g. Rhynchonella*) possess no canals traversing the calcareous layers.

The shell of the Inarticulata has a different structure. In *Lingula* it consists of alternating calcareous and chitinous layers, the calcareous material being mainly phosphate of lime. The canals which traverse these layers are more numerous and more minute than those found in the Articulate forms. The Brachiopods are divided into two orders, (1) Inarticulata, and (2) Articulata.

ORDER. INARTICULATA.

The valves are not provided with teeth but are held together by muscles only. The intestine is long and ends in an anus. There is no brachial skeleton.

Lingula. Shell thin, nearly equivalve, compressed, elongate-ovate or quadrilateral, tapering towards the umbones, slightly gaping at the extremities. Dorsal valve a little shorter than the ventral. Hinge-line slightly thickened. Twelve muscular impressions in each valve, but only feebly marked. Surface of shell smooth or concentrically or radiately striated. Fixation by means of a long peduncle passing between the umbones. Shell composed mainly of alternating layers of phosphate of lime and chitinous material. Cambrian to present day.

Lingulella. Separated from *Lingula* by the presence of a distinct slit in the ventral valve, and of a hinge-area. Cambrian to Ordovician.

Discina. Shell sub-orbicular, surface smooth or covered with striæ of growth. Valves conical, almost equal, the dorsal valve deeper than the ventral, the summits of both sub-central. Animal attached by a peduncle passing through a foramen just behind the summit of the ventral valve. Four adductor impressions, the anterior prominent, the posterior small and widely separated. Cambrian to present day.

Crania (fig. 35). Shell calcareous, quadrangular or subcircular, smooth or furnished with radiating ribs, fixed

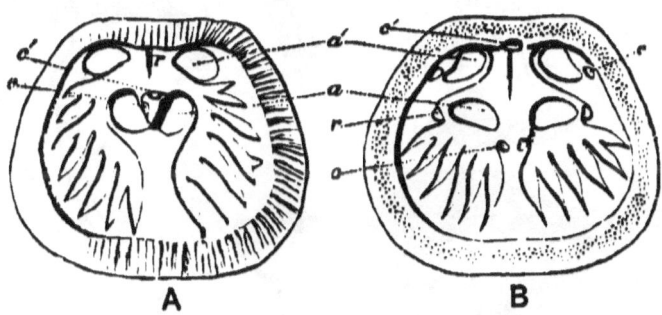

A   B

Fig. 35. *Crania anomala*, Recent. A, interior of ventral valve; B, dorsal valve. *a*, anterior adductors; *a'*, posterior adductors; *c*, posterior adjustors; *c'*, cardinal muscle; *r*, *o*, central and external adjustors. (From Woodward.)

by the ventral valve. Ventral valve depressed-conical; dorsal conical with a sub-central apex. Internal border of both valves covered with coarse granulations. Two pairs of well-marked adductor impressions in each valve (*aa'*); the posterior pair near the margin, the anterior near the centre of the valves and close together, especially so in the ventral valve. Also other smaller muscular impressions. Ordovician to present day.

ORDER. ARTICULATA.

The valves articulate by means of two teeth on the ventral valve which fit into sockets on the dorsal. The intestine is short and ends blindly. A brachial skeleton may or may not be present.

Productus (fig. 36). Shell free, generally transverse (*i.e.* broader than long) sometimes elongated, often produced into ears in the umbonal region. Dorsal valve

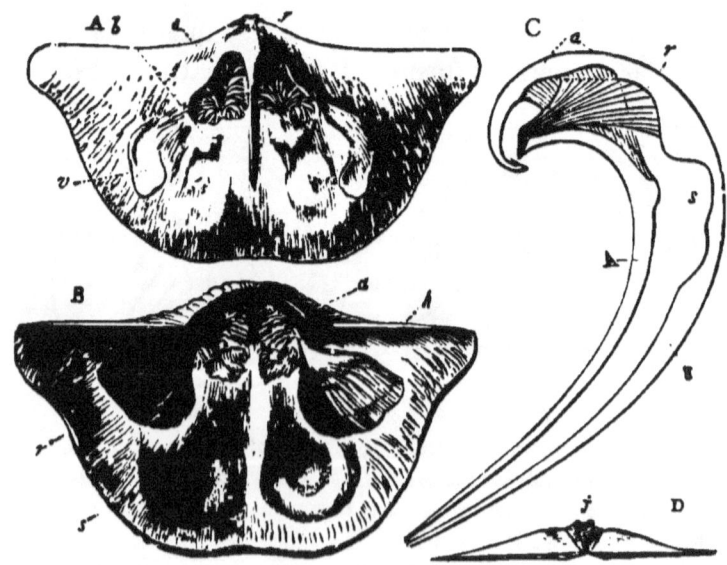

Fig. 36. *Productus giganteus*, Carboniferous Limestone. A, interior of dorsal valve; B, interior of ventral valve; C, ideal section of both valves; D, dorsal hinge-line. *j*, cardinal process; *a*, adductor; *r*, divaricator; *h*, ventral area; *b*, brachial prominence (?); *s*, hollows occupied by the spiral arms; *v*, reniform impressions. (From Woodward.)

concave. Ventral valve very convex, often geniculate, sometimes with a median sinus; umbone large, recurved, imperforate. Surface ornamented with radiating ribs, crossed by concentric folds, especially in the umbonal region. Hinge-line straight, teeth rudimentary. Area linear or absent. Tubular spines, especially in the region of the umbone and ears. Muscular impressions strongly marked. In the interior of the dorsal valve a median process. No brachial skeleton. Devonian to Permian.

Chonetes. Shell transverse, semicircular, concavo-convex, or sometimes plano-convex; area double. Hinge-line straight forming the greatest width of the shell. Teeth strong. Upper margin of area of ventral valve furnished with a row of hollow spines, which increase in length towards the terminations of the hinge-line. Surface ornamented with radial striæ. Silurian to Carboniferous.

Strophomena. Shell concavo-convex, semicircular or nearly quadrangular, ornamented with small radiating ribs, sometimes also concentric folds, rarely smooth. Space between the two valves very small. Hinge-line straight forming the greatest width of the shell. Area double, that of the dorsal valve linear, that of the ventral valve with a median notch covered by a pseudo-deltidium. Umbone of ventral valve perforated by a small circular foramen except in old age. Two strong diverging teeth in the ventral valve. Four muscular impressions. Ordovician to Carboniferous.

Leptæna. Shell concavo-convex, semicircular, ornamented with radiating ribs. Hinge-line straight forming the greatest width. Area double, the dorsal linear. Ventral valve very convex, with two diverging teeth. Dorsal valve with four strongly marked muscular impressions, which are elongated, extending nearly two-thirds of the length of the shell. Muscular impressions in the ventral valve very small. Radiating vascular impressions. Ordovician to Carboniferous ; perhaps also Lias.

Orthis (fig. 37). Outline circular or quadrate. Both valves convex, the dorsal sometimes flattened. Surface radiately ribbed or striated. Hinge-line straight, generally

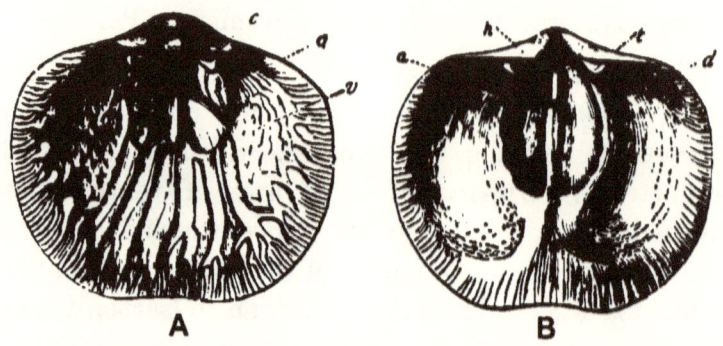

FIG. 37. *Orthis striatula*, Devonian. A, interior of dorsal valve; B, ventral valve. *c*, curved brachial processes (cruras) ; *v*, genital impressions; *h*, area ; *t*, teeth ; *a*, adductors; *d*, divaricators. (From Woodward.)

shorter than the width of the shell. Area double, each divided by a median triangular fissure. In the ventral valve, two large teeth, supported by dental plates. Four muscular impressions in the dorsal valve; two long narrow ones in the ventral. Cambrian to Carboniferous.

Spirifer (fig. 38). Shell transverse, more or less triangular, biconvex, smooth or ornamented with ribs or striæ. Often with a sinus on the ventral valve and a ridge on the dorsal. Hinge-line long and straight. Area double, that of the ventral valve triangular, often transversely striated, divided by a median triangular slit. Dorsal area small, also with a median slit. Teeth supported by dental plates in the ventral valve. Brachial skeleton often filling a great part of the interior of the

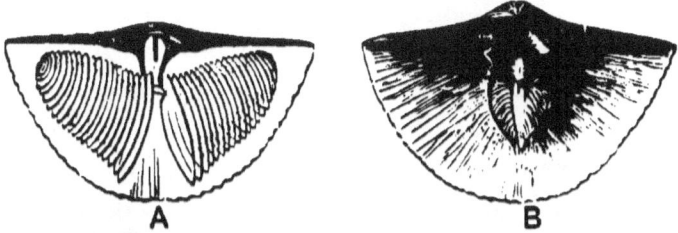

Fig. 38. *Spirifer striatus*, Carboniferous. A, interior of dorsal valve; showing brachial skeleton. B, interior of ventral valve. (From Woodward.)

shell, in the form of two spiral ribbons, with their apices directed laterally. Silurian to Permian. The sub-genus *Spiriferina* occurs in the Lias.

Uncites. Shell elongate-oval, biconvex, striated. Hinge-line curved, no area. Umbone of the ventral valve prominent and incurved, foramen closed in the adult. Apex of dorsal valve recurved and partly hidden in the ventral valve. Brachial skeleton spiral, the apices of the spires directed laterally. Devonian.

Atrypa (fig. 39). Shell sub-circular, biconvex, orna-

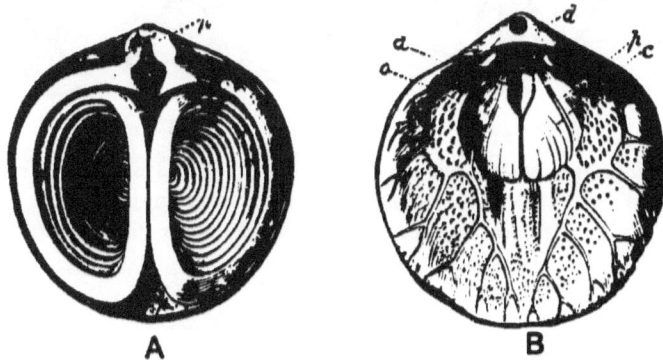

Fig. 39. *Atrypa reticularis*, Wenlock Limestone. A, dorsal valve showing brachial skeleton. B, interior of ventral valve. *a*, impressions of adductor muscles; *c*, divaricator muscles; *p*, muscles of peduncle; *o*, ovarian impression; *d*, deltidium. (From Woodward.)

mented with radiating ribs and often with lines of growth. Ventral valve depressed in front. Dorsal valve often much inflated. Hinge-line curved, no area. A small circular foramen, sometimes with a small deltidium often concealed. Ventral valve with two strong crenulate teeth, muscular impressions grouped in the centre of the valve. Brachial skeleton in the form of two spirals with their apices directed toward the centre of the dorsal valve. Ordovician to Trias.

Rhynchonella (fig. 40). Shell triangular, elongated or rounded, very convex, ornamented with radiating ribs. A sinus on the ventral valve and a corresponding ridge on the dorsal. Umbone small, acute, recurved;

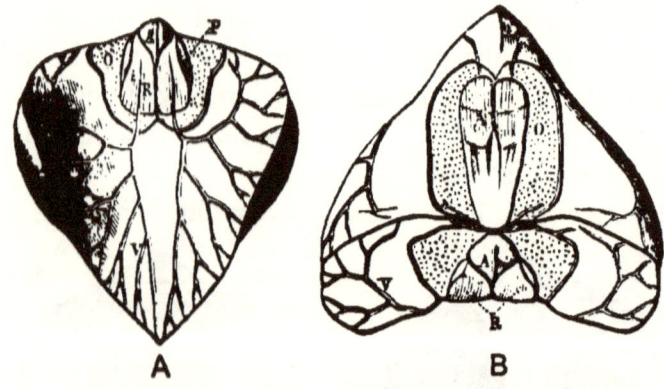

A   B

FIG. 40. *Rhynchonella acuminata*, Carboniferous Limestone. Internal casts. V, 'vascular' impressions; O, ovarian impressions; A, adductors; R, divaricators; P, muscles of the peduncle. (From Woodward.)

foramen enclosed by deltidium. Ventral valve with two strong teeth, muscular impression in middle of valve. Brachial skeleton reduced to two short, free, curved, lamellæ. Ordovician to present day.

Pentamerus (fig. 41). Shell oval, ornamented with ribs, rarely smooth. Ventral valve the most convex. Dorsal valve usually with a fold in front and on the ventral valve a corresponding depression. Umbone of

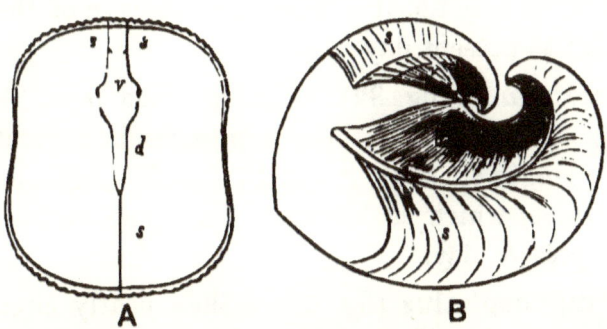

A   B

FIG. 41. *Pentamerus knighti,* Aymestry Limestone. A, longitudinal section; B, transverse section. *ss,* dorsal septa; *s,* ventral septum; *d,* dental plates. (From Woodward.)

ventral valve sharp, strongly incurved, usually touching the dorsal valve and concealing the triangular aperture. No area, nor deltidium. Dental-plates (*d*) trough-like, converging in the ventral valve to form a median septum (*s*), in the dorsal valve two contiguous septa (*ss*). Silurian to Devonian.

Terebratula (fig. 42). Shell biconvex; oval, elongate, or rounded; surface smooth. Often with two folds on

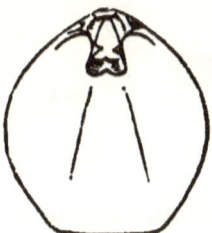

FIG. 42. *Terebratula vitrea,* Recent. Interior of dorsal valve, showing the brachial skeleton. (From Woodward.)

the dorsal valve and two corresponding sinuses on the ventral. Hinge-line curved. Umbone of ventral valve truncated by a circular foramen, having a deltidium at its base. Brachial skeleton in the form of a short loop extending to only about a third of the length of the shell. Devonian to present day.

Waldheimia (fig. 32). Distinguished from *Terebratula* by the longer brachial loop, extending to at least half the length of the shell, and by a median septum in the dorsal valve, which is however sometimes rudimentary. Lias to present day.

Stringocephalus (fig. 43). Shell nearly circular in outline; smooth. Ventral valve with a sharp prominent umbone, area present. Foramen large and triangular in the young individuals, smaller and oval in the adult on account of the development of the deltidium. Teeth large. Ventral valve with a median septum (*vs*), which

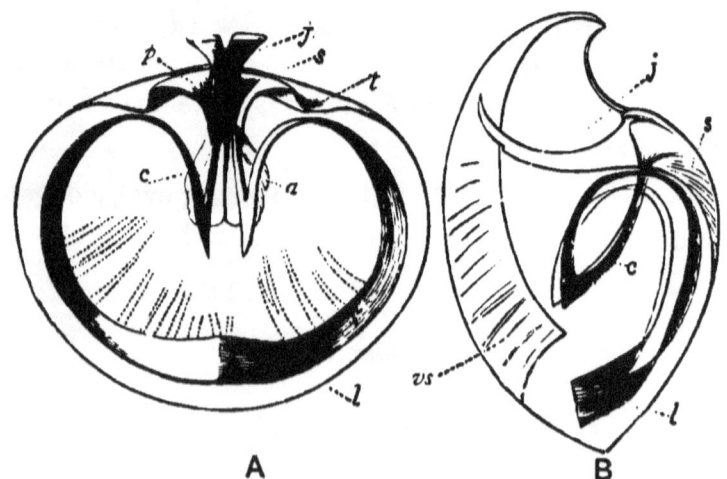

Fig. 43. *Stringocephalus burtini*, Devonian. A, Dorsal valve. B, Profile. *a*, adductor; *c*, crura; *l*, loop; *j*, cardinal process; *p*, hinge-plate; *s*, dorsal septum; *vs*, ventral septum; *t*, dental sockets. (From Woodward.)

extends from the umbone almost to the front of the valve, and increases in height towards the latter. Dorsal valve less convex, with a small septum (s), and a long slightly curved cardinal process (j), divided at its extremity to embrace the ventral septum. The brachial skeleton consists of two branches arising from the hinge-plate (p), which pass to the middle of the shell (c) and are then sharply bent back and form a ribbon (l) parallel to the margin of the valve. Silurian and Devonian.

Distribution of the Brachiopoda.

The Brachiopods are all marine and are found in all parts of the world; at the present time they are much less numerous than in former periods of the earth's history. About half of the existing species are found at depths of less than 100 fathoms, several of these do not extend beyond this limit. Below 150 fathoms they soon become comparatively rare, but a few species occur down to 2900 fathoms. Some genera, as for instance *Lingula*, do not occur below a depth of a few fathoms. A few species, as *Terebratulina caput-serpentis*, have a very wide geographical distribution, extending from polar to tropical regions, and these have also a great range in depth, the form mentioned being found from the shore down to 1180 fathoms.

Generally the species confined to shallow water have a much more limited geographical range than those found in deeper water; and the polar or boreal species have a wider range than the tropical, since they can find the same temperature in lower latitudes at great depths.

The Brachiopods are very abundant as fossils, the earliest forms occur in the Lower Cambrian beds. In the

Ordovician the Brachiopods are much more numerous than in the Cambrian, and they attain their maximum in the Silurian, their decline begins with the Devonian and becomes especially marked in the Mesozoic. The most important genera in the Cambrian are *Lingula, Obolella, Discina,* and *Orthis* (the last being the only representative of the Articulata); in the Ordovician, *Lingulella, Obolella, Orthis, Strophomena, Leptœna;* in the Silurian, *Lingula, Atrypa, Orthis, Meristella, Rhynchonella, Pentamerus, Strophomena, Chonetes;* in the Devonian, *Uncites, Stringocephalus, Atrypa, Orthis, Spirifer;* in the Carboniferous, *Chonetes, Athyris, Spirifer, Productus, Terebratula, Rhynchonella;* in the Permian, *Productus, Spirifer, Rhynchonella.* The majority of the Palæozoic genera die out before the commencement of the Mesozoic, the most important genera now being *Terebratula, Terebratulina, Waldheimia, Rhynchonella,* and *Crania.* In the Tertiary the Brachiopods are rare, the chief forms being *Terebratula, Waldheimia,* and *Rhynchonella.*

SUB-KINGDOM VII. MOLLUSCA.

Classes.	Orders.	Sections.
1. Lamellibranchiata.......	1. Asiphonida.	1. Monomyaria. 2. Heteromyaria. 3. Homomyaria.
	2. Siphonida.	1. Integripalliata. 2. Sinupalliata.
2. Gasteropoda.	1. Polyplacophora. 2. Prosobranchiata. 3. Opisthobranchiata. 4. Heteropoda. 5. Pulmonata. 6. Pteropoda.	
3. Scaphopoda.		Sub-Orders.
4. Cephalopoda.	1. Tetrabranchiata.........	1. Nautiloidea. 2. Ammonoidea.
	2. Dibranchiata............	1. Decapoda. 2. Octopoda.

THE majority of the mollusks (Oysters, Whelks, Cuttle-
fishes) are marine, but some live on land, others in
fresh-water. Unlike the worms and arthropods, they are
unsegmented animals and bear no appendages. Typically
the body is bilaterally symmetrical and there is consequently a repetition of the same organs on each side.
But in many gasteropods this symmetry is more or less
obliterated. From the dorsal surface there is a fold of the

skin forming what is known as the *mantle*; this generally secretes a calcareous shell, consisting of one or two pieces. There is a ventral protrusion of the body forming the *foot*, a muscular organ used generally in locomotion. Respiration takes place in most cases by means of gills; in some forms there is instead a pulmonary sac. A heart is present and is placed on the dorsal surface, and it is systemic (*i.e.* receives arterial blood). The mouth is situated anteriorly, and typically the anus is posterior, the former may or may not be provided with organs of mastication. Renal organs (nephridia) are present and communicate with the body-cavity. The nervous system consists of three pairs of ganglia connected by cords. Sexual reproduction only occurs; some forms being unisexual, others hermaphrodite.

The Mollusca are divided into four classes, (1) Lamellibranchiata, (2) Gasteropoda, (3) Scaphopoda, (4) Cephalopoda.

CLASS. LAMELLIBRANCHIATA.

In the lamellibranch as in the brachiopod the shell is generally calcareous and consists of two valves, but these instead of being dorsal and ventral as in the latter, are placed one on the right, the other on the left side of the animal, and the two are joined together by means of a hinge and ligament at the dorsal margin. The interior of the shell is lined by a fold of the skin, the *mantle* (fig. 44 *m*), which is divided into two lobes, one being placed in each valve. In the middle of the space enclosed by the mantle (the mantle-cavity) is the foot (*b*). This is a laterally flattened muscular organ, frequently hatchet[1] or

[1] Hence the name *Pelecypoda* used by some authors for this class.

plough-share shaped, and is used for crawling, or for burrowing in sand or mud. Sometimes as in the cases of *Trigonia* and *Cardium*, by means of a rapid movement, it

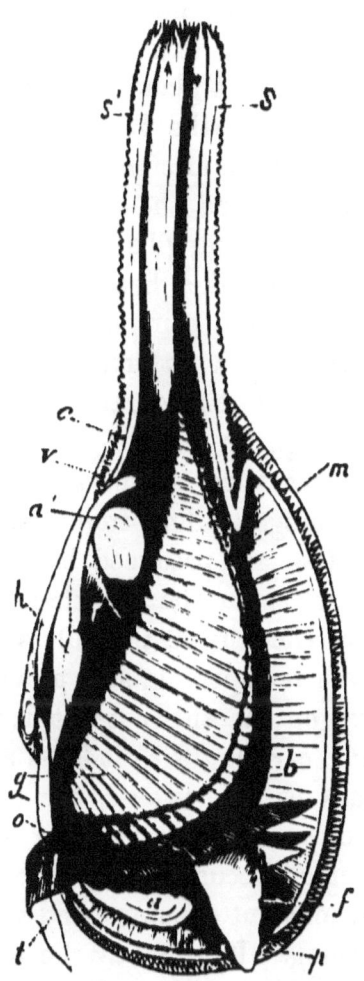

FIG. 44. *Mya arenaria.* The left valve and mantle, and also half the siphons, have been removed. *a*, anterior adductor muscle; *a'*, posterior adductor; *b*, visceral mass; *c*, cloacal chamber into which the anus opens; *f*, foot; *g*, branchiæ; *h*, heart; *m*, cut edge of the mantle; *o*, mouth; *s*, branchial siphon; *s'*, anal siphon; *t*, labial palps; *r*, anus. (From Woodward.)

enables the animal to jump to a considerable distance. In the genus *Mytilus* the foot is very much reduced; in others (*e.g. Ostrea*) it is absent altogether, but this occurs only in those forms which have lost the power of loco-motion. In some genera (*e.g. Mytilus*) there is on the posterior part of the foot a gland which secretes a bundle of horny fibres, known as the *byssus*, by means of which the animal moors itself to foreign objects. On each side of the foot, between it and the mantle, and attached to the body dorsally, are the gills or branchiæ (fig. 44 *g*). These are usually leaf-like, hence the name Lamelli-branchiata; there are two pairs, one on each side of the body, and they are covered with cilia.

In some forms, like *Anodon*, the margins of the two mantle-lobes although in contact are not united, and when this is the case, there are at the posterior margin, two adjoining openings leading from the exterior to the mantle-cavity; these are produced by the apposition of contiguous excavations in the mantle-lobes. A current of water caused by the cilia on the gills and mantle flows in through the ventral opening, and provides the animal with food and oxygen; another current flows out through the dorsal opening, carrying with it fæcal and indigestible matters. In many cases, however, the two lobes of the mantle are fused to a greater or less extent at their margins. This union occurs at two places, one between the exhalent and inhalent openings, and the other ventral to the latter opening. In this way the mantle comes to form a kind of bag, having three openings, a ventral for the protrusion of the foot, and two posterior for the in-halent and exhalent currents of water. Frequently the mantle is greatly produced at the posterior openings, so as to form two complete tubes, known as *siphons* (fig. 44

s, s'); these are sometimes free from one another, sometimes united, and they may be as much as four times the
length of the shell. The ventral is generally the longer,
it is furnished with tactile papillæ, and is known as the
branchial siphon (*s*), the dorsal being the *anal siphon* (*s'*).
In many forms the siphons can be withdrawn into the
shell by means of muscles. Occasionally, as in *Teredo*,
the siphons are surrounded by a calcareous tube.

The two valves of the shell can be closed by means of
the adductor muscles (*a, a'*), which pass from the interior
of one valve to the other. In many genera there are two
adductors, and these forms are frequently spoken of as
Dimyaria; others, known as the *Monomyaria*, possess one
only, and when this is the case it is the posterior which is
present, the anterior having atrophied; this occurs in the
oyster, but in this form the anterior muscle is found to be
present in the young state.

The mouth (*o*) is placed in the middle line of
the body, ventral to the anterior adductor muscle,
and it is not provided with organs of mastication or
prehension. At its sides, are two leaf-like processes,
the *labial palps* (*t*). The mouth leads into a short
œsophagus, which passes into a globular stomach surrounded by the liver; then comes the intestine, which
after undergoing many convolutions, reaches the dorsal
surface of the body, where it passes through the peri-
cardium and is surrounded by the ventricle of the heart,
and afterwards ends in an anus (*v*) situated dorsally to the
posterior adductor muscle. In the lamellibranchs there
is no head, hence the class is sometimes spoken of, as the
Acephala. The nervous system consists of three pairs of
ganglia. One pair is placed at the sides of the mouth and
is connected by cords with a pair in the foot, and with a

third pair placed beneath the posterior adductor muscle.
From these ganglia, nerves are given off to the muscles,
gills, etc. Tactile organs are present on the margin of
the mantle and especially on the ventral siphon. In some
forms, eyes occur at the ventral margin of the mantle-
lobes, they are especially well-developed in the genus
Pecten. The heart (*h*) is placed dorsally, just below the
hinge; it is surrounded by a large pericardial cavity,
and consists of two auricles, and a ventricle, which as
already mentioned, extends round the intestine. From
the ventricle, an anterior and a posterior aorta are given
off. In nearly all cases the blood is colourless. The renal
organs consist of a pair of glandular bodies underneath
the ventricle. In almost all forms the sexes are separate,
but a few are hermaphrodite.

As already mentioned the two valves of the shell are
placed on the sides of the animal and not dorsally and
ventrally as in the brachiopods. The margin near the
hinge (fig. 45 *d*) is dorsal, the opposite (*v*), where the
valves open, is ventral, that near the mouth is anterior (*a*),
that near the anus and siphons posterior (*p*). In the
majority of cases the two valves are equal or practically
equal, and each valve is generally inequilateral. But
in some (*e.g. Pectunculus*) the shell is equilateral, in
others (*e.g. Ostrea*) it is inequivalve. Each valve may be
regarded as a greatly depressed hollow cone, the apices of
which form the *umbones* (*u*); these are sometimes straight
(*e.g. Pecten*), but generally curved towards the anterior
margin. In a few genera (*e.g. Nucula, Trigonia*) they are
directed posteriorly. In *Diceras* the umbones are spiral.
There is sometimes, placed in front of the umbone and
bounded by a groove, an oval depressed area (*lu*), half
occurring on each valve, this is termed the *lunule*, and it

is important to remember that it is always anterior to the umbones. Behind the umbones there is sometimes a somewhat similar, but larger area, bounded by a ridge, and known as the *escutcheon*.

In the interior of the valves various markings will be noticed (fig. 45 *B*), these are produced by the union of the muscles with the shell. The adductors form prominent

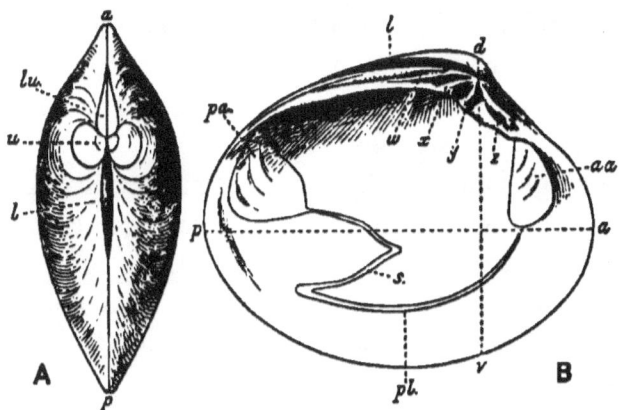

Fig. 45. *Cytherea chione.* Recent. *A*, dorsal view of the two valves. *B*, interior of left valve.

   a, anterior border; *p*, posterior; *d*, dorsal; *v*, ventral; *lu*, lunule; *u*, umbone; *l*, ligament; *aa*, anterior adductor impression; *pa*, posterior adductor; *pl*, pallial line; *s*, pallial sinus; *w*, *x*, *y*, cardinal teeth; *z*, anterior-lateral tooth.

oval or round, sometimes elongated, depressions (the *adductor impressions, aa, pa,*), there are two in each valve in the Dimyaria, one being anterior, the other posterior; sometimes they are of the same size, in others the anterior is smaller. In the Monomyaria there is one impression only which is then placed posteriorly or sometimes almost central. Less important than the adductor impressions are those produced by the muscles for the retraction of the foot, of which there are two in each valve; of these

9—2

one occurs close to the anterior adductor, the other just above the posterior adductor. Passing from one adductor to the other in each valve, is a linear depression, the *pallial line* (*pl*); this is caused by the attachment of the muscles of the mantle to the shell. In some forms this line runs evenly between the two adductor impressions and parallel to the margin of the valve, it is then said to be *simple* or *entire*. But in those genera which possess retractile siphons, there is a bending in of the pallial line just before reaching the posterior adductor, this indentation is known as the *pallial sinus* (*s*), and is caused by the muscles of the siphons.

The hinge is formed by means of projections known as teeth, which alternate in the two valves, the teeth of one valve fitting into depressions between those of the other. The teeth may be distinguished as *cardinal* and *lateral*. The cardinal are those which occur under the umbones (fig. 45 *w*, *x*, *y*); the lateral at the sides, those in front being the anterior-lateral (*z*), those behind, the posterior-lateral. In some genera cardinal teeth only are found, in others lateral or some of the lateral only. In a few forms the two kinds of teeth cannot be separated, thus *Arca* possesses a row of numerous small teeth, all of which are alike. Lastly some forms (*e.g. Anodon*) are without teeth. The margin on which the teeth occur is known as the *hinge-line*; generally it is curved, but in some genera like *Arca* it is straight. Sometimes (*e.g. Arca*) there is on each valve a flattened triangular space between the hinge-line and the umbone, known as the *area*; when this is present the umbones of the two valves are widely separated.

In the brachiopods the valves are opened by the divaricator muscles, but in the lamellibranchs the work of these muscles is performed by the ligament. This consists of two parts, the external (fig. 45 l), and the internal (sometimes erroneously termed the cartilage.) One or other may be absent. The external ligament is composed of horny material; it is placed outside the shell and is either under the umbones or posterior to them, it passes from one valve to the other and is frequently attached to more or less prominent ridges. When the valves of the shell are closed the external ligament is stretched, and consequently in order to open the shell, the animal has merely to relax its adductor muscles. The internal ligament consists of parallel elastic fibres, and is placed in grooves or sockets along the hinge-line, so that when the valves are closed it is compressed, and being elastic tends to force the valves apart. Its action is similar to that of a piece of india-rubber placed in the hinge-line of a door. Occasionally the ligament is preserved in fossil specimens. The length of a lamellibranch shell is measured from the anterior to the posterior margin (fig. 45 B, a—p), the breadth or height from the umbone to the ventral margin (d—v), the thickness from one valve to the other at right angles to the lines of length and breadth.

The shell is secreted by the mantle and consists of two calcareous layers, the inner is the *pearly* or *nacreous* layer, and consists of numerous lamellæ; the outer is the *prismatic* layer (fig. 46), and consists of prisms placed at right angles to the surface of the shell. The external surface is covered by a thin green or brownish epidermis. The prismatic layer is formed by the margin of the mantle only, the pearly layer by the whole of the rest of the mantle, and this layer gradually encroaches on the former, which consequently cannot afterwards increase in thickness, whereas the pearly layer may do so throughout the life of the animal. In some genera both layers consist of calcite, in others of aragonite, or one may be of calcite and the other of aragonite. The surface of the

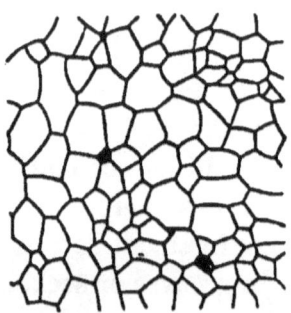

FIG. 46. Section of prismatic layer of recent *Pinna*, parallel to the surface of the shell and at right angles to the prisms. Magnified.

shell may be smooth, or may be ornamented with radiating or concentric ribs, with striæ or spines. Often the exterior shows concentric lamellæ which are considered to represent periods of growth. The part of the shell at the umbone is that which was first formed and it sometimes shows different characters to the other parts. The margins of the valves may be smooth or crenulated. In many genera the two valves can be completely closed, in others they are always open at some part, and are then said to be *gaping*; this gape occurs most frequently at the posterior part but sometimes also anteriorly.

It is of importance to be able to distinguish the right and left valves. In order to do this we must determine first the anterior and posterior margins. When the soft parts of the animal are present this is easily done. But when the shell only is before the observer the points to be noticed are these :—

(1)   The umbones are generally directed anteriorly.

(2)   The lunule is always anterior to the umbones.

(3)   The external ligament is never anterior.

(4)   The pallial sinus is posterior.

(5)   When one adductor impression only is present, it is the posterior.

Having found the anterior and posterior margins, the shell should be placed with the dorsal margin uppermost and the anterior margin pointing away from the observer, then the right and left valves will be on his right and left hand sides respectively.

Most of the lamellibranchs are free, but a few forms like the oyster are permanently attached by one valve. In some cases it is the right valve which is fixed, in others the left. In the free forms movement takes place usually by means of the foot, but some genera (*Pecten, Lima*) move by the alternate rapid opening and shutting of the valves. A few are capable of making borings into various substances; thus *Teredo*, the ship-worm, bores into wood, *Lithodomus* into limestone, and *Pholas* into various materials such as sandstone, limestone, gneiss, peat, and amber. Wood perforated by *Teredo* has been found fossil in various formations of Eocene and Oligocene age.

The features which more especially characterise the lamellibranchs as a class, are, the bilateral symmetry, the mantle being divided into two lobes, the bivalve shell, the lamellar gills, and the absence of a head and of organs of mastication. Although at first sight the shell appears to resemble closely that of the brachiopod, it differs in several important respects, namely, (1) in the valves being right and left, instead of dorsal and ventral, (2) in being generally inequilateral and equivalve, (3) in the presence of teeth on both valves, (4) in the presence of a ligament, (5) in the umbones never being perforated for a peduncle. The classification followed here is based on the presence or absence of siphons, and on the adductor muscles; this is not altogether a natural one, but it is convenient for palæontological purposes. There are two orders, (1) Asiphonida, (2) Siphonida.

ORDER. ASIPHONIDA.

Animal without siphons, mantle lobes free or united at one point only, pallial line simple.

Section 1. *Monomyaria.*

One adductor (the posterior) present only.

Ostrea*. Shell irregular, lamellar, inequivalve, slightly inequilateral, fixed by the left valve. Left valve convex, with radiating ribs or striæ, umbone prominent; right valve flat or concave, often smooth and without striæ or ribs. Ligamental cavity triangular or elongated. Hinge without teeth. Adductor impression sub-central; pallial line indistinct. Trias (? also Carboniferous) to present day.

Gryphæa. Shell inequivalve, free in the adult. Left valve large, with a prominent incurved umbone. Right valve flattened or concave. Lias to present day.

Exogyra. Shell fixed by the left (larger) valve. Right valve flat, operculiform. Umbones more or less spiral, directed posteriorly. Upper Jurassic to Chalk.

---

* All the genera of Mollusca described are marine unless otherwise stated.

Plicatula. Shell irregular, inequivalve, depressed; smooth, folded or scaly, without ears, fixed by the umbone of the right valve. Hinge-area obscure. Hinge with strong teeth in each valve; ligament internal, between the teeth. Adductor impression simple, excentral, near the pallial line. Trias to present day.

Lima. Shell obliquely oval, equivalve, compressed, with radiating striæ or ribs, the ribs scaly. Valves gaping anteriorly and sometimes posteriorly. Umbones distant, sharp, prominent, auriculate, the ears unequal. Hinge straight without teeth. A triangular hinge-area, furnished with a central ligamental cavity. Adductor impression large, divided, excentral. Two small pedal impressions. Carboniferous to present day.

Pecten. Shell suborbicular or oblong, free, closed, equilateral, inequivalve, umbones approximated. Surface usually with radiating ribs, auriculate, the anterior ears larger than the posterior, the right one with a byssal sinus. Right valve more convex than the left. Hinge-line straight. Ligamental cavity central, narrow, triangular, internal. Adductor impression large, sub-central. Lias to present day. (Possibly also Carboniferous.)

Aviculopecten. Shell a little inequilateral; right valve less convex than the left. Anterior ear smaller than the posterior; a byssal sinus beneath the anterior ear in the right valve. Ligament in a narrow groove parallel to the hinge-line. Adductor impression large, sub-central. Surface generally radiately ribbed. Devonian to Permian.

Section 2. *Heteromyaria.*

The anterior muscle small, the posterior large.

Avicula. Shell oblique, inequilateral, inequivalve, left valve more convex. Interior nacreous. Hinge straight, with one or two small cardinal teeth. Auriculate, the posterior ear, wing-like and longer than the anterior. A byssal sinus under the right anterior ear. Hinge-area small, striate. Ligament partly internal, partly external, the internal in a deep groove. Posterior adductor impression large, sub-central. Ordovician to present day.

Pterinea. Shell inequilateral, oblique, equivalve, auriculate, the anterior ear shorter than the posterior; a byssal sinus under the right anterior ear. Hinge-line long, straight; with anterior small teeth, and posterior elongated, laminar, teeth. Ligamental area large, longitudinally striated. Posterior muscular impression large, shallow; anterior impression small, deep, below the anterior ear. Ordovician to Carboniferous.

Gervillia. Shell obliquely elongated, slightly inequivalve, inequilateral, the left valve a little more convex. Umbones almost terminal. Hinge-line straight, broad, with numerous perpendicular widely separated ligamental pits; its posterior edge with two or more obscure teeth diverging behind. Ears not very distinct from the rest of the shell, anterior ear short, posterior long. Adductor impressions as in *Avicula.* Trias to Eocene.

Inoceramus. Shell variable in form, circular, oval, or oblong, inequilateral, inequivalve, ventricose or compressed, not auriculate. Umbones prominent. No teeth.

Surface with concentric (or rarely radiating) grooves. Hinge-line straight, or slightly curved, elongated. Numerous parallel close-set cartilage pits. Adductor impression rarely visible. Inner layer of shell thin and nacreous, outer layer thick, fibrous and prismatic. Trias to Chalk.

Perna. Shell nearly equivalve, inequilateral, compressed, subquadrate or sub-circular, auriculate. Hinge-line straight, no teeth. Hinge-area large. Cartilage pits numerous, parallel, close together and elongated. Right valve with a byssal sinus. Adductor impression large, sub-central, double. Posterior ear often large, anterior rudimentary. Trias to present day.

Mytilus. Shell equivalve, inequilateral, sub-triangular, posterior border rounded. Umbones sharp, terminal, anterior. Teeth small or obsolete. Ligament linear, marginal, sub-internal. Anterior adductor impression small, posterior large. Surface of shell with an epidermis. Trias to present day.

Modiola. Shell equivalve, inequilateral, oblong, inflated in front. Umbones obtuse, anterior, but not terminal. No teeth. Ligament linear, marginal. Adductor impressions like *Mytilus.* Devonian to present day.

Lithodomus. Shell sub-cylindrical, very inequilateral, rounded in front, wedge-like behind. Umbones anterior, not prominent. Ligament internal. No teeth. A thin nacreous layer. Carboniferous to present day.

Pinna. Shell equivalve, inequilateral, wedge-shaped, generally thin, not auriculate. Umbones sharp, anterior, terminal. Valves gaping posteriorly. Hinge-line straight, long. No teeth. Ligament linear, almost entirely internal, lodged in a groove. Posterior adductor large, sub-central; anterior apical. Devonian to present day.

Section 3. *Homomyaria.*

The two muscles of equal size. Mantle-lobes free or sometimes united posteriorly at one point.

Arca. Shell thick, generally equivalve, sub-quad-rangular, ventricose, costulate or cancellate. Margins smooth or dentate; closed or open ventrally. Hinge-line straight. Teeth numerous, equal, transverse. Umbones prominent, remote, separated by a lozenge-shaped area, which has numerous ligamental grooves converging from the hinge-margin to the umbones. Adductor impressions subequal, the anterior rounded, the posterior divided. Pallial line simple. Ordovician to present day.

Cucullæa. Shell rhombic or trapezoidal, ventricose, nearly or quite equivalve. Valves closed, ornamented with radiating striæ. Umbones incurved. Hinge-area large, well defined, with diverging ligamental grooves; hinge-line straight, with two short central transverse teeth, and two to five lateral teeth nearly parallel to the hinge-margin. Ligament external. Posterior adductor impression on a thin raised plate. Pallial line simple. Carbon-iferous to present day.

Cardiola. Shell thin, convex, oval, generally inequi-lateral; umbones prominent, incurved. Surface with radiating and concentric grooves. Hinge-line straight; ligamental area large, horizontally grooved. Muscular impressions unknown. Silurian and Devonian.

Pectunculus. Shell thick, solid, sub-orbicular, equi-valve, almost equilateral. Surface smooth or radiately striated. Ligament external. Umbones central, slightly curved towards each other, separated by a triangular ligamental area provided with diverging striæ. Hinge with a semi-circular row of numerous, small, strong, transverse teeth, obliterated at the centre in the older forms by the growth of the ligamental area. Margins crenulate inside, adductor impressions sub-equal. Pallial line simple. Lower Cretaceous to present day.

Nucula. Shell equivalve, trigonal, oval, closed, pos-terior side very short; umbones directed posteriorly. Surface smooth or ornamented. Interior nacreous. Margin of valves smooth or crenulated. Hinge-line angulated, with a median internal triangular ligamental pit, on each side of which is a row of numerous sharp teeth. Adductor impressions sub-equal. Pallial line simple. Silurian to present day.

Leda. Shell oblong, similar to *Nucula*, produced and pointed posteriorly. Surface smooth or striated. Teeth numerous. Ligamental pit internal. Pallial line slightly sinuated. Margins smooth. Lunule lanceolate. Silurian to present day.

Trigonia. Shell thick, ornamented with tubercles or with radiating or concentric ribs; trigonal, very inequi-lateral, anterior margin rounded, posterior produced and angular. Generally with a ridge extending from the umbones to the posterior border, cutting off an area which has a different ornamentation. Umbones anterior, directed posteriorly. Cardinal teeth diverging, striated, two in the right valve, three in the left, the central tooth in the latter being bifid. Ligament marginal, thick. Adductor impression deep, the anterior much smaller than the posterior, and placed near the umbones. Pedal impressions in front of the posterior adductor and one in the umbone of the left valve. Pallial line simple. Interior nacreous. Lias to present day.

Unio. Shell oval or elongated, with a thin epidermis. Surface smooth, striated or folded. Umbones more or less anterior, often corroded. Ligament external, elongated. In the right valve there are two anterior lateral teeth and a long lamellar posterior-lateral tooth; in the left valve one anterior-lateral, one cardinal, and two long lamellar posterior lateral teeth. Adductor impressions very deep, especially the anterior. Pallial line simple. Purbeck Beds to present day. Lives in freshwater.

Anthracosia. Shell elongate, oval, inequilateral. Umbones anterior, not prominent. A strong cardinal tooth in each valve. Ligament external in a linear groove. Muscular impressions deep. Pedal impression above the anterior adductor. Carboniferous and Permian.

Cardinia. Shell trigonal, oval or oblong, very inequilateral, compressed, thick, marked by striæ of growth. Umbones small, close together. Ligament external. Cardinal teeth small or obsolete; in the right valve one anterior-lateral tooth, in the left, one posterior-lateral. Impression of anterior adductor very deep. Pallial line simple. Trias to Lower Oolites.

ORDER. SIPHONIDA.

Animal with siphons. Mantle-lobes more or less united at the margins. Both muscles well developed.

Section 1. *Integripalliata.*

Siphons short, not retractile. Pallial line without sinus.

Cardita. Shell oblong, elongated, very inequilateral, ornamented with prominent radiating ribs. Often a little gaping and sinuous at its ventral margin. Lunule present. Ligament external. In the right valve two cardinal teeth and a small anterior-lateral tooth. In the left valve one cardinal and a posterior elongated lateral tooth. Adductor impressions very large. Pallial line simple. Trias to present day.

Astarte. Shell solid, inequilateral, compressed, closed, more or less trigonal or sub-orbicular. Surface smooth or with concentric furrows or striæ. A thick epidermis. Umbones prominent. Lunule distinct. Escutcheon elongated. Ligament external. Two cardinal teeth in each valve, lateral teeth rudimentary. Adductor impressions strongly marked, above the anterior one is a pedal impression. Pallial line simple. Silurian to present day. (Those in the Palæozoic doubtful.)

Opis. Shell trigonal, cordiform, convex, with an oblique keel extending from the umbone to the posterior border. Umbones prominent, incurved, or sub-spiral. Lunule large. Surface generally with concentric furrows. A cardinal tooth in each valve. Ligament external. Adductor impressions very deep. Pallial line simple. Trias to Chalk.

Crassatella. Shell solid, oblong or sub-trigonal, attenuated behind. Surface smooth or concentrically furrowed. Margins of valves smooth or crenulated. Umbones small, close together. Lunule distinct. Ligament internal. Hinge with two cardinal teeth, and one posterior-lateral and sometimes one anterior-lateral. Adductor impressions deep; pedal impressions small, distinct. Pallial line simple. Lower Cretaceous to present day.

Chama. Shell irregular, thick, inequivalve, fixed by the umbone of the larger valve (generally the left, sometimes the right). Umbones spiral or subspiral, that of the fixed valve longer than the other. Surface with concentric lamellæ or spines. The fixed valve larger and deeper than the other. In each valve a strong cardinal tooth, and sometimes in the inferior valve a narrow curved posterior tooth also. Ligament external, in a deep groove, prolonged towards the umbones. Adductor impressions large, often rough. Pallial line simple. Cretaceous to present day.

Hippurites. Shell large, massive, conical or sub-cylindrical, very inequivalve, fixed by the apex of the larger valve. The larger (right) valve, conical, striated or smooth, and with three parallel furrows on the cardinal side, and three corresponding folds in the interior. Smaller (left) valve flattened or slightly convex, operculiform, porous, the pores leading into canals; with a central umbone, two large cardinal teeth; two large adductor impressions; pallial line simple. The smaller valve is formed of two layers, the outer is thin and prismatic, the inner is porcellanous and traversed by numerous canals. The larger valve is also composed of two layers, the outer is formed of small prisms arranged in parallel layers obliquely to the surface of the shell, the inner is porcellanous, and formed of thin leaflets. Middle and Upper Cretaceous.

Lucina. Shell orbicular or oval, slightly inequilateral, more or less compressed. Lunule distinct. Umbonal area with an oblique posterior furrow. Hinge with usually two cardinal teeth and one or two lateral in each valve, the lateral and sometimes the cardinal are absent. Ligament external, sometimes partly internal. Adductor impressions well-marked, rugose, the anterior elongated within the pallial line, the posterior oblong. Margins of valves smooth or finely crenulated. Silurian to present day.

Cardium. Shell convex, nearly equilateral, cordate or oval, generally closed. Umbones prominent, incurved, nearly central. Surface with radiating ribs, which are often spiny. Margins of valves crenulated. Two cardinal teeth, and one anterior-lateral and one posterior-lateral in each valve. Ligament external. Adductor impressions shallow. Pallial line more or less sinuated. Trias to present day. (Perhaps also Palæozoic.)

Cyrena. Shell cordiform, oval or trigonal; umbones often eroded. Hinge with three cardinal teeth and one anterior- and one posterior-lateral in each valve. Ligament prominent, external. Pallial line usually entire. Lias to present day. Lives in fresh and brackish water.

Cyprina. Shell orbicular or oval, convex, with concentric striæ; a thick epidermis. Umbones prominent, incurved. Ligament external, prominent. No lunule. In each valve three cardinal teeth and one posterior-lateral. Adductor impressions oval. Pallial line entire. Margins of valves smooth. Lias to present day.

Section 2. Sinupalliata.

Siphons long, partly or completely retractile. Pallial line with a sinus.

Venus. Shell thick, oval, inflated; surface smooth or with ribs or concentric lamellæ; lunule distinct. Margin of valves finely crenulate. Hinge-plate wide with three cardinal teeth, often bifid. Ligament external, prominent. Pallial sinus small. Middle Jurassic to present day.

Cytherea (= *Meretrix*). Shell thick, ovate, sub-trigonal, smooth or with concentric furrows. Margin of valves not crenulate. Lunule well-marked. Ligament external. Hinge thick, with three cardinal teeth in each valve, two anterior-lateral in the right, and one in the left valve. Pallial sinus angular. Jurassic to present day.

Artemis (= *Dosinia*). Shell orbicular, compressed, with concentric striæ. Lunule depressed. Escutcheon narrow. Ligament sunk. Three cardinal teeth in each valve, one anterior-lateral in the left valve, and two (rudimentary) in the right. Margins smooth. Pallial sinus very deep. Cretaceous to present day.

Tellina. Shell transverse, oval, elongate, or sub-orbicular, slightly inequivalved, compressed, rounded in front, attenuated behind, and furnished with an oblique fold from the umbone to the posterior border. Margin of valves smooth. Two cardinal teeth in each valve, and one anterior- and one posterior-lateral which are often indistinct in the left valve. Ligament external, prominent. Pallial sinus very deep. Lower Cretaceous to present day.

Solen. Shell very long, sub-cylindrical, straight, smooth or finely striated, the dorsal and ventral margins parallel. Gaping at the anterior and posterior extremities. Margin of valves smooth. Umbones anterior, terminal. Hinge terminal, with one cardinal tooth in each valve. Ligament long, external. Anterior adductor impression elongated. Pallial sinus short, square. Trias (? also Devonian and Carboniferous) to present day.

Glycimeris (= *Panopea*). Shell equivalve, inequilateral, oblong, thick, concentrically striated, gaping at each end. Ligament external on a prominent ridge. One strong cardinal tooth in each valve. Pallial sinus very deep. Cretaceous to present day.

Pholadomya. Shell thin, translucent, oblong or oval, ventricose, equivalve, gaping posteriorly and sometimes anteriorly. Anterior side short and rounded. Surface with radiating ribs crossed by concentric striæ. Umbones prominent. Ligament external. Hinge without teeth or with a small transverse dentary tubercle in each valve. Adductor impressions very faint. Pallial sinus very deep. Lias to present day.

Goniomya. Shell ovate-elongate, nearly equilateral, gaping; surface with fine granulations and with V-shaped ribs pointing ventrally. Hinge without teeth. Ligament external. Adductor impressions near the dorsal margin. Lias to Cretaceous.

Myacites (= *Arcomya*). Shell thin, oblong, inequilateral, ventricose, gaping at the ends; surface granulated and often with concentric furrows. Umbones small, anterior. Ligament external. Hinge without teeth. Adductor impressions faint. Pallial line sinuous. Trias to Chalk.

10—2

Thracia. Shell oblong, slightly compressed, attenuated and gaping posteriorly; surface smooth, concentrically striated or somewhat granular. Right valve larger than the left. Hinge with a cartilage-process in each valve and a crescentic ossicle. External ligament short and prominent. Adductor impressions small. Pallial sinus deep. Trias to present day.

Mactra. Shell oval, trigonal, nearly equilateral, slightly gaping behind, smooth or with concentric striæ. Internal ligament in a large triangular pit. External ligament in a groove. In front of the internal ligament pit is a bifid cardinal tooth. Anterior- and posterior-lateral teeth well-marked, compressed. Adductor impressions semicircular. Pallial sinus round or angular. Corallian to present day.

Corbula. Shell oval, very inequivalve, closed, rounded in front, truncated behind. Surface generally with concentric grooves. Umbones prominent. Right valve larger and more convex than the left, and with a strong cardinal tooth in front of the cartilage pit, and a posterior cardinal tooth. Left valve with a projecting cartilage-process. Adductor impressions well-marked. Pallial sinus very small. Trias to present day.

Pholas. Shell elongate, cylindrical, gaping at both ends. Surface with spiny ridges, best marked in front. Dorsal region with accessory valves. No teeth; no ligament. In the interior under the umbones is a process for the insertion of the muscle of the foot. Pallial sinus very deep. Lias to present day.

Teredo. Shell more or less globular, gaping at the ends, valves tri-lobed, with concentric striæ. In the interior under the umbones is a long narrow plate for the insertion of the pedal muscle. Tube long, calcareous, sub-cylindrical, straight or curved, often with partitions. Jurassic (? Carboniferous) to present day.

Distribution of the Lamellibranchiata.

All the Lamellibranchs are aquatic animals, and by far the larger number are marine. The marine forms range from the shore down to a depth of 2900 fathoms; they are most abundant in shallow water, at depths greater than 500 fathoms they are scarce.

The lamellibranchs appear first in the Tremadoc Beds, and they gradually increase in importance, attaining their maximum at the present day. Many of the genera have a rather extended range in time. In the Palæozoic formations the Heteromyaria and the Homomyaria are predominant, the former attaining thus early its greatest development. In the Mesozoic, the Integripalliata reach their maximum, the Monomyaria are also abundant, whereas the Sinupalliata are represented by a few forms only. In the Tertiary, the Monomyaria and Heteromyaria are much less abundant, the prevailing forms belonging to the Sinupalliata.

The most important genera in the different systems are as follows :

Cambrian. *Modiolopsis, Glyptarca, Ctenodonta.*

Ordovician. *Ambonychia, Modiolopsis, Palæarca, Ctenodonta.*

Silurian. *Avicula, Pterinea, Modiolopsis, Cardiola, Ctenodonta, Grammysia.*

Devonian. *Pterinea, Cucullæa, Cardiola, Ctenodonta, Megalodon.*

Carboniferous. *Aviculopecten, Posidonomya, Anthracosia, Conocardium, Edmondia, Sanguinolites.*

Permian. *Monotis, Bakevellia, Axinus.*

Trias. *Ostrea, Lima, Pecten, Gervillia, Arca, Nucula, Myophoria, Cardita, Cardium.*

Jurassic. *Ostrea, Gryphæa, Lima, Pecten, Avicula, Gervillia, Trigonia, Modiola, Hippopodium, Pinna, Arca, Nucula, Cardinia, Myacites, Astarte, Cardium, Pholadomya, Thracia.*

Cretaceous. *Ostrea, Exogyra, Spondylus, Lima, Pecten, Gervillia, Inoceramus, Perna, Trigonia, Hippurites, Radiolites, Cardium.*

Eocene. *Pecten, Pectunculus, Astarte, Cardita, Crassatella, Chama, Lucina, Cardium, Cyprina, Cytherea, Panopæa, Pholadomya.*

Oligocene. *Ostrea, Mytilus, Cyrena, Cytherea, Psammobia, Corbula.*

Pliocene. *Pecten, Mytilus, Pectunculus, Nucula, Astarte, Lucina, Cardium, Cyprina, Venus, Artemis, Tellina, Mya.*

CLASS. GASTEROPODA.

The Gasteropoda contains even a larger number of animals than the preceding class; well-known examples are the snail, the whelk and the cowry. The bilateral symmetry, so characteristic of the lamellibranchs, is generally obliterated, owing to the twisting of the visceral-sac and the atrophy of some of the organs on one side of the body. There is a distinct head, which bears tentacles, and usually eyes. On the ventral surface of the body is a large fleshy foot; this is usually sole-like and used for crawling, but in the Heteropods it is in the form of a flattened fin, in the Pteropods it is wing-like. The mantle is never divided into two lobes. Respiration takes place by means of a pulmonary chamber, or by gills; the latter are placed in a sac formed by the mantle; sometimes they are present on both sides of the body, but very often those on the left have disappeared. In some forms the mantle at the opening of the gill-sac is produced into a tube, known as the *siphon*, by means of which water passes to the gills. The mouth is at the anterior end of the body; the anus is occasionally posterior, but as a rule it is placed near the opening of the gill chamber. Placed just within the mouth on the floor of the cavity is a dental apparatus, known as the *odontophore*; this consists of a chitinous ribbon, on which numerous teeth are placed in rows, it is moved by means of muscles and serves as a rasping organ. The arrangement of the teeth varies in different genera and is of considerable importance in the classification of recent gasteropods, but since the odontophore has never been definitely recognised in the fossil forms, it is of no service to the palæontologist. The nervous system consists of three pairs of ganglia united by cords. Some of the gasteropods are unisexual, others hermaphrodite.

In the majority of the gasteropods a shell is present, secreted by the mantle; in a few forms, as for instance the slugs, it is internal, but usually it is external. The shell, except in *Chiton*, and its allies, consists of a single piece, and is hence said to be *univalve*. In the limpet (*Patella*) it has the form of a hollow cone. But in most cases it consists of a long tube, open at one end, and tapering to a point at the other. This tube is generally coiled into a spiral, each coil being termed a *whorl*; in a few genera (*e.g. Vermetus, Siliquaria*) the whorls are separated, but as a rule they are in contact (fig. 47), the line between two contiguous whorls being known as the *suture* (*su*). All the whorls except the last one. form together the *spire* (*S*) of the shell, the point of which is termed the *apex* (*a*). The last whorl is nearly always larger than the preceding, frequently very much so, and the part of it farthest from the apex forms the *base* of the shell. The form of the spire varies in different genera and species, sometimes it is composed of a large number of whorls, sometimes of few, and it may be elongated, short, or depressed.   The angle of the spire (*spiral angle*) will consequently also vary; this is measured by lines drawn from the apex to the base of the shell on opposite sides of the exterior of the whorls.   The coiling of the shell is usually *dextral*; that is when the apex of the shell is pointed away from the observer (as in fig. 47), the aperture will be on the right hand-side; in a few cases it is *sinistral,* when the aperture will be on the left.

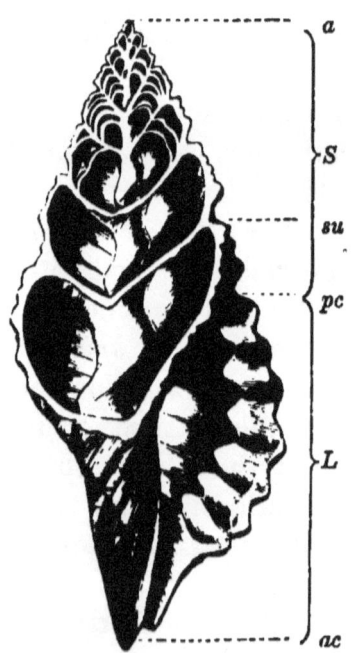

FIG. 47.   Longitudinal section of *Triton corrugatus.*   The upper part of the spire has been partitioned off many times successively.   *a,* apex; *su,* suture;   *S,* spire;   *L,* outer lip of the aperture;   *ac,* anterior canal;   *pc,* posterior canal.   (From Woodward.)

Frequently the inner parts of the whorls coalesce, and form an axial pillar extending from the apex to the base of the shell (fig. 47), and known as the *columella.*   In other cases the inner parts do not fuse and in the place of the columella there is left a space, extending from the base of the shell a greater or less distance towards the apex; the opening of this space at the base of the shell is called the *umbilicus*. When there is a columella the shell is said to be *imperforate*, when instead there is a space it is *perforate*; sometimes in the latter case the space becomes filled up with a shelly growth, known as *callus*.

Usually the cavity of the gasteropod shell is continuous from the apex to the aperture, but in a few cases partitions are thrown across the earlier parts of the shell (fig. 47), forming chambers which afterwards remain empty. The form of the aperture varies considerably in different genera and is of great importance in classification; in shape, it may be circular, oval, elongate, oblong, etc. Its margin is termed the *peristome*; the outer part of which forms the *outer lip* (*L*), the inner (that next the columella) the *inner lip*. As the gasteropod crawls along, the shell is carried on the dorsal surface of its body with the apex directed backwards; consequently the part of the aperture farthest from the apex is *anterior*, the opposite (nearest the apex) is *posterior*. Sometimes, as in *Natica*, there is no break in the aperture, it is then said to be entire or *holostomatous*; in others the anterior border is notched or produced into a tube (*ac*) in which the siphon is placed, these forms are said to be *siphonostomatous*; sometimes also there is at the posterior border another canal (*pc*), in which the excurrent or anal siphon is placed. The lip may be thin and sharp, or thickened. Sometimes it is curved outwards, and is then said to be *reflected*; or it is curved inwards and is *inflected*. It may be even, or crenulated, or produced into processes.

In many genera there is attached to the posterior part of the foot a calcareous or horny plate, the *operculum*; this is so arranged that when the animal withdraws into its shell, the operculum closes more or less completely the aperture. It has been considered by some as a second valve, but it probably represents the byssus of the lamellibranch, rather than this. The operculum is seldom preserved fossil; its form varies considerably in different genera, in some (*Turbo*) it is of very large size; it may be spiral, and is then sometimes formed of a large number of whorls (*multispiral*) as in *Trochus*, or of a few whorls (*paucispiral*) as in *Littorina*. When not spiral it may be *concentric* when growth is equal all round and it is marked with concentric lines, the nucleus being nearly central, as in *Paludina*; or it may be *unguiculate* or *claw-shaped* when the nucleus is at the apex as in *Fusus*.

The form of the shell in the spiral gasteropods varies considerably, depending on whether the whorls are in one plane or in a helicoid spiral, on the spiral angle, on the number and form of the whorls, on the size of the last whorl and whether it embraces the earlier whorls or not; the chief types are the following :—

1. *Discoidal;* the whorls all in one plane, as in *Planorbis.*

2. *Conical* or *trochiform;* conical with a flat base, as in *Trochus.*

3. *Turbinate;* conical with a convex base, as in *Turbo.*

4. *Turreted* or *elongated;* as in *Turritella.*

5. *Fusiform;* tapering to each end, as in *Fusus.*

6. *Cylindrical;* as in *Pupa.*

7. *Globular;* as in *Natica.*

8. *Convolute;* when the last whorl covers all the others and the aperture is consequently as long as the shell, as in *Cypræa.*

9. *Auriform;* aperture very large and spire very short, as in *Haliotis.* ·

The surface of the shell is frequently ornamented with spines, or with ribs and striæ, these are said to be longitudinal when they run parallel to the sutures from the aperture to the apex; they are transverse when they run across the whorls from suture to suture. When rows of spines or processes extend across all the whorls from the apex to the base of the shell, as in *Murex,* we have what are termed *varices.* The colours with which the shells of recent gasteropods are provided are only preserved fossil in rare cases. The shell consists of an outer epidermal layer, and of a thick porcellanous layer; in some cases there is also an inner nacreous or pearly layer.

The Gasteropoda are divided into the following six orders, (1) Polyplacophora, (2) Prosobranchiata, (3) Opisthobranchiata, (4) Hcteropoda, (5) Pulmonata, (6) Pteropoda.

ORDER. POLYPLACOPHORA.

The body is bilaterally symmetrical, and the shell is formed of eight calcareous plates. This includes the genus *Chiton* and allied forms. The order is only poorly represented in the fossil state; the earliest representatives occurring in the Ordovician rocks.

ORDER. PROSOBRANCHIATA.

The gills and auricle are in front of the ventricle of the heart; there is always a shell.

Patella. Shell conical, oval or sub-circular; apex sub-central or excentral, recurved anteriorly; surface with radiating ribs or striæ, rarely smooth. Margin simple or spinose. Muscular impression horse-shoe shaped, open in front. Jurassic to present day.

Emarginula. Shell conical, surface cancellated, apex recurved posteriorly. Anterior border with a well-marked slit. Muscular impression horse-shoe shaped. Carboniferous Limestone to present day.

Pleurotomaria. Shell trochiform, conical, turbinate, or discoidal; interior nacreous. Umbilicus present or absent. Aperture subquadrate or oval, outer lip sharp, with a slit, which as the shell grows becomes filled up, leaving a band on the whorls, toward which the lines of growth converge, being directed obliquely backwards. Operculum horny. Upper Cambrian to present day.

Murchisonia. Shell turreted, with many whorls, provided with a band as in *Pleurotomaria*. Aperture oval, with a slit, and a short anterior canal. Ordovician to Permian.

Bellerophon. Shell globular or discoidal; whorls few, symmetrically coiled in one plane. Aperture sub-circular or oval, with a deep median sinus, which is replaced by a band or keel dividing the shell into two similar parts; columellar edge often with callus. Upper Cambrian to Permian.

Phasianella. Shell elongated, oval or oblong, smooth, polished, imperforate, interior not nacreous. Aperture oval, entire, rounded anteriorly, angular posteriorly; outer lip thin, simple, sharp. Columella flattened. Operculum calcareous, convex externally, concave internally. Devonian to present day.

Turbo. Shell solid, turbinate or conical, whorls convex, interior nacreous. Aperture large, circular, entire, slightly produced anteriorly; outer lip sharp. Imperforate or with a small umbilicus. Operculum thick, calcareous, exterior convex, interior flat and spiral, nucleus central or sub-central. Silurian to present day.

Trochus. Shell conical, whorls numerous and flat or slightly convex, the last whorl angular; base flat or nearly so. Aperture oblique, rhomboidal, outer lip sharp. Columella twisted, with a prominent anterior protuberance. Operculum horny, multispiral. Silurian to present day.

Nerita. Shell thick, solid, ovoid or semiglobose, imperforate. Spire short. Surface smooth or with spiral ribs. Aperture semicircular; outer lip thick, denticulate; inner lip callous, flattened with a straight denticulate border. Operculum calcareous. Cretaceous to present day.

Solarium. Shell conical, depressed, angular at the periphery. Aperture entire, subquadrate; lip sharp. Umbilicus wide and deep, limited by a crenulated margin. Operculum horny, spiral. Cretaceous to present day.

Euomphalus. Shell depressed, discoidal, with a wide and large umbilicus; whorls convex with a ridge on the upper surface. Aperture polygonal; outer lip with a sinus on its upper surface. Silurian to Carboniferous.

Scalaria. Shell more or less umbilicate, turreted, spire elongate; whorls numerous, convex, sometimes separated, ornamented with transverse ribs or sometimes with longitudinal lamellæ. Aperture circular, entire, margin thickened. Operculum horny, paucispiral. Trias to present day.

Turritella. Shell imperforate, turreted, many-whorled, whorls flat or slightly convex, ornamented with spiral ribs and with striæ of growth; spire very long. Aperture oval or subquadrate, entire, outer lip thin. Operculum horny. Trias to present day.

Calyptræa. Shell conical, limpet-shaped, spiral, apex central; interior with a half-cup shaped process under the apex and attached posteriorly. Cretaceous to present day.

Natica. Shell oval, globular, generally smooth, spire short, last whorl very large. Aperture semilunar or oval, entire; outer lip sharp, inner lip callous, not crenulate. Frequently an umbilicus, often filled with callus. Operculum of same size as aperture, horny or calcareous, paucispiral, nucleus excentric. Carboniferous (perhaps Silurian) to present day.

Paludina. Shell thin, turbinate; whorls convex, smooth or with faint ribs. Aperture entire, oval, slightly angulated behind. Operculum horny with concentric striæ. Lower Cretaceous to present day. Lives in freshwater.

Littorina. Shell thick, not nacreous internally, turbinate, few-whorled, imperforate. Aperture rounded, angular behind, outer lip sharp. Columella flattened. Operculum horny, paucispiral. Lias to present day.

Pseudomelania. Shell many-whorled, elongate, turriculate, imperforate, spire long. Aperture oval, entire, a little inflated in front, narrowed behind; outer lip sharp. Columella smooth. Lias to Tertiary.

Melania. Shell elongate, turreted, many-whorled, imperforate, apex sharp but usually corroded. Surface smooth, ribbed or spiny. Aperture entire, narrow behind, rounded in front; outer lip sharp, slightly sinuous. Operculum horny, subspiral. Wealden to present day. Lives in freshwater.

Nerinea. Shell elongate, perforate or not, whorls numerous. Aperture sub-quadrangular, oval or elongate, with a short anterior canal and a posterior slit near the suture, which forms as it becomes filled up a continuous band. Columella and also the interior of the whorls furnished with folds which are continuous to the apex. Inferior Oolite to Upper Cretaceous.

Cerithium. Shell imperforate, turreted, without epidermis. Whorls numerous, the last whorl always shorter than the spire. Aperture oblong or semi-oval, with a short posterior canal and a well-marked recurved anterior canal; outer lip expanded. Operculum horny, oval, paucispiral. Trias to present day.

Strombus. Shell ovoid, ventricose, tuberculate or spiny, imperforate. Spire with numerous whorls, the last very large. Aperture long, narrow, with a short anterior canal; often canaliculate posteriorly; outer lip expanded, thick, often lobed, with a deep notch near the anterior canal. Operculum small, horny, claw-shaped, edge serrated. Lower Cretaceous to present day.

Rostellaria. Shell fusiform, spire elongated, composed of many whorls, which are smooth or faintly ribbed. Aperture oblong with a long straight or slightly curved anterior canal and a posterior canal applied to the spire; outer lip expanded, thick or crenulate, with a notch in front. Operculum small, oval or claw-shaped, edge not serrated. Eocene to present day.

Cypræa. Shell ovoid or elongate, convex, convolute, surface covered with shining enamel. Spire concealed. Aperture long and narrow, with a short canal at each end; outer lip, inflected and crenulated; inner lip crenulated. In the young forms the outer lip is thin and the spire prominent. Cretaceous to present day.

Buccinum. Shell oval or elongate, imperforate. Spire long. Whorls ventricose, smooth or with longitudinal folds. Aperture oval, large; outer lip simple; anterior canal short, truncated, a little reflected. Operculum small. Cretaceous to present day.

Nassa. Shell ovate, ventricose, generally ornamented. Aperture oval, with a short reflected anterior canal. Inner lip callous, forming a tooth-like projection near the anterior canal; outer lip crenulate internally. Columella with an oblique fold at its base. Cretaceous to present day.

Purpura. Shell tuberculate, striated or lamellar, not varicose. Spire short, last whorl large. Aperture oval, large, with an oblique groove in front. Columella flattened, callous. Operculum lamellar, nucleus external. Pliocene to present day.

Fusus. Shell imperforate, fusiform, elongate, spire many-whorled. Aperture oval; outer lip simple. A long straight anterior canal, not closed. Columella smooth, without folds. Operculum oval. Cretaceous to present day.

MOLLUSCA. GASTEROPODA. 161

Murex. Shell oval or elongate, solid, spire prominent, whorls convex, carrying three or more continuous longitudinal varices, which may be spiny, foliaceous, or tubercular. Aperture rounded, anterior canal more or less long, narrow and tubular, often partly closed; no posterior canal; outer lip thick. Operculum oval, nucleus subapical. Upper Cretaceous to present day.

Mitra. Shell fusiform, thick. Spire elevated, summit acute. Aperture narrow, elongate, notched in front. Columella with oblique folds, of which the posterior are the stronger; outer lip not reflected, thickened internally. No operculum. Eocene to present day.

Voluta. Shell ovate or fusiform, solid, thick, summit of spire mammilated. Last whorl very large, aperture elongate, oval; canal very short, recurved; outer lip simple, often thick, rarely reflected. Columella with oblique folds, of which the anterior are the stronger. No operculum. Upper Cretaceous to present day.

Pleurotoma. Shell turreted, fusiform, spire long. Aperture oval; outer lip curved, provided with a deep slit near the suture; inner lip smooth. Canal long, straight, narrow. Operculum horny, ovate, acute, nucleus apical. Cretaceous to present day.

Conus. Shell inversely conical, generally smooth. Spire short, many-whorled. Aperture narrow, straight, with parallel or sub-parallel borders; outer lip thin, simple, no folds or teeth, notched at the suture. Columella straight, smooth. Operculum horny, much smaller than the aperture. Cretaceous to present day.

ORDER. OPISTHOBRANCHIATA.

The gills and auricle are placed behind the ventricle. A shell is absent in some forms. All are hermaphrodite and all marine.

Bulla. Shell solid, smooth, sub-globular or ovoid, convolute. Spire concave. Aperture as long as the last whorl, rounded at the ends, widest in front; outer lip sharp. Cretaceous to present day.

ORDER. HETEROPODA.

The forms included in this order live in the open ocean at the surface. The foot is modified so as to form a vertical fin; a shell is absent in some and when present is always thin. Only a very few forms occur fossil.

ORDER. PULMONATA.

Respiration takes place by means of a pulmonary chamber. A shell may be present or absent, and is holostomatous. All the genera are hermaphrodite, and nearly all live on land or in fresh water.

Limnæa. Shell spiral, thin, horny; last whorl very large, spire sharp. Aperture large, oval, rounded in front. Columella more or less twisted. Peristome sharp, entire. Purbeck Beds to present day. Lives in fresh water.

Planorbis. Shell discoidal, horny, whorls numerous. Aperture oblique; peristome simple, sharp. Jurassic to present day. Freshwater.

Helix. Shell variable, conical, discoidal, or globular; perforate or not; aperture oblique. Peristome simple or reflected. Eocene to present day. Lives on land.

ORDER. PTEROPODA.

The Pteropods are all pelagic animals. The head is not well marked, and the foot is represented by two lateral wing-like fins. A shell may or may not be present.

Hyolithes (= *Theca*). Shell straight, rarely curved, pyramidal, triangular in section, smooth or striated; posterior part sometimes crossed by walls. Aperture sometimes oblique; provided with an operculum having the form of a half cone. Upper Cambrian to Permian.

Conularia. Shell generally straight, pyramidal, section quadrangular, each lateral face with a median longitudinal groove; posterior part of shell sometimes provided with concave partitions. Surface ornamented with numerous transverse, parallel, angulated ridges. Aperture partly closed by triangular or lobed processes. Ordovician to Trias.

Tentaculites. Shell thick, solid, in the form of a greatly elongated cone, straight or slightly curved, section circular, posterior extremity sharp or with a vesicular enlargement. Surface provided with prominent, transverse, parallel rings, and with transverse and longitudinal striæ. Ordovician to Devonian.

Distribution of the Gasteropoda.

Some of the Gasteropoda live on land, others in fresh water, but the majority are marine; they are found in the seas of all parts of the world, but are especially abundant in warm regions and in comparatively shallow water. A few forms can exist both on land and in water, *e.g.* *Ampullaria*, which commonly lives in lakes and rivers, is also found on land. Some marine genera, such as *Littorina*, *Cerithium*, and *Purpura*, are able to live in fresh as well as in salt water; on the other hand some freshwater forms are at times found living in the sea, *e.g.* *Limnœa*, *Neritina*, *Bithynia*, and *Planorbis*; this is especially the case in places where the water is less salt than the main mass of the ocean, as for instance in the Baltic, where we find the genera just mentioned living side by side with *Littorina* and with the marine lamellibranchs *Cardium*, *Tellina*, and *Mya*. Of the six orders of the Gasteropoda, four are entirely marine, viz. the Polyplacophora, Heteropoda, Opisthobranchiata, and Pteropoda; and the Prosobranchiata are mainly marine. The Pulmonata are found only on land and in fresh water. The Heteropoda and Pteropoda live in mid-ocean at or near the surface, whereas the other marine forms occur mainly at no very great distance from the coasts and in comparatively shallow water.

In connection with the Gasteropoda a few words may be said with regard to the distribution of the marine Mollusca generally. Just as we find on land, that the surface of the earth can be divided into regions, each characterised by the presence of certain animals not found elsewhere, so also in the oceans we have similar life-provinces, caused mainly by conditions of climate and food supply. These are marked by the abundance of certain genera and the presence of some species which do not extend into other provinces; but they are less distinct than the terrestrial regions, since very few of the genera are confined to one province. In the European region the chief provinces are: the *Arctic*, which includes the polar seas and extends as far south as the North of Iceland and the North Cape; the *Boreal*, extending from the last down to near the southern end of Norway and including

the Shetland Islands; the *Celtic*, including the coasts of
Southern Sweden, the Baltic, Denmark, Northern France
and the British Isles; and the *Lusitanian*, the coasts of
the Bay of Biscay, Portugal, the Mediterranean, and North-
west Africa. In each province the character of the
molluscan fauna also varies with the nature of the sea-
bottom, some genera (*e.g. Mya, Lutraria, Scrobicularia*)
being found especially on muddy bottoms, others (*e.g.
Natica, Turritella, Cyprœa, Cardium*) on sandy, and others
(*e.g. Buccinum, Littorina, Patella, Arca*) on rocky. There
is also a distribution according to depth, caused by
temperature (which as a whole decreases with the depth),
and by the absence of light; in this respect five zones
have been traced:—

(1) *Littoral Zone*, extending between high and low
water marks; in Europe this is especially characterised
by the abundance of the genera *Littorina, Trochus,
Patella, Hydrobia, Haliotis, Fissurella, Solen, Mya*, and
Cardium.

(2) *Laminarian Zone*, ranging from low water down
to about 14 fathoms; in it algæ (*Laminaria, etc.*) are
particularly luxuriant, and afford food for numerous phyto-
phagous mollusks. Some of the commonest genera met
with are *Trochus, Nassa, Rissoa,* and *Ostrea.* Nudibranchs
are also very numerous.

(3) *Zone of Nullipores or Corallines*, from 14 to about
35 fathoms, where the calcareous algæ (Nullipores) are
very abundant. It is characterised by the abundance of
*Pleurotoma, Fusus, Buccinum, Natica, Eulima, Venus,
Dosinia, Astarte, Nucula, Arca, Lima*, and *Pecten.*

(4) *Zone of Brachiopods and deep-sea Corals*, from
35 to about 230 fathoms; off Europe *Oculina* is the
common coral; brachiopods and Polyzoa are also abundant.

Some of the chief mollusks are *Turritella, Odostomia, Dentalium, Tellina, Neæra,* and *Yoldia.*

(5) *Abysmal Zone,* extending from the last down to the greatest depths at which life has been found. In this zone the shells are mostly thin, colourless, transparent and of small size; it is especially characterised by numerous Scaphopods; other common forms are *Pleurotoma, Fusus, Actæon, Scaphander, Philine, Arca, Nucula, Limopsis, Leda, Lima,* and *Pecten.* The remains of Pteropods which have fallen from the surface of the ocean after death are also numerous.

In the fossil state gasteropods are less numerous than lamellibranchs, although they exceed them at the present day. The earliest forms occur in the Upper Cambrian, they belong to the holostomatous Prosobranchiata, and throughout the Palæozoic this is the predominant group, no genera belonging to the siphonostomatous section are known with certainty until the Trias is reached; the latter become more abundant in the Oolites, still more so in the Cretaceous, and in the Tertiary they are the predominant forms. The other orders are not nearly so well represented as the Prosobranchiata. The Polyplacophora range from the Ordovician to the present day, but they are more abundant in the Palæozoic than in later formations. The Heteropoda are represented by a few forms only, the first occurring in the Miocene. The Opisthobranchiata range from the Carboniferous to the present day, they are moderately well represented in the Jurassic and Cretaceous and become more abundant in the Tertiary. The Pulmonata are first found in the Carboniferous, but they are quite rare until the Tertiary is reached. The Pteropoda occur first in the Lower Cambrian, but the nature of some of the earlier forms (*Hyolithes, Conularia, Tentaculites*) is somewhat doubtful; it is possible that they may not be Pteropods; but representatives of the order certainly occur in the Silurian and Devonian.

The most important genera found in the different systems are :—

Cambrian. *Bellerophon, Hyolithes, Conularia.*

Ordovician. *Bellerophon, Holopœa, Cyclonema, Maclurea, Conularia, Tentaculites.*

Silurian. *Pleurotomaria, Murchisonia, Bellerophon, Euomphalus, Holopella, Acroculia.*

Devonian. *Pleurotomaria, Murchisonia, Bellerophon, Loxonema, Euomphalus, Macrocheilus, Tentaculites.*

Carboniferous. *Pleurotomaria, Murchisonia, Bellerophon, Loxonema, Euomphalus, Naticopsis, Macrocheilus, Conularia.*

Permian. *Pleurotomaria, Murchisonia, Turbo, Loxonema, Macrocheilus.*

Trias. *Pleurotomaria, Turbo, Loxonema, Natica, Turritella.*

Jurassic. *Pleurotomaria, Amberleya, Cirrus, Phasianella, Trochus, Natica, Pseudomelania, Nerinea, Cerithium, Alaria, Purpuroidea.*

Cretaceous. *Pleurotomaria, Solarium, Turritella, Natica, Paludina, Cerithium, Aporrhais, Cinulia.*

Eocene. *Phorus, Calyptrœa, Natica, Melania, Cerithium, Rostellaria, Cyprœa, Cassidaria, Triton, Fusus, Pyrula, Murex, Typhis, Voluta, Oliva, Pleurotoma, Conus.*

Oligocene. *Neritina, Natica, Paludina, Melania, Cerithium, Potamides, Murex, Voluta, Ancillaria, Pleurotoma, Limnœa, Planorbis, Rissoa, Helix, Bulimus.*

Pliocene. *Trochus, Scalaria, Turritella, Emarginula, Natica, Littorina, Cerithium, Buccinum, Nassa, Purpura, Fusus, Voluta.*

CLASS. SCAPHOPODA.

The Scaphopoda include only a few genera, which in some respects resemble the lamellibranchs. The body is bilaterally symmetrical; the mantle is cylindrical and open at both ends, and it secretes a straight or slightly curved tubular shell which is also open at both ends. The foot is greatly elongated and can be protruded through the larger aperture of the mantle and shell. The animal is attached to the posterior part of the shell by means of a muscle; an odontophore is present, but the head is not well marked, and eyes and heart are absent. The sexes are separate. All the Scaphopods are marine, and they often live buried in sand or mud. The earliest forms occur in the Ordovician rocks.

Dentalium. Shell conical or sub-cylindrical, attenuated posteriorly, slightly curved. Anterior aperture simple, not constricted; posterior aperture smaller. Surface smooth, annulated or ornamented with longitudinal striæ or ribs. Devonian to present day.

CLASS. CEPHALOPODA.

The Cephalopods are more highly organised than any of the other mollusks; well-known forms are the cuttle-fishes, belemnites, ammonites, and the nautilus. They are always bilaterally symmetrical. The head is well marked, it is separated from the body by a constriction, and is especially characterised by the fact that the fore-

foot extends round the mouth, and its margin is produced
into eight or ten (many in *Nautilus*) processes or arms
(fig. 48 *e*, *f*), which are provided either with sucking discs
or tentacles, and are used in prehension and locomotion.
The mid-foot is in the form of a tube termed the *funnel*
(*d*) which opens in front to the exterior, and behind into

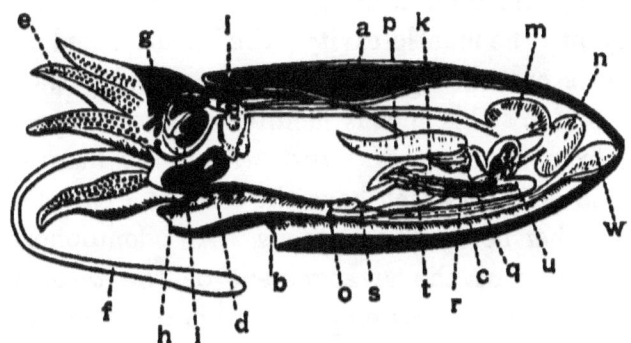

Fig. 48. Diagram of a vertical median antero-posterior section of *Sepia
officinalis*. *a*, shell; *b*, mouth of mantle-cavity; *c*, mantle-cavity;
d, funnel; *e*, lobes (arms) of the fore-foot; *f*, long arm of the fore-
foot; *g*, the upper beak or jaw; *h*, the lower beak or jaw; *i*, odontophore; *k*, the viscero-pericardial sac; *l*, the nerve-collar; *m*, the
crop; *n*, the gizzard; *o*, the anus; *p*, left gill; *q*, ventricle of the
heart; *r*, renal glandular mass; *s*, left nephridial aperture; *t*, viscero-
pericardial aperture; *u*, branchial heart; *w*, ink-sac. (After Lan-
kester, *Zool. Art. Encyc. Britt.*)

the mantle-cavity (*c*). The funnel may be either a perfect
tube or may be formed by the apposition of two troughs.
The hind-foot is absent. On the upper surface of the
head there are two large eyes, which, except in *Nautilus*,
are almost as highly developed as in vertebrate animals.
The mantle is formed by a single fold of the integument,
which passes quite round the body of the animal; but
dorsally the fold is very shallow so that the mantle-cavity
exists mainly on the ventral surface. The gills (*p*) are placed

in the mantle-cavity, in some forms there is one pair, in others two. A current of water flows in at the sides of the mantle-cavity, and passes out through the funnel, by means of the contraction of the walls of the mantle-cavity. In the forms belonging to the order Dibranchiata, a gland (known as the *ink-sac, w*) which secretes a black fluid (sepia) is present; the duct from this opens together with the anus (*o*) into the mantle-cavity; the ink is ejected at times and passes out through the funnel, rendering the water cloudy, and by this means facilitating the escape of the animal from its enemies. Just within the mouth there are two jaws (*g, h*) which have the form of a parrot's beak, and are either horny or calcareous. An odontophore (*i*) is also present, but the arrangement of the teeth is less variable than in the gasteropods, and is of little value for systematic purposes. The heart consists of a median ventricle (*q*), and of lateral auricles, which are either two or four in number, according as there are two or four gills; it gives off in front an artery to the head, and one behind to the viscera. The nervous system is remarkable in that the three pairs of ganglia are placed close together, forming a central mass (*l*); one part is placed above the œsophagus, and is connected by cords with the other part beneath it. This central nervous system is enclosed in a cartilaginous box and gives off nerves to the arms, viscera, etc. The sexes are always separate, and the genital ducts open into the mantle-cavity. The shell may be external or internal (*a*), in the latter case it is usually placed in a sac in the mantle on the dorsal side; in some forms it is absent.

ORDER. TETRABRANCHIATA.

The only genus of the Tetrabranchiata existing at the present day is *Nautilus*, but in past geological times the order was represented by very numerous and varied forms, such as *Orthoceras*, *Nautilus*, and *Ammonites*. The Tetrabranchs are characterised by possessing two pairs of gills, two pairs of auricles, and two pairs of kidneys. An ink-sac is absent; the funnel is not a complete tube, but is formed by the apposition of two troughs. The arms are numerous and do not bear sucking-discs.

A shell is present in all forms and is always external. It consists of a tube, which tapers to a point at one end, and may be straight, arched, or spiral; in the spiral forms the whorls may be separate, or partly free, or in contact throughout; in some cases they are placed all in one plane, in others arranged obliquely. The cavity of the shell, unlike that in the gasteropods, is not continuous throughout from the aperture to the apex, but is divided up into

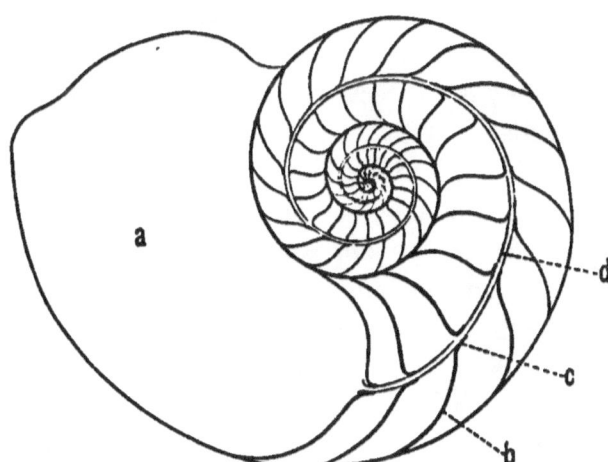

Fig. 49. Section of shell of *Nautilus*. *a*, body-chamber; *b*, septum; *c*, septal neck; *d*, siphuncle.

a number of chambers by means of partitions termed *septa* (fig. 49 *b*); the size of the chambers increases towards the aperture of the shell. The body of the animal was placed in the last chamber (*a*), all the earlier ones being filled with air only. Originally the earlier chambers were occupied by the animal, but as growth went on, it successively withdrew to the larger parts of the shell, each time depositing behind it a septum and thus forming a new chamber. All the chambers are traversed by a tube known as the *siphuncle* (*d*), which is given off from the posterior part of the animal. The position of the siphuncle varies in different genera; in some (*Nautilus*) it pierces the septa at or near their centre, in others (*Ammonites*) at the external margin, in others (*Clymenia*) at the internal margin. In the modern *Nautilus* the siphuncle is membranous, except that it is coated with calcareous granules; but in some fossil forms it was completely invested by a calcareous tube. In addition to this the septa are frequently produced in the form of funnels around the siphuncle, so as to more or less completely ensheathe it. These funnels are termed *septal necks* (*c*); in some genera (*Nautilus*) they are directed backwards, in others (*Ammonites*) forwards.

In the genus *Nautilus*, the outer convex portion of the shell is the ventral side, and the inner the dorsal; but in some fossil forms the opposite was the case, the outer being dorsal, and the inner ventral. It will therefore be more convenient to speak of the external and internal margins, instead of the dorsal and ventral. The margin of the aperture is in some cases even all round; in others a process is given off from the external margin, or the lateral margins are produced into 'ears,' or the external margin may possess a sinus. In a few forms the aperture is constricted. The line where the edges of the septa unite with the shell is known as the *suture* (fig. 50), obviously this will only be seen when the shell is removed; but the fossil forms frequently occur as casts and in these the sutures are admirably shown. The form of the sutures varies considerably in different genera and is of great

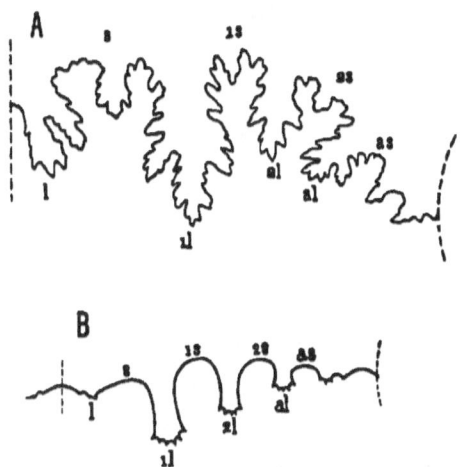

Fig. 50. *A*, suture of an Ammonite (*Parkinsonia parkinsoni*) from the Inferior Oolite. *B*, Suture of *Ceratites nodosus*, from the Muschel-kalk. *l*, external lobe; 1*l*, 2*l*, superior and inferior lateral lobes; *al*, auxiliary lobes; *s*, external saddle; 1*s*, 2*s*, superior and inferior lateral saddles; *as*, auxiliary saddles. In each case the straight line on the left represents the position of the siphuncle, and the curved one on the right the line of contact with the next whorl.

importance for systematic purposes; in some cases they are straight or only slightly curved, in others they are folded many times, the portions which are convex towards the mouth of the shell being termed the *saddles* (fig. 50 *s*), whilst the intervening concave portions are known as the *lobes* (*l*). In many forms the lobes and saddles exhibit secondary foldings, these may be slight, producing merely a denticulate suture, or they may be deep and provided with other foldings, giving a foliaceous appearance to the

suture. The lobes and saddles are similar on opposite
sides of the shell ; commonly there is first the external lobe
(fig. 50 *l*) on the external margin, then the superior and
inferior lateral lobes (1 *l*, 2 *l*), and other lobes known as
auxiliary lobes (*al*). The saddles are arranged in a similar
manner, we have the external saddle (*s*), the lateral saddles
(1 *s*, 2 *s*), and auxiliary saddles (*as*).

The surface of the shell may be smooth or variously
ornamented with striæ, ribs, tubercles or spines.

There are two sub-orders (1) Nautiloidea, (2) Ammonoidea.

The form of the shell is variable ; it may be straight,
arched, or spiral. The sutures are usually simple, but
occasionally undulate or denticulate. The septal necks
are (except in the genera *Bathmoceras* and *Nothoceras*)
directed backwards. The position of the siphuncle is
variable ; its interior is frequently contracted by calcareous deposits.

Orthoceras. Shell straight, occasionally slightly
curved, conical, transverse section usually circular. Septa
simple, concave ; the last chamber large ; aperture not
contracted. Siphuncle usually slender, cylindrical, and
central, or sub-central, sometimes ex-central. Ornamentation variable. Tremadoc Beds to Trias.

Actinoceras. Similar to the preceding, but the
siphuncle is large and is inflated between the septa, and
contains in the interior a large amount of calcareous
deposit. Ordovician to Carboniferous Limestone.

Gomphoceras (= *Phragmoceras*). Shell fusiform,
straight or slightly curved ; section circular, sometimes
oval; last chamber very long, aperture contracted, T-shaped.

Siphuncle sub-central, placed towards the ventral (usually) convex side. Surface smooth or with transverse ribs or striæ. Silurian (perhaps also Ordovician, Devonian and Carboniferous).

Cyrtoceras. Like *Orthoceras* but always curved, and with the siphuncle usually sub-marginal. Cambrian to Carboniferous.

Nautilus. Shell spiral, coiled in one plane, whorls few and more or less embracing. Last chamber large, aperture simple, with an external sinus. Septa concave, sutures simple or with slight lobes and saddles. Siphuncle sub-central, septal necks short and directed backwards. Surface of shell smooth or ornamented with striæ or ribs. Ordovician to present day.

Aturia. Shell discoidal, whorls completely embracing; suture-line zig-zag, with a deep lateral lobe on each side. Siphuncle on the internal margin; septal necks elongated, completely covering the siphuncle. Eocene and Miocene.

SUB-ORDER. AMMONOIDEA.

The shell is generally coiled into a plane spiral. The sutures are undulated or bent into lobes and saddles. The siphuncle is marginal and does not contain internal deposits. The septal necks (except in *Clymenia* and *Goniatites*) are directed forwards.

Clymenia. Shell discoidal; whorls numerous, all visible, but each partly embraces the preceding one; the last chamber is long, generally occupying three-quarters of the last whorl. Aperture with a ventral sinus. Sutures simply lobed. Siphuncle on the internal margin; septal necks directed backwards. Surface usually ornamented with transverse striæ. Upper Devonian.

Goniatites. Shell discoidal; whorls embracing, umbilicus sometimes narrow, sometimes wide. ˙ Last chamber usually large, aperture with a ventral sinus. Sutures never foliaceous, sometimes angular, sometimes rounded; siphuncle small, on the external margin; septal necks usually directed backwards. Upper Silurian to Carboniferous.

Ceratites. Shell discoidal, ornamented with ribs or tubercles; umbilicus large; last chamber short. Saddles rounded, lobes denticulate. Trias, especially Muschelkalk.

Ammonites. Shell coiled in a plane spiral; the whorls sometimes embracing. Sutures lobed and foliaceous. Siphuncle on the external margin. Surface smooth, or ornamented with striæ, ribs, tubercles or spines. The external margin of the shell may be rounded or provided with a ridge or keel. Lias to Chalk.

In the last chamber of some *Ammonites* and a few other genera, a pair of calcareous or horny plates, known as the *Aptychus*, are occasionally found; in shape they are triangular or semicircular, and the edges where the two plates are in contact are straight, the others curved. The *Aptychus* is thought to have served as an operculum.

The species of *Ammonites* are very numerous and differ so much from one another that they are now regarded as representing many distinct genera; these are based mainly on the length of the last chamber, on the form of the sutures, and the presence or absence of an aptychus, and on the aperture. But in an elementary work like the present it will be convenient to retain the old genus *Ammonites*.

Hamites. Shell bent upon itself three times, the parts not in contact; the last chamber long. Suture-line with the saddles and lobes deeply incised, the superior-lateral lobe and often the inferior-lateral lobe being divided into two paired parts. Surface smooth or ornamented with ribs, tubercles, or spines. Lower Greensand to Chalk.

Turrilites. Shell spiral, turreted, usually sinistral, all the whorls in contact. Sutures with the lateral lobes symmetrically divided. Surface ornamented with ribs or tubercles. Gault to Chalk.

Baculites. Shell straight, elongate-conical; last chamber large, aperture produced ventrally. Sutures with the lobes symmetrically divided. Lower Greensand to Upper Chalk.

Scaphites. Shell coiled in a plane spiral; the whorls in contact and embracing, except the last, which is detached from the spiral and then recurved. Last chamber long. Surface ornamented with simple or nodular ribs. Gault to Chalk.

Crioceras. Shell coiled in a plane spiral; the whorls not in contact. Surface ornamented with ribs and often with tubercles and spines. Lower Greensand to Gault.

Ancyloceras. Like *Crioceras*, but the last whorl is produced in a straight line and then bent back in the form of a hook. Inferior Oolite to Lower Greensand.

ORDER. DIBRANCHIATA.

The Dibranchiates are represented at the present day by the various forms of cuttle-fishes; but they are of much less importance geologically than the Tetrabranchs, the only really common fossil genus being *Belemnites*. Some of the modern cuttle-fishes attain an enormous size, for instance *Loligo* sometimes has a length of forty feet or more.

The Dibranchiata, as the name indicates, possess one pair of gills only; there is also one pair of auricles and one pair of kidneys. The number of arms is limited to eight or ten; and on the inner side—that facing the mouth—they are provided with rows of sucking discs, which sometimes possess horny hooks. The jaws are not calcified. An ink-sac is always present and is occasionally found preserved fossil; and even in this condition it is capable of being used for artistic purposes. The funnel is in the form of a complete tube. A skeleton is absent in some forms; when present it is internal, with the single exception of the genus *Argonauta*; it may be either horny or calcareous. In some (*Sepia* etc.) it has the form of a flattened spoon-like body, known as the *pen*, which is composed mainly of laminated calcareous material; occasionally at the posterior end there is a small chambered portion. The pen is placed on the dorsal surface of the animal in a sac formed by the mantle. In *Spirula* the shell is situated in the posterior part of the body, and consists of a tube coiled in a plane spiral and divided up into chambers by means of septa, which are traversed by a siphuncle placed near the inner margin. In *Belemnites* it consists of a solid portion (the "guard") and of a chambered part with a siphuncle. The shell in *Argonauta* is of quite a different nature to that found in other forms; it is spiral but not chambered, and is secreted, not by the mantle, but by the two dorsal arms, and is found only in the female, serving for the reception of the eggs.

The Dibranchiata are divided into two sub-orders (1) the Decapoda, (2) the Octopoda.

SUB-ORDER. DECAPODA.

There are ten arms, eight of equal length and two longer than the others: the suckers are stalked and are provided with a horny ring. An internal shell is always present. The genera *Spirula* and *Sepia* already mentioned belong to this sub-order; the former does not occur fossil and the latter only rarely. Allied to *Sepia* is the genus *Belosepia* found in the Eocene. The most important fossil form is *Belemnites*.

Belemnites. The shell in this genus consists of two parts—the guard (fig. 51 *a*) and the phragmocone (*b*). The former is solid and is much more commonly preserved than the latter; it varies considerably in shape and size, being cylindrical, fusiform, conical, etc. The posterior end is always pointed; at the anterior end there is a conical cavity, termed the alveolus. The length of the guard varies from one to fifteen inches.

When sliced transversely or longitudinally it is seen to be formed of a number of layers arranged concentrically around an axial line, which is not quite central but is placed nearer the ventral surface; these

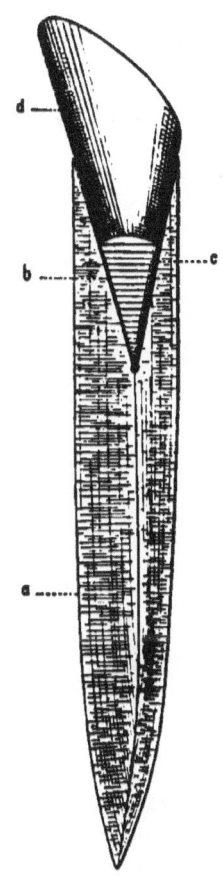

Fig. 51. Diagram-section of *Belemnites*. *a*, guard; *b*, phragmocone; *c*, siphuncle traversing the chambers of the phragmocone; *d*, pro-ostracum.

layers are not of uniform thickness along the whole length of the guard, they become thicker towards the posterior end and thinner towards the anterior. Each layer is formed of minute prisms of calcite, which are placed perpendicular to the axial line, thus producing a radiating fibrous appearance. The surface of the guard is sometimes smooth, or it may be granular, or furnished with ramifying vascular impressions; in some species there is a longitudinal groove on the ventral surface.

The phragmocone (*b*) is a conical tube which fits into the alveolus at the anterior end of the guard, it is divided up into chambers by septa which are concave in front; a siphuncle (*c*) traverses the chambers along the ventral margin. The wall of the phragmocone (sometimes termed the *conotheca*) is very thin, and in well preserved specimens the dorsal surface (or sometimes the lateral) is found to be produced in front into a large laminar expansion (*d*); this prolongation is known as the *pro-ostracum*, and corresponds to the "pen" of the cuttle-fish. The suckers on the tentacles were provided with horny hooks, which are occasionally preserved fossil; the ink-sac and mandibles have also been found in a few specimens. Lias to Upper Cretaceous.

Belemnitella. This differs from the preceding genus in having a slit in the guard on the ventral side of the alveolus. There are well-marked vascular impressions on the ventral surface. Chalk.

SUB-ORDER. OCTOPODA.

There are eight arms only; the suckers are sessile and possess no horny ring. The shell is rudimentary or absent. This sub-order is very poorly represented in the fossil state; examples of it are *Octopus* and *Argonauta*, the latter has been found in the Pliocene Beds.

Distribution of the Cephalopoda.

The Nautiloidea at the present day are represented by four species of *Nautilus* only; these occur in comparatively shallow water in the Indian Ocean, the Persian Gulf, the China Sea, and off New Guinea and Fiji. The group appears much earlier in the geological series than either the Ammonoidea or the Dibranchiata, and soon attained its maximum development. Two genera, *Orthoceras* and *Cyrtoceras*, are found in the Cambrian (Upper Tremadoc Beds), and these, especially the first, continue to be important in the succeeding Palæozoic formations as far as the Carboniferous. In the Ordovician the group is very much better represented than in the Cambrian, the chief genera being *Orthoceras, Cyrtoceras, Endoceras,* and *Nautilus*; but it is most abundant in the Silurian, where the number of species is very great; afterwards in the Devonian and Carboniferous, although still very numerous, there is a slight decline. In the Permian it is poorly represented; and only two genera extend beyond the Palæozoic, of these, one (*Orthoceras*) becomes extinct in the Trias, the other (*Nautilus*) lives on to the present day, and becomes especially abundant in the Cretaceous, in the Tertiary it is rare, and is associated with one other form only, namely, *Aturia*.

The distribution of the Ammonoidea differs from that of the Nautiloidea in that the former are mainly Mesozoic. In the Palæozoic the only genera are *Goniatites, Clymenia,* and (in the Carboniferous of India) *Ammonites*. Throughout the Mesozoic the Ammonites are extremely abundant;

in the Trias *Ceratites* is characteristic; in the Cretaceous we get a remarkable development of new genera, *Turrilites, Hamites, Scaphites, Crioceras,* and *Baculites,* all of these except the first, being evolute forms. At the end of the Cretaceous, the Ammonoids become extinct in a remarkably sudden manner, except in California, where some Ammonites have been found in the lower Tertiary beds.

The Dibranchiata are more numerous and more varied in existing seas, than they were at any former period. They are most abundant in littoral regions and are distributed in provinces similar to the other mollusks; typical littoral genera are *Octopus, Sepia* and *Loligo.* Some forms are pelagic, others abyssal. The Dibranchiata are unknown in the Palæozoic, the earliest examples appearing in the Trias. Throughout the Mesozoic, *Belemnites* is the chief form, and is very abundant especially in the clayey beds. In the Jurassic, *Geoteuthis* and *Belemnoteuthis* also occur; and in the Upper Cretaceous, *Belemnitella.* In the Tertiary, *Belosepia* and *Beloptera,* are the principal genera.

SUB-KINGDOM VIII. ARTHROPODA.

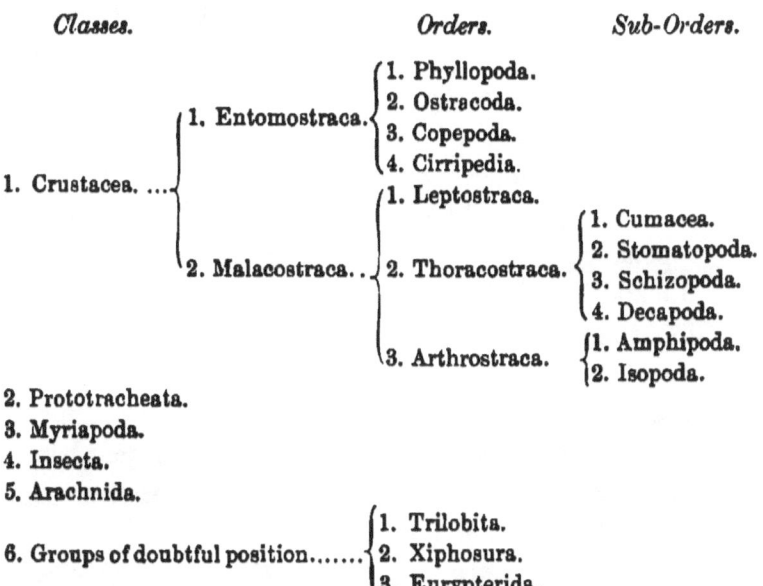

| *Classes.* | *Orders.* | *Sub-Orders.* |

1. Crustacea. ...
- 1. Entomostraca.
  1. Phyllopoda.
  2. Ostracoda.
  3. Copepoda.
  4. Cirripedia.
- 2. Malacostraca..
  1. Leptostraca.
  2. Thoracostraca.
    1. Cumacea.
    2. Stomatopoda.
    3. Schizopoda.
    4. Decapoda.
  3. Arthrostraca.
    1. Amphipoda.
    2. Isopoda.

2. Prototracheata.
3. Myriapoda.
4. Insecta.
5. Arachnida.
6. Groups of doubtful position.......
  1. Trilobita.
  2. Xiphosura.
  3. Eurypterida.

IN the Arthropods the body is bilaterally symmetrical
and segmented, and some or all of the segments bear a
pair of appendages each, which differ from those of the
worms in being jointed. Some of the appendages near
the mouth are modified so as to function in mastication
and prehension. A chitinous exoskeleton is always present
and is often strengthened by the deposition of carbonate

or phosphate of lime. A heart is found in most forms; it is placed dorsally, and is provided with paired slits, termed ostia. The body-cavity contains blood. In some forms respiration takes place by means of the general surface of the body; others are provided with special organs—gills (or branchiæ), tracheæ, pulmonary sacs (or lung-books). The gills are generally processes given off from some of the appendages; the tracheæ are branching tubes filled with air and opening to the exterior; the pulmonary sacs are infoldings of the integument. The nervous system consists of a supra-œsophageal ganglion, a ring round the œsophagus, and a ventral cord, usually with ganglia, placed beneath the intestine. Cilia are absent in all members of the sub-kingdom, with the exception of *Peripatus*. The sexes are separate in almost all forms.

The Arthropoda are divided into the following classes, (1) Crustacea, (2) Prototracheata, (3) Myriapoda, (4) Insecta, (5) Arachnida. The last four breathe by means of tracheæ or pulmonary sacs, and are therefore often grouped together as the Tracheata, the Crustacea which breathe by means of gills, forming the Branchiata. The Tracheate forms are comparatively rare as fossils, and consequently no description of them will be given here: the Myriapoda include the millipedes and centipedes, the oldest form is from the Old Red Sandstone; the Insects occur first in the Upper Silurian, they become more abundant in the Coal Measures, and are fairly common in some of the Mesozoic and Cainozoic deposits, as for instance the Lias, the Solenhofen Slates, the Purbeck, and the Bembridge Beds; the Arachnida include amongst others the scorpions and spiders, the earliest scorpion is found in the Silurian, the earliest spider in the Coal Measures.

CLASS. CRUSTACEA.

The members of this class are mainly aquatic and are very abundant as fossils; they breathe generally by means of gills, but in some cases by the general surface of the body. The chitinous exoskeleton is frequently hardened by a calcareous deposit, hence the name Crustacea. Segmentation is usually well-marked, but is absent in the Ostracoda. Three regions may be distinguished in the body:—the head, the thorax, and the abdomen. There are five segments in the head, but these are indicated only by the appendages; the number in the thorax and abdomen is variable in one of the two great divisions, namely the Entomostraca, but is constant in the other, the Malacostraca. In most forms some or all of the segments of the thorax (and sometimes also the anterior segments of the abdomen) fuse with those of the head to form a *cephalothorax*, this is covered dorsally by a large, unsegmented shield or carapace, termed the *cephalothoracic shield*. The head usually bears five pairs of appendages, viz. two pairs of antennæ, one of mandibles, and two of maxillæ. The thorax is also provided with appendages, and very often the abdomen too. The mandibles and maxillæ serve as jaws, and often also some of the anterior thoracic appendages. Eyes are generally present and are placed on the head; in some cases they are simple, in others compound, consisting of a number of lenses. The sexes are separate except in some cirripeds and isopods. In some cases development is direct, that is to say, the young individual has the same form as the adult, but generally this is not the case, the young undergoing a metamorphosis before reaching the adult stage. The two chief larval forms are known as the *Nauplius* and the *Zoœa*. In the *Nauplius*

form the body is unsegmented and possesses three pairs
of appendages representing the two pairs of antennæ and
the mandibles. In the *Zoœa* stage some of the thoracic
appendages are also present, and the abdomen is segmented but possesses no appendages.

The Crustacea are divided into two large groups,
(1) the Entomostraca, (2) the Malacostraca.

ENTOMOSTRACA.

The forms included in this group are mostly of small
size and of comparatively simple organisation. The number of segments in the body is variable, and also the
number and form of the appendages. In the development
there is nearly always a *Nauplius* stage. There are four
orders, (1) Phyllopoda, (2) Ostracoda, (3) Copepoda,
(4) Cirripedia. The Copepods are not definitely known
as fossils.

ORDER. PHYLLOPODA.

The Phyllopoda includes the water-fleas (*Daphnia*)
and other forms. The body is segmented and the greater
part of it is covered by a shield-like carapace or by a
bivalved shell. The number of segments in the abdomen
and thorax varies very widely. On the head there are
generally two pairs of antennæ, one of mandibles, and one
or two of maxillæ. The thorax bears four or more pairs
of swimming-feet, which are leaf-like. The abdomen is
frequently without appendages; it often ends in a caudal
fork. Two large eyes are present and often also a small
unpaired eye. The Phyllopods live mainly in fresh or
brackish water. Only a very few genera are found fossil;
the earliest occur in the Devonian.

Estheria. Valves thin, horny; ovate, oblong or quadrilateral, united at the straight dorsal border, and with the apices placed anteriorly or nearly central. Surface generally covered with concentric striæ. Devonian to present day. Living in fresh or brackish water.

ORDER. OSTRACODA.

The Ostracods are generally minute. The body is not segmented and is usually compressed laterally and completely enclosed in a bivalved shell (or carapace), which may be horny or calcareous; one valve is placed on each side of the animal. Dorsally the two valves are joined together by means of an elastic ligament which serves to open the shell; an adductor muscle passes from the interior of one valve to the other. There are seven pairs of appendages which can be protruded when the shell is opened. In the marine forms the shell is notched anteriorly so as to allow the antennæ to pass through when the shell is closed. The head carries two pairs of antennæ, one of mandibles, two of maxillæ. The thorax has two or three pairs of appendages, which are not leaf-like. The abdomen is rudimentary and is without appendages; it terminates either in a fork or a spiny plate. Respiration takes place by means of the general surface of the body. The carapace is in almost all cases the only part which occurs fossil; its surface may be smooth or variously ornamented.

Leperditia. Carapace smooth, convex, elongated, a little wider posteriorly. The right valve larger than the left. Hinge-line straight. There is a small tubercle (eye-spot) placed anteriorly near the hinge; and posterior to it is a slightly elevated circular area. Ordovician to Carboniferous.

Primitia. Carapace equivalve, convex, oblong. Hinge-line straight. Each valve has a dorsal groove which starts from the hinge-line. Cambrian to Carboniferous.

Beyrichia. Carapace elongated, inflated; dorsal border straight, ventral border semicircular. On the surface there are two or three large furrows which pass from the dorsal towards the ventral edge, the parts between being convex and often tuberculate. Cambrian to Devonian.

Cypris. Carapace thin, smooth or punctate, kidney-shaped or oval; ventral edge often concave. Oligocene to present day. Freshwater.

Cypridea. Differs from *Cypris* in having a beak-like process at the anterior ventral angle. Purbeck and Wealden.

Distribution of the Ostracoda.

The Ostracods have a very wide distribution at the present day; they are mainly marine, and often occur in shoals. They are most abundant in shallow water, only fifty-two species being found below the 500 fathom line. The fossil forms are very numerous, the earliest occurring in the Cambrian.

ORDER. CIRRIPEDIA.

The Cirripeds include the barnacles, acorn-shells, etc.; forms which differ considerably in appearance from the other crustaceans, and which were for a long time regarded as mollusks. The body is completely enclosed in a fold of the integument, which commonly forms a calcareous shell. The animal, in the adult state, is fixed to a foreign object by the anterior end of the head, either directly or by means of a stalk or peduncle. The head is not well-marked off from the thorax; it bears two pairs of antennæ, one pair of mandibles, and two pairs of maxillæ. The thorax has usually six pairs of bira-mous feathery limbs. The abdomen is rudimentary. A heart and vascular system are absent; nearly all forms are hermaphrodite. The shell consists of several pieces; in *Lepas* (which possesses a stalk) there are five, two are placed on each side of the body, those near the stalk being termed the *scuta* (fig. 52 *a*), those at the upper end the *terga* (*b*), and there is also one unpaired part placed dorsally, the *carina* (*c*). *Balanus* has no stalk; in this the shell consists of a tube formed of six pieces, in the upper part of which the scuta and terga are placed.

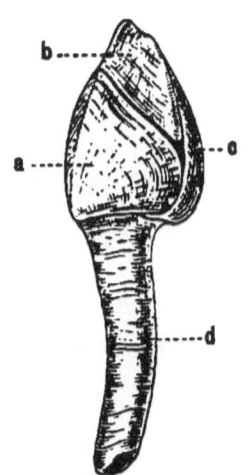

FIG. 52. *Lepas austra-lis*, Recent. *a*, scutum; *b*, tergum; *c*, carina; *d*, peduncle. Natural size. (After Darwin.)

Distribution of the Cirripedia.

The Cirripeds are all marine, and the greater number are found in shallow water. *Balanus* is especially characteristic of littoral regions. At a depth of greater than 1000 fathoms, only two genera, *Scalpellum* and *Verrucosa* have been found, but these are not confined to deep water. The earliest genus is *Turrilepas*, which ranges from the Ordovician to the Devonian. *Pollicipes* commences in the Rhætic, *Scalpellum* in the Cretaceous, and *Balanus* in the Eocene; all three are still living.

MALACOSTRACA.

The Malacostraca are of large or moderate size and more highly organised than the Entomostraca. The number of segments is constant throughout the group, there being five in the head, eight in the thorax, and six in the abdomen; each segment bears one pair of appendages. In some cases the development is direct, in a few the Nauplius stage occurs, but most commonly the Zoæa larva is found.

There are three Orders, (1) Leptostraca, (2) Thoracostraca, (3) Arthrostraca.

ORDER. LEPTOSTRACA (PHYLLOCARIDA).

This order forms a transition between the Phyllopoda and the Malacostraca; in the Palæozoic formations it is represented by numerous forms, but only three genera are now living, the most important being *Nebalia*. They are provided with a large carapace which is usually bivalved and covers the thoracic and some of the abdominal segments; in front it possesses a movable rostrum. There are twenty-one segments in the body—five in the head, eight in the thorax, eight in the abdomen, the last segment being forked or spined. There are nineteen pairs of appendages, as in the Malacostraca: the head bears two pairs of antennæ, one of mandibles, two of maxillæ; on the thorax there are eight pairs of leaf-like feet similar to those of the Phyllopods; the abdomen has six pairs of appendages, the first four being large, the last two small. The two posterior segments are without appendages. The eyes are compound and stalked.

Hymenocaris. Carapace semi-oval, smooth, not bi-valved. Abdomen formed of eight segments and four or five caudal spines. Appendages unknown. Lingula Flags.

Ceratiocaris. Carapace bivalved, often marked with striæ, oval, truncated behind and with a lanceolate rostrum in front. Body formed of fourteen or more segments, the first six or seven being covered by the carapace; the last segment is produced into a strong spine and provided with two smaller spines. Ordovician to Carboniferous.

Distribution of the Leptostraca.

The three living genera are all marine. The earliest representative is *Ceratiocaris* which occurs in the Tremadoc Beds and ranges on to the Devonian. *Hymenocaris* is found in the Lingula Flags; *Echinocaris* in the Devonian; and *Dithyrocaris* in the Carboniferous.

ORDER. THORACOSTRACA.

In this order there is a cephalothorax formed by the fusion of the head with some or all of the segments of the thorax, and this is covered dorsally by a shield or carapace. There are thirteen segments in the cephalothorax, six in the abdomen and a terminal telson. The eyes are compound and are usually placed on movable stalks. The Thoracostraca includes four sub-orders, (1) Cumacea, (2) Stomatopoda, (3) Schizopoda, (4) Decapoda. The first and third are unknown in the fossil state; and only a few forms of the Stomatopoda have been found.

SUB-ORDER. DECAPODA.

The Decapods include the lobsters, crayfishes, and the crabs. The head and in almost all cases all the segments of the thorax are covered by the large and usually strong cephalothoracic shield; this is frequently marked out into anterior and posterior portions by a groove,—the cervical suture, the anterior belonging to the head, the posterior to the thorax. Anteriorly the shield is produced into a spine, the rostrum. The gills are placed in a chamber formed by the downward prolongation of the cephalothoracic shield. The cephalothorax bears thirteen pairs of appendages, five belonging to the head, eight to the thorax. On the head there are (1) antennules, (2) antennæ, (3) mandibles, (4 and 5) maxillæ, the last three pairs serving as jaws. On the thorax the three first pairs (maxillipedes) serve in locomotion and also in mastication; the posterior five pairs are the ambulatory limbs, the first pair being the large chelæ. The abdomen bears six or fewer pairs of small appendages.

There are two sections, (1) Macrura, (2) Brachyura.

Section 1. Macrura.

This includes the lobsters and crayfishes. The abdomen is long, well developed, and provided with four or five pairs of appendages. There is a large caudal fin.

Meyeria. Cephalothorax laterally compressed, with a sharp rostrum, and a deep V-shaped cervical suture; the posterior part of the cephalothorax covered with sharp granules. Abdomen semicylindrical, longer than the cephalothorax, and ornamented with rows of granules. Lower Greensand.

Section 2. Brachyura.

This includes the crabs. The abdomen is short and more or less rudimentary; it is curved up underneath the thorax, and bears from one to four pairs of appendages. There is no caudal fin.

Xanthopsis. Cephalothorax rounded, convex, surface punctate, the posterior portion with rounded elevations; the frontal border with four, and the anterior-laterals with one to three, tooth-like processes. Orbital cavities deep, without fissures. Chelæ unequal. Abdomen of the male narrow and formed of five segments, owing to the fusion of the third, fourth, and fifth segments. Abdomen of female broad, composed of seven segments. London Clay.

Distribution of the Decapoda.

All the Brachyura, and most of the Macrura, are marine. The latter are the first to appear in the geological series, a few genera being found in the Upper Palæozoic; the earliest is *Palæopalæmon* from the Upper Devonian; in the Carboniferous *Anthrapalæmon* and others occur. The section becomes much more abundant in the Mesozoic, attaining its maximum in the Jurassic, where we get, amongst others, the genera *Glyphœa, Eryon, Æger,* and *Eryma.* In the Cretaceous, *Enoploclytia, Hoploparia,* and *Meyeria* occur. Only a few forms are found in the Tertiary. The Brachyura are represented by one or two genera only in the Jurassic; in the Cretaceous by *Palæocorystes* and several others; the Eocene forms are much more numerous, *Xanthopsis* being the commonest genus; but the section attains its maximum at the present day.

ORDER. ARTHROSTRACA.

There is no cephalothoracic shield; there are usually seven (sometimes fewer) segments in the thorax; and usually six in the abdomen, and a telson, but the abdomen is sometimes rudimentary. The head carries two pairs of antennæ, one of mandibles, two of maxillæ, and one of maxillipedes. The thorax has seven, and the abdomen six, pairs of appendages. The eyes are sessile. There are two sub-orders, (1) Amphipoda, (2) Isopoda.

SUB-ORDER. AMPHIPODA.

The Amphipods (*e.g. Gammarus, Talitrus*) are usually of small size and the body is laterally compressed. There are seven segments in the thorax, the appendages of which bear the gills. The abdomen is elongated and bears six pairs of appendages, the three anterior serve for swimming, the three posterior for jumping. Some of the Amphipods are marine, others fresh water; the fossil forms are rare, a few doubtful examples occur in the Palæozoic; those found in the Tertiary are mainly fresh water genera.

SUB-ORDER. ISOPODA.

The body is flattened dorso-ventrally. In the thorax there are six or seven segments, each with a pair of ambulatory appendages. The abdomen is often short, and is formed of six segments (frequently fused) and a telson; some of the appendages function as gills. Many Isopods are marine, others fresh water, whilst a few live on land; the fossil forms are rare. A specimen, named *Prearcturus*, from the Old Red Sandstone of Herefordshire, has been referred to this group, but two undoubted examples occur in the Solenhofen Slates; in England the earliest form (with the possible exception of *Prearcturus*) is *Archæoniscus* from the Purbeck Beds.

GROUPS OF DOUBTFUL POSITION.

ORDER. TRILOBITA.

The trilobites derive their name from the fact that the body is divided into three parts, by means of two furrows, which extend from the anterior to the posterior extremities; in a few genera, however (*Homalonotus, Illænus*),

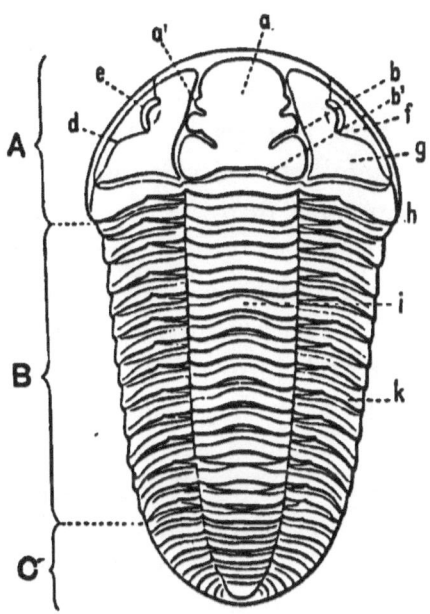

FIG. 53. *Calymene blumenbachi*, from the Wenlock Limestone. *A*, head, *B*, thorax, *C*, pygidium. *a*, glabella; *a'*, axal furrow; *b*, one of the glabella furrows; *b'*, neck furrow; *d*, facial suture; *e*, eye; *f*, free cheek; *g*, fixed cheek; *h*, genal angle; *i*, axis of thorax; *k*, pleura. Natural size.

this trilobation is only very feebly shown, or almost absent. In a longitudinal direction, three regions can be distinguished in the body, the head (fig. 53 *A*), the thorax (*B*), and the pygidium[1] (*C*); each of these three regions is covered dorsally by a calcareous shell. That covering the head, and known as the head-shield or cephalic shield, is semicircular or triangular in shape and is not segmented; in it may be distinguished a median and two lateral portions; the former is the more convex and is termed the *glabella* (*a*), the latter are the *cheeks*. The glabella is marked off from the cheeks by means of a furrow on each side, known as the *axal furrow* (*a′*). The form of the glabella varies in different genera, in some it extends quite to the anterior margin of the head-shield, in others only a part of the way; sometimes it is wider behind than in front, at others *vice versa*, or it may be uniform throughout. Generally it is divided at the sides into lobes by means of transverse furrows (*b*), usually three on each side; in some cases the furrows from the two sides meet in the middle of the glabella. On the posterior part of the glabella there is another furrow, which extends quite across, this is the neck-furrow (*b′*). The cheeks are each more or less triangular in shape and less convex than the glabella, they are frequently bordered by a flattened margin. The posterior angles of the cheeks, often spoken of as the genal angles (*h*), may be rounded (*e.g. Calymene*) but are often pointed or produced into spines (*e.g. Tri-nucleus*). Each cheek is divided into two portions by means of a suture (the *facial suture, d*). The inner part, that is, that between the facial suture and the glabella, is termed the *fixed cheek* (*g*) and is immovable; the outer part, known as the *free cheek* (*f*), is movable on the fixed cheek. The course of the facial suture varies in different forms; it may commence at the genal angle (*h*), or

---

[1] These are by some authors regarded as cephalothorax, abdomen, and post-abdomen respectively.

on the posterior border inside the genal angle, or on the external border just in front of the genal angle; it passes anteriorly and may be continuous with the suture of the other cheek in front of the glabella, or it may cut the anterior margin of the head-shield, in which case it is often united with the other suture on the inferior surface of the head. When the sutures are continuous in front of the glabella, it is obvious that the cheeks will also be continuous. In some genera (*Agnostus, Trinucleus*) the facial suture is absent. The eyes (*e*) are placed on the upper surface of the head, one on each free cheek near the facial suture, and generally near the middle of the cheek; they are compound, each consisting of a number of lenses; in a few genera (*Agnostus, Ampyx*) eyes are absent. The head-shield is continued on the under surface of the head forming a marginal rim (fig. 54 *a*); attached to this in the median line is a plate, usually oval in shape, situated just in front of the mouth and known as the *hypostome* (*b*).

The thorax (fig. 53 *B*) is formed of a series of segments, which vary in number, from two to twenty-six; these are movable upon one another, in some cases sufficiently to enable the animal to roll itself up like a wood-louse. Each segment is divided into a central and two lateral parts by means of two furrows. The central part is more convex than the lateral and forms the axis (*i*), the lateral parts being known as the pleuræ (*k*). The anterior part of the axis of each segment is not visible when the animal is unrolled, since it is overlapped by the preceding segment, with which it forms an articulating surface. The pleuræ in some genera possess a longitudinal ridge, in others a groove; a few forms have smooth pleuræ. Each pleura at some distance from the axis is curved downwards and usually also backwards, the point where this

curvature occurs is known as the fulcrum; generally each
pleura overlaps the anterior part of the succeeding one,
and often the fulcrum is rounded so as to form an articulating facet.   The terminations of the pleuræ are in some
cases rounded, in others produced into spines.

The pygidium (fig. 53 C) is usually triangular or semicircular in shape, it is formed of a variable number of
segments, which differ from those of the thorax in being
fused together and immovable; the segmentation being
shown by grooves.   Just as in the thorax, the pygidium
possesses a central part or axis, and lateral portions; the
axis may reach quite to the posterior extremity or only
part of the way.   The margin of the pygidium may be
even or entire, or it may be provided with a posterior
spine or with lateral spines.

The appendages of the trilobites were for a long time
unknown, since only a very few specimens showing the
ventral surface have been found; the most satisfactory of
these is *Asaphus megistos* (fig. 54) from the Ordovician
Beds of Ohio.   In this each segment of the thorax and
pygidium was found to bear a pair of jointed appendages.
Further information on this subject has been obtained by
Mr C. D. Walcott, by means of cutting thin sections of
rolled up specimens of *Calymene* and *Cheirurus*.   In this
way he found that on the ventral surface of the body there
was a thin membrane, which was strengthened by transverse arches to which the appendages of the thorax and
pygidium were attached; these each consisted of six or
seven joints, and at the base a spiral gill was attached.
The head also carried four pairs of jointed appendages.

The Trilobites are more closely related to the Xiphosurans than to any other Arthropods, and since these are
now regarded by many zoologists as belonging to the

Arachnida, rather than to the Crustacea, it is possible that the Trilobites will also have to be placed in that class.

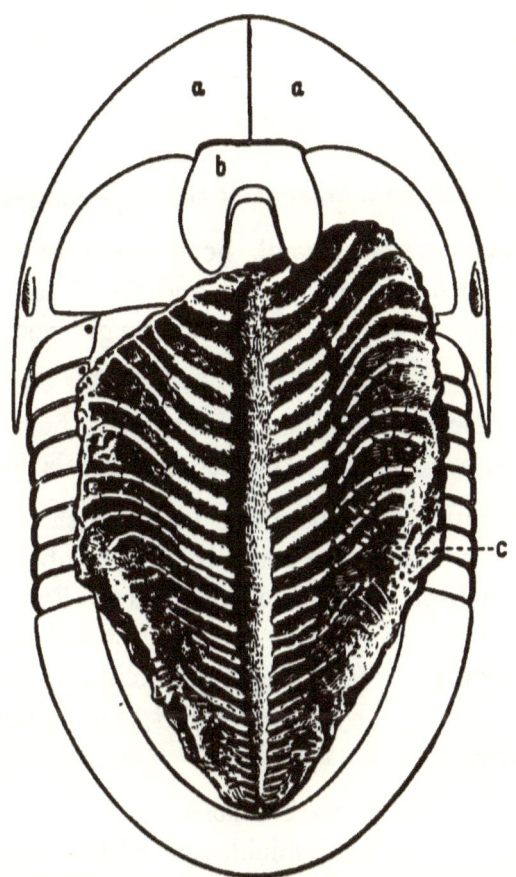

Fig. 54. Under surface of *Asaphus megistos*, from the Ordovician rocks of Ohio, showing a pair of appendages attached to each segment. The shaded part represents the actual specimen. *a*, infolded margin of the head-shield; *b*, hypostome; *c*, branchial filaments? (After Walcott.)

They agree with *Limulus* in the trilobation of the body and in the possession of a similar shield covering the anterior part of the body; with the Palæozoic Xiphosurans the resemblance is more marked, since some of these possess facial sutures and have the segments of the thorax and abdomen free. The larval form of *Limulus* presents a great resemblance to some trilobites, in this stage the caudal spine is absent and the segmentation is better marked. The trilobites differ from the Xiphosurans in the absence of ocelli, in the possession of a hypostome, and in the form and arrangement of the appendages.

Agnostus. Body small, head-shield and pygidium similar in form and size; eyes and facial suture absent. Thorax formed of two segments, pleuræ grooved. Harlech to Bala Beds.

Microdiscus. Similar to *Agnostus* but with four segments in the thorax. Harlech to Lingula Flags.

Trinucleus. Head-shield large, with long genal spines, and a broad punctate border; glabella inflated, pyriform, furrows absent, or indistinct. Eyes generally absent. No facial suture. Thorax formed of six segments, pleuræ grooved, straight, but slightly curved near their extremities. Pygidium short, triangular, margin entire. Arenig to Bala Beds.

Ampyx. Similar to *Trinucleus*, but without a punctate border to the head-shield, and with a long straight spine given off from the front of the glabella, and also with discontinuous facial sutures. Tremadoc to Bala Beds.

Olenus. Body oval; head-shield larger than the pygidium, with a narrow border, and genal spines; glabella usually a little contracted in front, separated from the anterior border by a flat space; facial sutures discontinuous in front; eyes well-developed, placed forward and

united to the front of the glabella by a straight ridge.
Thorax of from twelve to fifteen segments, pleuræ
pointed. Pygidium small. Lingula Flags to Tremadoc
Beds.

Paradoxides. Body large, elongated, narrowed posteriorly. Head-shield broad, semicircular, with a border,
and long genal spines; glabella elongated in front, with
two to four furrows on each side. Facial sutures extend
from the posterior to the anterior border. Eyes well
developed. Thorax long, formed of sixteen to twenty
segments; pleuræ grooved and produced into long backwardly directed spines. Pygidium very small, axis of two
to eight segments. Harlech Beds to Lingula Flags.

Olenellus. Similar to *Paradoxides*; but differs in
the glabella not expanding in front, in the facial suture
being invisible, in having only thirteen or fourteen segments in the thorax, and in the absence of lateral lobes on
the pygidium. Lower Cambrian.

Conocoryphe (= *Conocephalites*). Head-shield semicircular, without genal spines; axal furrows deep, glabella narrow in front, and with three or four backwardly
directed furrows; free cheeks small. Facial sutures not
continuous in front and ending near the genal angles.
Thorax with fourteen or fifteen segments. Pygidium
small, margin entire, axis with from two to eight segments.
Harlech to Tremadoc Beds.

Angelina. Body oval. Head-shield with long genal
spines, glabella without furrows; eyes small, near the
middle of the cheeks. Thorax with fourteen or fifteen
segments, pleuræ facetted. Pygidium short, margin provided with two teeth, axis formed of four or five segments.
Tremadoc Beds.

Calymene. Head-shield semicircular, genal angles rounded, occasionally pointed; glabella greatly inflated, broadest behind, with three pairs of lateral furrows, forming three globular lobes on each side. Eyes prominent. Facial suture extending from the genal angle to the anterior border. Thorax formed of thirteen segments, axis prominent, pleuræ grooved and facetted. Pygidium with six to eleven segments, margin entire. Arenig to Upper Ludlow.

Homalonotus. Body large, elongated, trilobation indistinct. Head-shield broad, genal angles rounded, furrows on the glabella indistinct or absent. Eyes small. Facial suture passing from the genal angles to the front margin, but often continuous in front. Thorax with thirteen segments; axis wide, not well-marked. Pygidium rather small, triangular, axis with ten to fourteen segments. Arenig to Devonian.

Ogygia. Body large, nearly flat. Head-shield large, semicircular; glabella distinct, wider in front, with four lateral furrows. Eyes large. Hypostome not notched. Facial suture starting from the posterior border, sometimes cutting the front margin, but generally continuous. Thorax consisting of eight segments, axis narrow, distinct; pleuræ grooved. Pygidium large, semicircular, margin entire, axis of numerous segments. Tremadoc to Llandeilo Beds.

Asaphus. Body oval, surface smooth or with striæ. Head-shield semicircular, with a flattened border, genal angles rounded or spinose; glabella wide in front and usually without lateral furrows. Eyes large. Hypostome notched posteriorly. Thorax formed of eight segments, pleuræ obliquely grooved, with rounded extremities.

Pygidium of about the same size as the head, rounded, margin entire; formed of numerous segments which are usually visible on the axis only. Tremadoc to Bala Beds.

Illænus. Body oval, convex. Head-shield large, semicircular; glabella indistinctly marked, without furrows externally, but within the test there are four pairs. Eyes remote from one another. Facial sutures commence on the posterior border, cut the anterior border in front of eye and unite on the inferior surface. Thorax with usually ten segments, pleuræ not grooved or ridged. Pygidium large, semicircular, axis rudimentary, segments not visible externally. Arenig to Wenlock.

Æglina. Head-shield large; glabella large, convex, projecting beyond the margin in front. Cheeks narrow; eyes very large. Facial suture discontinuous, nearly parallel to the axis of the body. Thorax with five or six segments, pleuræ grooved. Pygidium rounded, axis reduced. Arenig to Bala Beds.

Bronteus. Head-shield large, semicircular, genal angles pointed. Glabella very wide in front, three lateral furrows in some species, none in others. Facial sutures discontinuous in front, eyes sickle-shaped, placed near the posterior border. Thorax with ten segments, axis narrow, pleuræ ridged. Pygidium very large, fan-shaped, axis short, lateral lobes large with radiating grooves. Bala Beds to Devonian.

Phacops. Head-shield nearly semicircular, glabella prominent, broadest in front, with three or four furrows; facial sutures commencing on the lateral border of the cheek in front of the genal angle, and continuous in front of the glabella. Eyes generally large, granulated, formed of large facets. Thorax with eleven segments, pleuræ grooved. Pygidium variable. Ordovician to Devonian.

Cheirurus. Head-shield semicircular, genal angles pointed; glabella convex, with three pairs of furrows, the last uniting with the neck-furrow. Facial sutures continuous in front and ending on the external margin. Eyes prominent. Thorax with usually eleven segments, pleuræ grooved, and produced into spines. Pygidium with four segments, lateral lobes with backwardly-directed spines. Tremadoc to Devonian.

Encrinurus. Head-shield covered with tubercles; glabella pyriform, eyes small, placed on short peduncles. Facial sutures not continuous, ending on the lateral margin. Thorax with eleven segments, pleuræ ridged. Pygidium narrow, triangular, pleuræ bent backwards. Bala to Upper Ludlow.

Acidaspis. Head-shield broad, trilobation not well-marked, genal angles spined; glabella with a pair of longitudinal furrows parallel to the axal furrows, and with two or three lateral furrows. Eyes connected with the glabella by a ridge. Facial sutures continuous in front and ending on the lateral margins. Thorax with nine or ten segments, pleuræ produced into long spines. Pygidium small, with long spines. Llandeilo Beds to Devonian.

Phillipsia. Body oval; glabella with nearly parallel sides, with two or three lateral furrows, the posterior one being directed backwards and united to the deep neck-furrow, thus cutting off a basal lobe. Eyes large, reniform. Facial sutures not continuous in front ending on posterior border. Thorax with seven segments, pleuræ grooved.

Pygidium semicircular, formed of from twelve to eighteen segments, margin entire. Devonian to Permian.

Griffithides. Body oval; glabella pyriform without lateral furrows, with inflated basal lobes; eyes small. Thorax with nine segments. Pygidium rounded, formed of about thirteen segments. Carboniferous.

Distribution of the Trilobita.

The Trilobites form one of the most important and striking features in the Palæozoic faunas, they occur first in the Lower Cambrian Beds, and reach their maximum in the Ordovician; they are still abundant in the Silurian, but become less important in the Devonian, and in the Carboniferous are represented by four genera only. In Europe they do not extend beyond the Carboniferous Limestone, but in North America one species of *Phillipsia* has been found in the Permian.

The most important genera are :—

Cambrian. *Agnostus, Microdiscus, Paradoxides, Olenellus, Olenus, Conocoryphe, Niobe, Asaphus, Angelina.*

Ordovician. *Ogygia, Ampyx, Trinucleus, Illænus, Asaphus, Æglina, Calymene.*

Silurian. *Phacops, Homalonotus, Calymene, Acidaspis, Cheirurus, Proetus, Illænus, Lichas.*

Devonian. *Phacops, Homalonotus, Cheirurus, Bronteus.*

Carboniferous. *Phillipsia, Griffithides, Brachymetopus.*

ORDER. XIPHOSURA.

The only living representative of the Xiphosura is *Limulus*, the king-crab, found on the eastern shores of North America and Asia, and in the Malay Archipelago. The body is protected by a chitinous shell, which shows a fairly well marked trilobation; the cephalothorax is covered dorsally by a large horse-shoe shaped shield, which carries on its upper surface two pairs of eyes, one compound, near the middle of the lateral parts, the other simple and placed close together near the anterior margin. Behind the cephalothorax, and movably articulated with it, comes the abdominal shield; this is composed of six fused segments, the segmentation being shown by grooves; at the sides it bears movable spines, and posteriorly it is provided with a long caudal spine. The cephalothorax bears six pairs of appendages on its under surface, the anterior pair only being placed in front of the mouth; the basal joints of the five posterior pairs function in mastication. The abdomen carries six pairs of appendages, the anterior pair are plate-like and serve as an operculum to cover the remaining five pairs, these bear the gills which consist of a large number of thin plates.

The earliest Xiphosurans (*Hemiaspis, Neolimulus*) are found in the Silurian; in the Carboniferous, *Prestwichia, Belinurus* and others occur. *Limulus* appears first in the Trias. The Palæozoic genera differ in some respects from the later ones; the head-shield is not fused with the thoracic shield, and the former sometimes possesses a facial suture; generally also, some or all of the segments of the thorax and abdomen remain free and movable. Thus in *Hemiaspis* there are six segments in the thorax and three in the abdomen, all of which are free: in *Belinurus* there are five free thoracic segments and three fused abdominal ones; in *Prestwichia* all the segments of both thorax and abdomen are fused.

ORDER. EURYPTERIDA.

The Eurypterids are quite extinct and form a very remarkable group of the Arthropoda; they are usually of large size, some having a length of several feet; trilobation is either absent or only very faintly shown. The body is protected by a chitinous skeleton (fig. 55), the anterior part (cephalothorax) consisting of a large quadrate or semicircular shield; this is followed posteriorly by thirteen

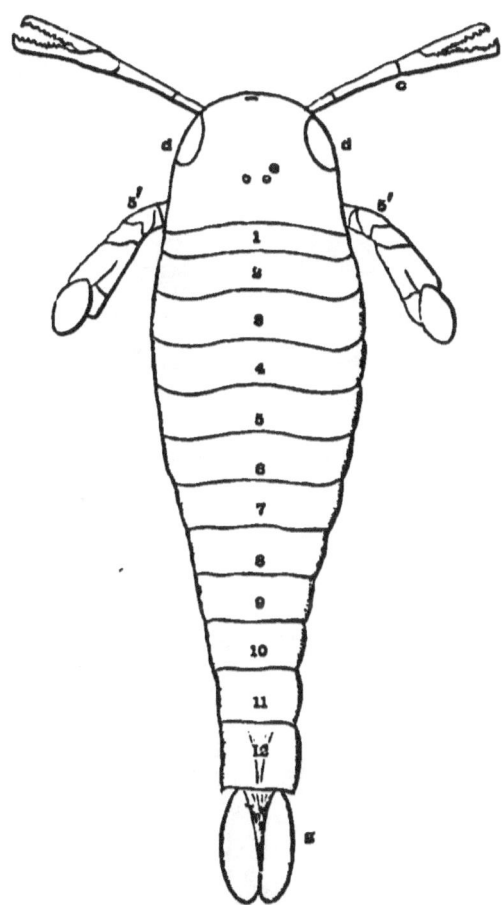

FIG. 55. Dorsal surface of *Pterygotus osiliensis*, from the Upper Silurian, Rootziküll. *c*, first pair of appendages; *d*, compound eyes; *e*, ocelli; *g*, telson; 5′, fifth pair of appendages; 1—6, segments of the abdomen; 7—12, segments of the post-abdomen. Reduced. (After Schmidt.)

free and movable segments which taper towards the
posterior extremity. The first six free segments (1—6)
are regarded by some as the abdomen, by others as the
thorax, and the remaining seven (7—12, *g*) as either the
abdomen or post-abdomen; the last segment is usually an
oval pointed plate, the telson (*g*). The cephalothoracic

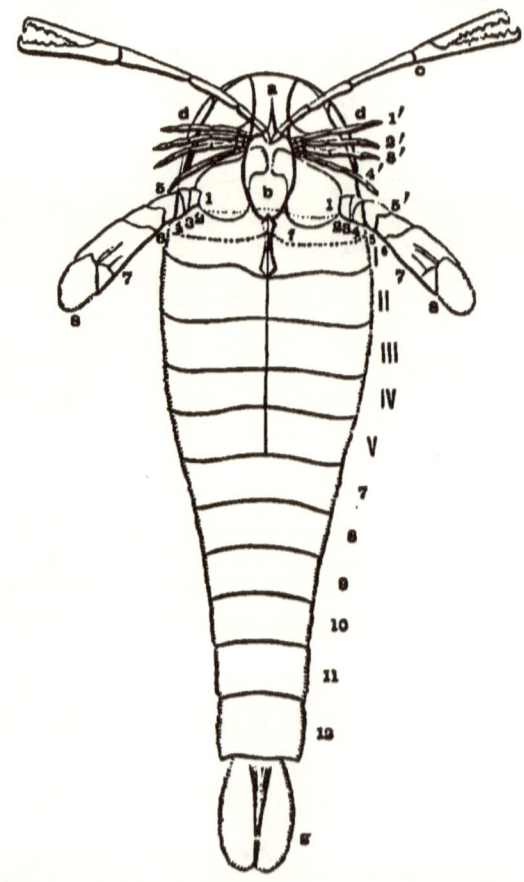

Fɪɢ. 56. Ventral surface of *Pterygotus osiliensis*, from the Upper Silurian,
Rootziküll. *a*, epistome; *b*, metastoma; *c*, first pair of appendages;
d, compound eyes; *f*, operculum; *g*, telson; 1′—5′, second to sixth
pairs of appendages; I.—V., ventral plates of the abdomen; 7—12,
segments of the post-abdomen. Reduced. (After Schmidt.)

shield carries on its upper surface two pairs of eyes; a large compound pair (d) placed laterally or at the anterior angles, and a pair of simple ocelli (e) placed close together near the centre of the shield. The mouth is on the under surface of the cephalothorax (fig. 56); in front of the mouth there is one pair of appendages only (c), they are jointed and often end in chelæ, and are considered to represent the antennæ; the other four or five pairs of appendages (1'—5') consist of seven or eight joints each and are sometimes chelate, they function both in mastication and swimming, the posterior pair (5') is often very much larger than the others. Placed just behind the mouth, in the median line, is an oval or heart-shaped plate —the *metastoma* (b). The six segments of the abdomen are not continued round on the ventral surface as would at first sight appear. But there are instead five plate-like appendages which cover the gills (I.—V.); the first, known as the operculum, is often divided into two parts by a median process, and corresponds with that of *Limulus*. The segments of the post-abdomen (7—12) are continued on the under surface and bear no appendages.

The Eurypterids agree with the Xiphosura in many points, but differ in the abdominal segments being always free, in the possession of a metastoma, and in the absence of trilobation.

Eurypterus. Cephalothoracic shield quadrate; the compound eyes are not at the margin, but a little in front of the median lateral point on each side. The telson is greatly elongated. The pre-oral appendages are small and not chelate; of the five other pairs of appendages the posterior is very much the larger. The metastoma is oval. Lower Ludlow to Carboniferous.

Pterygotus. Cephalothoracic shield rounded in front; the compound eyes are marginal, at the anterior angles. The telson is oval with a pointed extremity. The pre-oral appendages are long and chelate. Metastoma oval. The examples of this genus are usually of enormous size, *P. anglicus* sometimes reaching a length of nearly six feet. Lower Ludlow to Old Red Sandstone.

Slimonia. Cephalothoracic shield quadrate ; the compound eyes at the anterior angles. The telson is oval, ending in a point. Metastoma heart-shaped. The pre-oral appendages short and not chelate. Upper Ludlow and Passage Beds.

Distribution of the Eurypterida.

The order ranges from the Ordovician to the Permian, and is most abundant in the Upper Silurian and Old Red Sandstone. The chief genera are *Eurypterus, Pterygotus, Slimonia,* and *Stylonurus.*

LIST OF SOME IMPORTANT PALÆONTOLOGICAL WORKS.

GENERAL.

K. A. von Zittel. Handbuch der Palæontologie. 4 vols. 1876– .
(There is a French translation by Barrois.)

G. Steinmann and *L. Döderlein.* Elemente der Paläontologie.
1888–1890.

H. A. Nicholson and *R. Lydekker.* Manual of Palæontology. Third
edition. 2 vols. 1889.

J. Morris. A Catalogue of British Fossils. Second edition. 1854.

PROTOZOA.

W. B. Carpenter. Introduction to the Study of the Foraminifera.
1862. (Ray Society.)

H. B. Brady. Report on the Foraminifera. (Challenger Report)
1884.

T. R. Jones, W. K. Parker, and *H. B. Brady.* A Monograph of the
Foraminifera of the Crag. 1866. (Palæont. Soc.)

H. B. Brady. A Monograph of Carboniferous and Permian Foraminifera. 1876. (Palæont. Soc.)

E. Haeckel. Report on the Radiolaria. (Challenger Report) 1887.

G. J. Hinde. Notes on Radiolaria from the Lower Palæozoic Rocks
(Llandeilo-Caradoc) of the South of Scotland. Ann. Mag. Nat.
Hist. ser. 6, Vol. VL (1890), p. 40.

Rüst. Beiträge zur Kenntniss der fossilien Radiolarien aus Gesteinen
des Jura. Palæontographica. Band XXXI. 1885.

14—2

PORIFERA.

G. J. Hinde. Catalogue of the Sponges in the Geological Depart-
ment of the British Museum (Natural History). 1883.
G. J. Hinde. A Monograph of British Fossil Sponges. 1887- .
(Palæont. Soc.)
W. J. Sollas. On the structure and affinities of the Genus
Siphonia. Quart. Journ. Geol. Soc. Vol. xxxiii. (1877), p. 790.

HYDROZOA.

C. Lapworth. On the geological distribution of the Rhabdophora.
Ann. Mag. Nat. Hist. ser. 5, Vol. iii. (1879), pp. 245, 449 ;
Vol. iv. (1879), pp. 333, 423 ; Vol. v. (1880), pp. 45, 273, 358 ;
Vol. vi. (1881), pp. 16, 185.
C. Lapworth. On Scottish Monograptidæ. Geol. Mag. dec. 2,
Vol. ii. (1876), pp. 308, 350, 499, 544.
J. Hopkinson and *C. Lapworth.* Descriptions of the Graptolites of
the Arenig and Llandeilo Rocks of St David's. Quart. Journ.
Geol. Soc. Vol. xxxi. (1875), p. 631.
H. A. Nicholson. A Monograph of the British Graptolitidæ. Part I.
General Introduction. 1872.
J. Hall. Graptolites of the Quebec group. (Figures and descrip-
tions of Canadian Organic Remains. Dec. ii.). 1865.
H. A. Nicholson. A Monograph of the British Stromatoporoidea.
1886-1892. (Palæont. Soc.)

ACTINOZOA.

H. M. Edwards and *J. Haime.* A Monograph of the British Fossil
Corals. 1850-54. (Palæont. Soc.)
P. M. Duncan. A Monograph of the British Fossil Corals. (Sup-
plement to the preceding.) 1866-72. (Palæont. Soc.)
P. M. Duncan. A Revision of the families and genera of the Sclero-
dermic Zoantharia, or Madreporaria. Journ. Linn. Soc. (Zool.)
Vol. xviii. (1885), pp. 1-204.
H. A. Nicholson. On the structure and affinities of the "Tabulate
Corals" of the Palæozoic Period. 1879.

H. A. Nicholson. On the structure and affinities of the Genus Monticulipora and its sub-genera. 1881.

ECHINODERMATA.

T. Wright. Monograph on the British Fossil Echinodermata from the Cretaceous Formations. Vol. I. Echinoidea. 1864–1882. (Palæont. Soc.)

W. P. Sladen. A Monograph of the British Fossil Echinodermata. Vol. II. Asteroidea. 1891– . (Palæont. Soc.)

T. Wright. A Monograph on the British Fossil Echinodermata of the Oolitic Formations. Vol. I. Echinoidea. (1857–1878.) Vol. II. Asteroidea and Ophiuroidea (1863–1880). (Palæont. Soc.)

P. M. Duncan. A Revision of the Genera and great Groups of the Echinoidea. Journ. Linn. Soc. (Zool.), Vol. XXIII. (1889), p. 1.

E. Forbes. Monograph of the Echinodermata of the British Tertiaries. 1852. (Palæont. Soc.)

J. W. Gregory. A Revision of the British Fossil Cainozoic Echinoidea. Proc. Geol. Assoc., Vol. XII. (1891), p. 16.

F. A. Bather. British Fossil Crinoids. Ann. Mag. Nat. Hist. ser. 6, Vol. V. (1890), pp. 306, 373, 485 ; Vol. VI. (1890), p. 222 ; Vol. VII. (1891), pp. 35, 389 ; Vol. IX. (1892), pp. 189–202.

R. Etheridge and *P. H. Carpenter.* Catalogue of the Blastoidea in the Geological Department of the British Museum (Natural History). 1886.

E. Forbes. On the Cystideæ of the Silurian Rocks of the British Islands. Mem. Geol. Survey, Vol. II., Part II. 1848.

J. Barrande. Système Silurien du centre de la Bohême. (Cystidées par *W. Waagen.*) 1888.

VERMES.

G. J. Hinde. On Annelid Jaws from the Cambro-Silurian, Silurian, and Devonian Formations in Canada, and from the Lower Carboniferous in Scotland. Quart. Journ. Geol. Soc., Vol. XXXV. (1879), p. 370.

G. J. Hinde. On Annelid Jaws from the Wenlock and Ludlow Formations of the West of England. Quart. Journ. Geol. Soc., Vol. XXXVI. (1880), p. 368.

POLYZOA.

G. Busk. Report on the Polyzoa. (Challenger Report) 1886.

G. Busk. A Monograph of the Fossil Polyzoa of the Crag. 1859. (Palæont. Soc.)

T. Hincks. History of the British Marine Polyzoa. 1880.

G. W. Shrubsole. A Review of the British Carboniferous Fenestellidæ. Quart. Journ. Geol. Soc., Vol. xxxv. (1879), p. 275.

G. W. Shrubsole. A Review and Description of the various species of British Upper Silurian Fenestellidæ. Quart. Journ. Geol. Soc., Vol. xxxvi. (1880), p. 241.

G. R. Vine. Reports on Fossil Polyzoa. Rep. Brit. Assoc. 1880-92.

BRACHIOPODA.

P. Fischer. Manuel de Conchyliologie. 1887. [Brachiopods, by D. P. Œhlert.]

T. Davidson. British Fossil Brachiopoda. Six vols. 1851-1886. (Palæont. Soc.)

J. Hall and *J. M. Clarke.* An Introduction to the Study of the Genera of the Palæozoic Brachiopoda. (Geol. Survey New York, Palæontology. Vol. viii.) 1892.

MOLLUSCA.

S. P. Woodward. Manual of the Mollusca. Fourth edition by R. Tate. 1880.

P. Fischer. Manuel de Conchyliologie. 1887.

J. Sowerby. Mineral Conchology of Great Britain. 1812-29.

W. Carpenter. Report on the Microscopic Structure of Shells. Rep. Brit. Assoc. for 1844 (1845), p. 24, and for 1847 (1848), p. 93.

J. Lycett. British Fossil Trigoniæ. 1872-79. (Palæont. Soc.)

S. V. Wood. A Monograph of Eocene Bivalves of England. 1861-71. (Palæont. Soc.)

S. V. Wood. A Monograph of the Crag Mollusca. Vol. i. Univalves, 1848. Vol. ii. Bivalves 1850, and supplements. (Palæont. Soc.)

J. Morris and *J. Lycett.* Mollusca from the Great Oolite, with supplement, 1850–63. (Palæont. Soc.)

W. H. Hudleston. British Jurassic Gasteropoda. 1887– . (Palæont. Soc.)

A. H. Foord. Catalogue of the British Fossil Cephalopoda in the British Museum. Parts I. and II. 1888–91.

T. H. Huxley. On the structure of the Belemnitidæ. (Mem. Geol. Survey.) 1864.

J. Phillips. A Monograph of the British Belemnitidæ. 1865. (Palæont. Soc.)

S. S. Buckman. A Monograph of Inferior Oolite Ammonites of the British Islands. 1887– . (Palæont. Soc.)

T. Wright. Monograph of the Lias Ammonites. 1878–86. (Palæont. Soc.)

J. F. Blake. British Fossil Cephalopoda. Part I. 1882.

D. Sharpe. Mollusca in the Chalk of England. Parts I. and II., Cephalopoda. 1853–4. (Palæont. Soc.)

ARTHROPODA.

H. Woodward. Catalogue of British Fossil Crustacea. 1877.

T. R. Jones. A Monograph of the Fossil Estheriæ. 1862. (Palæont. Soc.)

T. R. Jones. A Monograph of the Tertiary Entomostraca of England. 1856. (Palæont. Soc.)

T. R. Jones, J. W. Kirkby and *G. S. Brady.* A Monograph of the British Fossil Bivalved Entomostraca from the Carboniferous Formations. 1874–84. (Palæont. Soc.)

T. R. Jones. A Monograph of the Entomostraca of the Cretaceous Formations of England. 1849. (Palæont. Soc.)

C. Darwin. A Monograph on the Fossil Lepadidæ. 1851. (Palæont. Soc.)

C. Darwin. A Monograph on the Fossil Balanidæ. 1854. (Palæont. Soc.)

T. R. Jones and *H. Woodward.* A Monograph of the British Palæozoic Phyllocarida. 1888–92. (Palæont. Soc.)

T. Bell. A Monograph of the Fossil Malacostracous Crustacea. 1857–62. (Palæont. Soc.)

216   PALÆONTOLOGICAL WORKS.

<mark>bibliography</mark> *J. Carter.* On the Decapod Crustacea of the Oxford Clay. Quart.
Journ. Geol. Soc., Vol. XLII. (1886), p. 542.

B. N. Peach. On some new Crustaceans from the Lower Carboniferous Rocks of Eskdale and Liddesdale. Trans. Roy. Soc. Edin.,
Vol. XXV. (1880–83), pp. 73, 511.

J. W. Salter. A Monograph of the British Trilobites from the
Cambrian, Silurian, and Devonian Formations. 1864–1883.
(Palæont. Soc.)

H. Woodward. A Monograph of the British Carboniferous Trilobites. 1883–4. (Palæont. Soc.)

J. Barrande. Système Silurien du centre de la Bohême. Trilobites. 1852.

C. Lapworth. On *Olenellus callavei* and its geological relationships.
Geol. Mag. dec. 3, Vol. VIII. (1891), p. 529, plates xiv. and xv.

C. D. Walcott. The Fauna of the Lower Cambrian or Olenellus
zone. 1890. (Ann. Rep. U. S. Geol. Survey.)

C. D. Walcott. The Trilobite : New and Old Evidence relating to
its Organization. (Bull. Mus. Comp. Zool., Vol. VIII.), 1881.

H. Woodward. A Monograph of the British Fossil Crustacea
belonging to the order Merostomata. 1866–78. (Palæont.
Soc.)

T. H. Huxley and *J. W. Salter.* On Pterygotus. 1859. (Mem.
Geol. Survey, Organic Remains.)

INDEX.

CAMBRIDGE: PRINTED BY C. J. CLAY, M.A. & SONS, AT THE UNIVERSITY PRESS.

www.ingramcontent.com/pod-product-compliance
Lightning Source LLC
Chambersburg PA
CBHW030107030726
47498CB00007B/2284